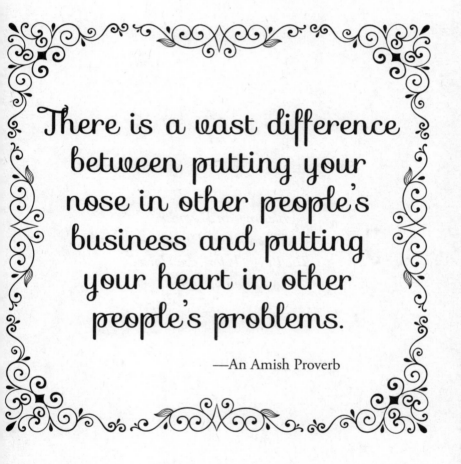

There is a vast difference between putting your nose in other people's business and putting your heart in other people's problems.

—An Amish Proverb

SUGARCREEK AMISH MYSTERIES

Blessings in Disguise
Where Hope Dwells
The Buggy before the Horse
A Season of Secrets

A Season

OF SECRETS

ELIZABETH ADAMS

Guideposts

New York

Published by Guideposts Books & Inspirational Media
110 William Street
New York, NY 10038
Guideposts.org

Cover and interior design by Müllerhaus
Cover illustration by Bill Bruning, represented by Deborah Wolfe, LTD.
Typeset by Aptara, Inc.

Printed and bound in the United States of America
10 9 8 7 6 5 4

CHAPTER ONE

The door of the Swiss Miss flew open just as Cheryl Cooper finished hanging hand-blown glass balls on the small fir tree by the front window. She put the ornament box down and turned to see Lydia Troyer walk inside and slam the door against the cold late November wind.

"I am sorry," Lydia said as she crossed the floor and hung her coat in the office at the back. She returned, tying a red Swiss Miss apron around her waist. "It is very chilly out there today." Lydia warmed her hands in front of the potbellied stove for a moment.

"It definitely feels like winter is on its way," Cheryl said. Thanksgiving had just passed, and she was looking forward to the cheer and warmth of the Christmas season, but she was not looking forward to the cold that came with it.

Lydia pulled her cell phone out of her pocket and looked at the screen. Then she put it away and turned to Cheryl. "What should I do?"

Cheryl had to laugh. Lydia—the best friend of her other part-time employee, Esther Miller—was Amish, but she was on *rumspringa,* her running-around years where the rules were relaxed and Amish teens could experience the outside world. Lydia had embraced that freedom wholeheartedly. She dressed *Englisch*—not in the traditional Amish style—and carried her cell phone with her everywhere, just like most teenagers in America. And, like a typical teen, she checked it constantly. But Lydia was a hard worker as well as bright and outgoing, and Cheryl was glad to have her around.

"There are some boxes I was going to unpack over behind the counter," Cheryl said gesturing to the back of the shop. "Maybe you could inventory those and set them out?"

"I will start there," Lydia said and headed off. During the holiday season, Cheryl had asked Lydia to pick up more hours. Lydia was eager to make some extra money while Cheryl was thankful that she'd have more help around the shop in the busy coming weeks.

Cheryl turned back to the small Christmas tree, adjusted the placement of a few of the ornaments, and then looked around the store. The shelves were well stocked with handmade soaps, candles, jams, and cheese, as well as hand-carved wooden toys and other small souvenirs. Cheryl ran the Swiss Miss, a gift shop right in the heart of Ohio Amish country, and she tried her best to make the shop warm and welcoming as well as fill it with the finest merchandise she could find. And now, with the holiday season in full swing, Cheryl knew that it was especially important for the store to look its best. The Amish may not be extravagant in celebrating the holiday, but the tourists who came through Sugarcreek would be looking for gifts, and Cheryl was happy to help. A few customers were currently browsing the candy bins, but they seemed quite content selecting between pastel-colored saltwater taffy, spicy peppermints, and bitter horehound.

Satisfied that all was in good order, she carried the empty box toward the back of the shop and set it down on the counter. She'd take the box back out to her car, and then she'd spend some time working on putting together a care package for her aunt Mitzi, who owned and had run the Swiss Miss before she moved to Papua New Guinea to follow God's call to the mission field earlier this year. Aunt Mitzi's latest letter had said that everything was going well, but she missed some of her favorite things from home, like peanut butter and Greta Yoder's famous cinnamon rolls, so Cheryl had decided to put together a care package filled with her aunt's favorite things. She'd include some of Naomi Miller's jams for sure, and also a bag of the taffy Rebekah Byler made that Mitzi loved so much, and...

Cheryl looked up as Lydia gasped.

"What's wrong?" she said.

Lydia was staring down at her phone, her long black hair falling around her face. "What could this mean?" she muttered.

"What is it?" Cheryl's heart beat faster. Could something be wrong with one of Lydia's family members?

"I just got this weird text," Lydia said and held out her cell phone.

Cheryl looked at it and squinted to read the letters on the small screen: *I know what happened to Mark.*

She looked back up at Lydia, trying to make sense of the words. Lydia's face had drained of color.

"Who is Mark?"

"My cousin," Lydia said. She pulled the phone back toward herself and read the message again. "He disappeared a little over three years ago. No one ever knew what happened to him. Except now"—she looked up at Cheryl, her eyes wide—"it looks like someone does know after all."

Cheryl looked back down at the cell phone Lydia held out and tried to make sense of what she had just told her. Lydia's fingers flew across the screen, typing a response: *Who is this?*

"Wait, what do you mean your cousin Mark disappeared three years ago?"

They both stared at the screen, waiting for a response, but none came.

"Just that. He left his job at Weaver Lumber one night, in late September three years ago, and he never made it home. The police were brought in, and there were all kinds of theories about where he went, but they never found out what happened to him."

Cheryl's thoughts raced around in her head. She had only lived in Sugarcreek a short time, and she had never heard about this before. How had an Amish boy simply disappeared? Wasn't this the kind of thing people still talked about years later? What could have happened to him?

"Back up. Tell me more about what happened," Cheryl said.

Lydia took a deep breath and nodded. Her eyes were wide, but Cheryl could see she was trying to stay calm. "Mark was eighteen, in his running-around time, but still very devoted to his family and the church. But then one night he left his job to drive home and that was that. He vanished. They found his car outside the bus station in Columbus a few weeks later."

Cheryl tried to make sense of this. "What did the police say?" she finally asked. She looked down at the phone, but there was still no response.

"They say he ran away. That he took a bus somewhere and just left." Lydia sent another text back asking, *What happened?* "They talked to a few people and found out that he was interested in art, which is true, and that he liked many things about the Englisch life, which is also true, and they said he must have driven to the bus station, gotten on a bus, and run away."

She looked up from the phone and set it down gently on the counter. "But he did not run away. He would not have. Not without saying good-bye."

Lydia could be a bit flighty, but Cheryl heard nothing but earnestness in her voice.

"Mark *was* pretty interested in the Englisch life, and yes, he was trying to decide whether to join the church or not..."

This, Cheryl had come to understand, was the purpose of the running-around time, or rumspringa. The strict rules the Amish lived by were relaxed so that kids could see the outside world and make an informed decision about whether they wanted to remain Amish and join their church, or whether they would leave the church behind and become Englisch. An overwhelming number did choose to stay Amish in the end, but each teenager had to make his or her own choice.

"But just because Mark was interested in the Englisch world, it does not mean he just left. Mark would have told me if he was planning to go somewhere. We were close. He was always one of my favorite cousins. And he would have said good-bye to his parents. He would never have just vanished like that. I am positive."

Cheryl could see Lydia was getting worked up, and she could certainly understand why. Lydia felt very strongly that Mark hadn't run away. But that only left one alternative...

"So what do you think happened to him?" Cheryl asked.

Lydia shook her head. "I do not know. I do not..." She hesitated. "I hate to think about it, but I wonder if something horrible happened to him. I hope not, but I do not know what else it could have been. Especially with the bloody shirt they found behind the Honey Bee. I mean, what else could..."

"The bloody what?" Goodness. This was getting gruesome.

Lydia stopped. "Oh, right. I am sorry. I forgot you do not know any of this." She took a deep breath and then continued. "They found one of Mark's shirts in a trash bin behind the Honey Bee the day after he disappeared. It had blood on it. So it seems likely..."

Lydia gulped, taking in air. She was getting worked up again, so Cheryl waited a moment. Lydia was sure something bad had happened to her cousin, but Cheryl didn't know what to believe. But whatever the truth was, someone out there now knew, or claimed to know, what had happened to Mark. But who was it?

She looked down at Lydia's phone, lying on the counter. It was a standard cell phone with a touch screen. There was still no answer. "Do you have any idea who could have sent the message?"

"I do not know." Lydia pointed to the number at the top of the screen. It was a local number, but not one she had stored in her phone, so there was no name attached to it. "I do not recognize this number."

A text like this would most likely have come from someone Lydia knew. After all, whoever sent it must have known that Lydia and Mark had been close. But it hadn't come from someone whose number Lydia was familiar with. Since it was a text, it could only have come from a cell phone or tablet, and as only teens on rumspringa were allowed to use such devices, the number of potential senders was limited.

Unless it came from an *Englischer*, of course. In which case, it could be just about anyone.

But even if someone really did know what had happened to Mark, why send a text about it? If this was real—and Cheryl wasn't sure it was—why not simply tell Lydia directly?

And if this wasn't real… Cheryl shook her head. If this wasn't real, it was a very cruel joke.

"This person is not responding to my questions," Lydia said, looking at the screen again. "Is there any way to find out whose number this is?"

"Probably," Cheryl answered. That challenge didn't seem too difficult. How hard could it be to find out who a specific phone number belonged to? If they found that, they'd find the person who sent the text, and, if that person was telling the truth, it would hopefully lead to answers about Mark. "I'm not sure how, but I bet there's a way."

"Oh, Cheryl, if there is a way to find this out, it would mean so much. Could you help me?"

Cheryl didn't know what to say. She already had plenty going on—with the store during holiday season and getting the gift box for Mitzi—but then she saw Lydia's pained, earnest face and realized there was only one thing she could do.

"Of course I'll help you."

CHAPTER TWO

A busload of tourists arrived shortly after Cheryl's conversation with Lydia, and she spent the next hour ringing up purchases for a giddy group of older women shopping for their grandkids' Christmas stockings. By the time the shop had cleared out, Esther Miller, her friend Naomi's daughter and Lydia's best friend, had shown up for her shift and was helping Lydia restock the suddenly depleted shelves.

The girls were chattering in Pennsylvania Dutch as they worked, and Cheryl couldn't understand a word of it, but by the way Lydia pulled out her phone to show Esther, Cheryl assumed she was filling her in on the anonymous text. As far as Cheryl knew, whoever sent it had not yet responded with more information about who they were or what had happened to Mark.

Speaking of which... Cheryl decided things were under control and that she could take a few minutes to see what she could find out about the mysterious phone number. She sat down on the stool behind the counter and pulled out the scrap of paper where she had written the number down. First, she used the store's phone to call the number and held her breath while it rang. There was no answer. Next, she tried it with her cell phone, but again, no one picked up. Her call was dumped into an anonymous voice-mail box. She left a message asking the owner of the phone to please call her back. Well, that would have been too easy, she supposed.

Next, she went into the small office at the back of the shop, turned on the store's computer, and pulled up a browser window. She had heard there were Web sites that could tell you who a particular phone was registered to—or, more specifically, who the monthly bill was sent to—and she quickly found a site and typed the number in eagerly. The Web site returned that the number was blocked.

Cheryl refreshed the page and typed in her own phone number, just to make sure the site worked, and it confirmed that the account her phone number was registered to was paid by a Cheryl Cooper in Sugarcreek, Ohio. So she knew the site worked, but it hadn't gotten her any closer to finding out who owned the number.

Next, she searched online directories and tried Googling the number itself, but she came up with nothing.

Cheryl's fingers hovered over the computer keyboard. There had to be some way to trace the number. The police did this all the time on TV, so there must be some...

And then it was so obvious what to do next she couldn't believe she hadn't thought of it before.

"Lydia, I have an idea," Cheryl said, stepping back out into the front of the shop.

Lydia set down the stack of wrapped fudge squares she'd been arranging and walked toward Cheryl.

"Would it be all right with you if I checked with the police to see what they can tell me about this phone number?" Cheryl asked as Lydia stopped in front of her. "I think they might be able to trace the number."

Lydia's eyes widened. "That would be wonderful. Please, talk to whoever you need to if it will help us find who sent this."

"All right then." Cheryl looked around the shop. Between Lydia and Esther, they seemed to have things covered. "I'm going to run out for a few minutes."

Both girls nodded, and then Lydia walked back toward Esther, and they continued chattering in Pennsylvania Dutch while they worked. Cheryl slipped on her coat, grabbed her purse, and went out the back door of the shop to the parking lot. A few minutes later, she was walking into the lobby of the Sugarcreek Police Station.

Cheryl said hello to Delores, the receptionist at the front desk, and Delores buzzed the police chief's office. They chatted for a few minutes, and then Delores's phone buzzed, and she said the police chief was ready to see Cheryl. She walked through the frosted glass door and into the police chief's office.

Chief Twitchell looked up from his computer when Cheryl stepped into his office.

"Hello, Cheryl." He quickly closed the window on his screen, but not before Cheryl saw that he'd been playing a matching game. "What can I do for you?" Cheryl had worked with the police chief on a few other puzzles that had come her way since she'd moved to Sugarcreek, and he was friendly. She felt confident he would help her if he could.

"Hi, Chief Twitchell. I was wondering if you could help me with something."

He nodded and gestured for her to sit in one of the green vinyl chairs across from his desk.

"I'm trying to trace the owner of a certain cell phone number. Could you help me find that?"

Chief Twitchell sat back in his chair. "Can I ask why?" The police chief was in his mid-forties with salt-and-pepper hair and a long nose, but he had a smile on his face.

Cheryl nodded. "Do you remember a Troyer?"

The policeman nodded. "Yes I do. We looked into that case thoroughly, Cheryl, and it was a clear-cut case of a runaway. He was wantin' to start a new life, away from the Amish, and so he did it."

"That may be. But his cousin Lydia just got a text from someone at this number"—she slid the paper where she'd written the number across his desk toward him—"saying they know what happened to him. And Lydia would very much like to find out who sent it and what they know."

He cocked an eyebrow, but Cheryl rushed on. "I tried tracking the number online, but it's blocked. I was hoping you could contact the phone company and help me find out whose number it is."

She pasted a hopeful smile on to her face. He smiled and shook his head.

"Do you know which carrier this number is with?"

"No," she admitted. She had no way to know which phone company the phone was tied to.

"It's goin' to be a lot of work in that case."

"I'm sorry about that," Cheryl said. "But I really would be grateful. It would mean so much to her to find out if someone really does know what happened to her cousin."

He tented his hands. He seemed to be considering. "The texts could be from a disposable phone."

Cheryl hadn't thought about that. She had seen those phones for sale at drugstores. They were cheap to buy and easy to activate and came with no contract. You could simply use one and dispose of it when you were done. If the text had come from a phone like that, it would be very hard to track. But surely the police had their ways.

"Well, that would be harder," she admitted. "But would you be willing to try anyway?"

"Did you try callin' the number?"

"Yes, I did. No one picked up."

He hesitated. "Cheryl, it's probably a joke. Someone tryin' to get a laugh."

Cheryl nodded. "I thought about that. But at least if you tracked it, then we'd know, right?"

He stared at her for a moment and then sighed. "I'll see what I can do. But it will take some time to work with all the different phone companies. And I just want to make sure you realize that you may not like what you find."

"I know Lydia will be glad for any answers you can give her," Cheryl said. "And I would be so thankful."

"I'll see what I can find out." He gave her a weary smile.

She said good-bye and walked out of his office, but instead of heading straight back to her store, she decided to pay a visit to her friend Naomi Miller. Cheryl had some money to give Naomi from the sale of her jams, and this would be a good time to do that as well as get Naomi's take on the whole Mark situation. Naomi had a cool head, and she also knew just about everyone in the area. She would no doubt be able to tell Cheryl more about Mark's disappearance. Lydia had said she could talk to anyone she needed to about this, so she knew Lydia wouldn't mind.

It was close to time for Esther's shift to be over, so Cheryl called the store to ask if she wanted a ride home, and Esther accepted gratefully. Lydia would handle the shop until Cheryl came back.

Cheryl put Esther's bike in her trunk, and then she and Esther climbed into Cheryl's car and drove down the long country road that led toward the Millers' farm. As she drove, Cheryl took in the beauty of the rolling hills and the charm of the animals at pasture. The fields were mostly picked clean by this point in the year, but they still looked starkly beautiful under the brilliantly blue late-autumn sky. Every time she drove down these roads, Cheryl thought about how different her life was now than it had been just a few months ago, before she had quit her high-pressure banking job in Columbus and come out here to take over the Swiss Miss. She missed some things about the city, but when she took in the serene beauty that surrounded her daily, she was so thankful to be here.

Cheryl turned into the Millers' long dirt driveway and pulled up in front of the solid, squat farmhouse. The corn had been gathered in for the year, so the corn maze had been razed, and the animals for their petting zoo were safely tucked away in the barn. Off in the distance she could see someone—was it Levi?—splitting logs, no doubt stocking the wood pile in preparation for the long winter ahead. Esther led Cheryl up onto the wooden porch, and just as Esther was about to reach for the handle, the solid wood door swung open. Naomi's teenage daughter Elizabeth stood just inside.

"Hello. We heard your car drive up." Elizabeth was eighteen and very pretty with dark brown hair, wide brown eyes, and an easy laugh. She looked particularly charming today in her dark green dress, and she had a soothing voice and dreamy artistic temperament.

Cheryl had to laugh. No doubt most of the Millers' visitors arrived on bike or by buggy, and her car probably stood out.

"Please come inside," Elizabeth said, gesturing for Cheryl to step in. Esther followed behind her. "Esther, when you get cleaned up, we could use your help. We are working on pie crusts."

"I will be right there," Esther said and tromped up the stairs toward the bedrooms.

"We are in here." The strings of Elizabeth's *kapp* trailed behind her as she led Cheryl to the kitchen. Naomi was working behind a long butcher-block counter in the middle of the room. The stove and sink were behind her along one wall, and a well-used dining table took up most of the far side of the room. On the wall hung framed verses from one of Naomi's favorite hymns, which Elizabeth had written out in calligraphy and decorated with beautifully drawn floral vines. The scent of spicy apple cider hung in the air.

"Hello, Cheryl," Naomi said, looking up from a large bowl of flour on the counter in front of her.

"Goodness. You weren't kidding about making pie crusts." Cheryl laughed. The majority of the counter was covered with bowls and piles of flour and butter. They must be cooking for a crowd.

"There will be a fund-raiser on Saturday for a boy in our church," Naomi explained as she used two knives to cut butter into the bowl of flour. "We are making pies." Naomi gestured for her friend to come in and sit down in one of the sturdy wooden dining chairs. "Would you like some hot cider?"

"That sounds wonderful," Cheryl said, settling into the unpadded chair. She was amazed at how comfortable and welcoming this kitchen always felt. Elizabeth moved to the propane stove and ladled hot cider into an earthenware mug and then moved around the counter and set it in front of Cheryl. Cheryl felt a sense of calm settle over her. Somehow despite the three teenagers who lived under Naomi's roof, plus her two older stepsons—Levi and Caleb, as well as the extended family and friends who were always in and out, this kitchen always felt peaceful. Cheryl soaked it in.

"This smells delicious," Cheryl said, wrapping her cold fingers around the mug. As Elizabeth returned to her task, Cheryl looked at the bowls of dough spread across the counter. "The pies will still be good by Saturday?" Cheryl didn't know all that much about cooking, but she was surprised to hear the pies would last that long.

Naomi smiled, and Elizabeth laughed as she resumed her work on her own bowl. "We are just making the dough for the crusts today. We will keep it in the refrigerator until later in the week. When you are making this many pies, it pays to get started early."

"Got it." When Cheryl had first met Naomi, she had been surprised to learn that they had a small, propane-fueled refrigerator, but she had come to learn that the Amish in this district weren't against all technology, but tended to avoid appliances and conveniences that plugged them into the power grid.

"That makes more sense." She watched Naomi and Elizabeth work for a moment, in awe of their quiet efficiency. These were women who had plenty of experience making pies.

"Thank you for bringing Esther home. You have saved her a bike ride," Naomi said.

"It wasn't a problem." Cheryl took a sip of the cider. It was hot and sweet and delicious. "Besides, I wanted to talk to you anyway."

"Oh, really? Talk to me about what?"

"Well, for one thing, your spiced cranberry jam." Cheryl dug into her purse and pulled out an envelope of cash. "People are going crazy for it in the shop. I can barely keep it in stock. When can you bring in more?"

Naomi gestured with her flour-covered hands for her to leave the envelope on the table.

"I am so glad to hear it. I can certainly make more next week, after this fund-raiser is over," Naomi said, smiling. "It was my *grossmudder's* recipe, and I love to make it at this time of year."

"That would be wonderful." Cheryl took another sip of the cider. "I also wanted to let you know I'm putting together a care package to send to Aunt Mitzi," Cheryl said. "I wanted to send her some of her favorite things, and I was hoping you might be willing to include some jam in that."

"Of course." Naomi nodded. "I would be happy to. She always seemed to enjoy my apricot preserves. I will get you a couple of jars of that to put in the package."

"That would be wonderful." Cheryl looked down at her mug of cider, trying to figure out how to broach the main reason she'd come, when Esther came stomping down the stairs and into the kitchen.

"Cheryl, did you tell them what happened today?" Esther said, lifting an apron off the hook by the door to the pantry and tying the strings around her waist.

"What's this?" Naomi turned to Cheryl, her eyebrows raised.

"That's the other thing I wanted to talk to you about," Cheryl said. Esther stepped behind the counter with her mother and sister. "Do you know anything about a boy named Mark Troyer?"

"Oh yes," Naomi said, nodding. "That was a very sad story."

Esther reached for a bowl and the canister of flour. Elizabeth nodded and then turned away to bring her bowl to the sink. She started sprinkling in cold water as Naomi continued.

"He disappeared one day, and his poor family never found out where he went," Naomi said. She abandoned the knives and began to work the dough with her hands. "It was so terrible. I cannot even imagine what poor Joanna must have gone through. She never found out what happened to her son." Her hands worked quickly, using her fingers to break up the butter and spread it through the flour.

"But it turns out someone *does* know what happened to him," Esther said, her eyes wide as she measured flour out of a large ceramic crock with a metal measuring cup.

"What do you mean?" Naomi stopped working the dough.

"Lydia Troyer got a text today," Esther said eagerly. Cheryl had never seen her so animated before. But then again, Mark's disappearance had been big news around here a few years back. No doubt everyone who'd heard about the story then would be interested to hear what had happened today. Even quiet, dreamy Elizabeth had paused her work and was listening. "She doesn't know who it came from, but whoever sent it said they knew what happened to Mark."

Naomi turned back to her bowl and began pressing the dough with her fingers again. "Did this text"—Cheryl noted the discomfort with which Naomi used the word *text*—"say anything more?"

"That was all," Cheryl said. "And when we tried calling the number to see who sent it, no one picked up. Lydia asked me to help her figure out the sender, hoping it might lead to some real information about Mark. And she told me a bit about what happened when he disappeared, but she was excited, and I wasn't sure I was getting the whole story."

"Ah. I see. You were hoping I could fill in the holes," Naomi said.

"Exactly." Cheryl was relieved that it was out there now. She just hoped Naomi would say yes. She knew her friend tried not to gossip, but she hoped Naomi would see this as a way to help find answers.

"I only know what I heard," Naomi finally said, her hands moving quickly in the bowl. "But it would mean so much to

Joanna to find answers, so I'll tell you what I know. But why don't you start with what Lydia told you."

Cheryl nodded. "Lydia told me some people think he ran away, and others worry that something bad happened to him. She said he left his job at Weaver Lumber and was headed home, but he never made it. They found his car outside the bus station in Columbus a few weeks later. And she said something about a bloody shirt in the trash outside the Honey Bee."

"So she didn't tell you about Jessica Stockton?" Esther volunteered as she dumped a stick of butter into her bowl.

"What?" Cheryl blew on her cider. "No, she didn't mention anything about Jessica." Cheryl had met Jessica Stockton; she was a "Yoder Toter" or an Englisch driver the Amish hired to take them places farther away than a horse and buggy could go. It was strange that Lydia hadn't mentioned this bit to Cheryl.

"From what we heard, it's not true that no one saw him again after he left work that day," Naomi said. "Jessica Stockton says she was driving along Cherry Ridge Drive and saw a car stopped at the shoulder. It was a rainy night, and she worried that the car had broken down and someone needed help, so she pulled over."

"Mark was behind the wheel, and there was a *girl* in the car with him," Esther said. Naomi gave her daughter a harsh look, no doubt warning her to watch her tone, though again, Cheryl could see why teenagers would have taken special note of the facts of the case. It was one of their peers who had disappeared, after all.

"Who was it?" Cheryl asked.

"No one knows," Naomi said. "Jessica did not recognize her. Some people suggested it was a sign he had run off with the girl, but we do not know who she was, so no one can say."

"But then, Mark was kind of a player," Esther said.

"A *player*?" Naomi narrowed her eyes at her daughter.

"He flirted with a lot of different girls," Esther translated for her mother.

"Where did you learn a word like that?" Naomi said, shaking her head. Cheryl stifled a smile. She knew her friend worried about her children being exposed to the world too much, but Cheryl secretly thought it was funny to see Amish teens, especially someone as reserved and responsible as Esther, experimenting with Englisch slang.

"Lydia," Esther said. "Anyway, Mark was seen with a girl the night he disappeared. No one knows who she was. And then they found his car at the bus station, so people think he got on a bus and ran away."

"But if he had a car, why would he go to the bus station to run away?" Cheryl asked. "Why wouldn't he simply have driven wherever he wanted to go?"

"You did not see his car," Esther volunteered. "He is lucky he made it as far as Columbus. If he was trying to go any farther, he definitely needed a better way to do it."

"It was a rather old vehicle," Naomi added. "It broke down a lot."

Elizabeth giggled. "That is like saying babies make a little bit of noise."

Cheryl supposed that theory made some sense. If Mark had been trying to run away, he wouldn't want to risk breaking down on the way. And it sounded as if he'd already had car trouble the night he disappeared. Maybe he really had abandoned his car at the bus station and gotten on a bus to somewhere else far away. Cheryl hoped that was the case. Because the other option...

Well, she didn't like to think about it, but she'd lived in Columbus long enough to know that cars were often found near the bus station for other reasons. Often, when the police found an abandoned vehicle in that area, they were likely to find a body turn up somewhere nearby soon afterward.

But that hadn't happened in this case, she reminded herself. Just because his car had been found there didn't mean anything bad had happened to him. The police had taken it as evidence that he'd run away. She would continue to hope that was the case. But why would he simply abandon his car? If he no longer needed it, why not try to sell it?

Something else had been nagging at her ever since she'd heard that Mark had a car. She hadn't met too many Amish teens who drove.

"Isn't it unusual for an Amish teenager to have a car?" she ventured.

"It is not common, but it happens," Naomi said.

"Lydia is saving up for a car," Esther volunteered. Naomi ignored that comment.

"It is allowed during the running-around time, just like cell phones and other things that are generally *verboten*. But cars are costly—not only to purchase, but to maintain. And it is often difficult to get the paperwork necessary to get a license. An Amish teen would first need to apply for a social security number, and that means getting a birth certificate," Naomi said. Cheryl knew that the Amish did not, as a rule, obtain these things like most Englisch did. "And then you must learn to drive and find a car to practice in. You have to want it pretty badly to go through all the steps required to make it happen. Thankfully, my children have not been so motivated."

"Yet." Esther smiled. Cheryl could see she was teasing her mother, but Naomi didn't seem to think it was funny.

"So Mark must have wanted a car pretty badly to go through all it took to get one," Cheryl said. "Do you know why?"

"I do not know why anyone would want to own one of those things," Naomi said. "They may be convenient, but they are expensive and dangerous." She smiled shyly at Cheryl. "No offense."

"I can understand why you'd want one," Esther said. "It would have taken me at least half an hour to get home after work today. It took only a few minutes in Cheryl's car."

Naomi's lips were pressed into a line.

"I heard he was taking art classes," Elizabeth volunteered. "That is why he wanted the car, so he could get to his art classes."

Elizabeth was still facing toward the sink, though she turned her head toward the room as she offered this piece of information. She had been so quiet that Cheryl had almost forgotten she was there, but this was an interesting bit of information she hadn't heard before.

"How did you hear that?" Esther asked.

Elizabeth shrugged. "I do not remember. I think someone must have mentioned it at one of the singings."

"What sort of art classes?" Cheryl said. "Do you know where he took them?"

"I do not know," Elizabeth said. "It is just what I heard."

Cheryl made a mental note to ask Lydia whether she knew anything about art classes later. She relished the warmth of the cider through the ceramic mug and thought through what else Lydia had told her.

"Lydia also said something about a shirt with blood on it?" Cheryl said.

"Yes, Kathy Snyder found it in the trash can behind the Honey Bee. That was one of the things that made people believe something bad had happened to him." Naomi squished the dough through her fingers, squashing the butter into smaller and smaller pieces.

"They never figured out how it came to be there?"

"Not that I know of." Naomi's voice was quiet. "Of course no one wanted to believe..."

"How did they know it was Mark's shirt?" Cheryl asked.

"I am not sure. You would have to ask Kathy."

Cheryl decided to change her line of questioning. "Do you think Mark ran away?"

Naomi's hands stilled. "It is not for me to say. I do not know."

"I heard he was into gambling and ran up a big debt at the racetrack that came due," Esther said. "That is why he ran off."

Naomi gave Esther a serious look. "Where did you hear that?"

Esther shrugged. "I do not know. It is what people say."

"We do not repeat what people say," Naomi said sternly. "We do not spread gossip."

Esther ducked her head, acknowledging her mother's words.

"I cannot believe he ran off because of a gambling debt," Elizabeth said. Her voice was soft, but her words were firm. "I think someone has watched too many movies. Besides, how would you know what he would do? You were only a kid at the time."

"I was thirteen. Old enough to know what was going on," Esther said defiantly.

Elizabeth shrugged and went back to washing out the bowl.

"Elizabeth, if it wasn't gambling, what do you think happened?" Cheryl said.

Elizabeth thought for a moment, and then she shut off the faucet. "I cannot say. But I do hope someone will find out," she finally said. "If this person who sent the text to Lydia really does know what happened, I hope you will try to find him."

"How about you, Naomi? If you had to guess, what would you say?"

Naomi wiped her hands on her apron and twisted the fabric in her hands.

"I do not know," she said again. "But no one has heard from him this whole time. If he were out there somewhere, wouldn't he have tried to contact his *maam*, if only to let her know he was okay?" She looked down at the counter. She seemed to consider her words carefully. "All I know is, it would be such a gift to Joanna to finally have answers. Even if it is bad news, at least she would know."

Cheryl nodded. "I think the texts may well be a joke, but I'll do my best to find the person who sent them anyway. Then she would know. And if anyone out there really does know what happened, I'll do everything I can to find out."

For a moment, there was only quiet in the kitchen.

"And we will do everything we can to help you," Naomi finally said. "As I have often heard you say, together we will get to the bottom of this."

CHAPTER THREE

A few minutes later, Cheryl and Naomi climbed into Cheryl's car and started off down the road. Naomi had offered to introduce Cheryl to Mark's parents so she could ask them about what happened when Mark disappeared. Cheryl had called the shop, and Lydia said she could handle watching the store for a while longer, so Naomi and Cheryl decided now was as good a time for their visit as any.

"The Troyers' farm is just a few miles down the road," Naomi said, pointing away from town. "It is that big white farmhouse with the maple in front that blazes so orange every fall."

That could describe just about every house in the district—half of which were owned by families named Troyer—but Naomi promised to tell her where to turn, and as they drove, she filled Cheryl in on this branch of the Troyer family. Mark's father, Saul, was the elder brother of Lydia's father. Mark was the eldest of eight children, born less than a year after Joanna and Saul had married. The youngest child was not even one year old. Elizabeth, Naomi said, had gone to stay with the family and help Joanna after the birth. It was not uncommon for a teenage girl to help take care of the family while the mother cared for the new baby. Joanna and Naomi attended school together and had always been friendly, though they were not especially close. Saul was well respected in their community and was among the most faithful to the *Ordnung*, or set of rules the community agreed to live by.

After Mark disappeared, Naomi said, Joanna had gone to the police, begging for help to find her son. Saul had been upset as well, but he quickly came to the conclusion that Mark had left them without a word, and after not too many months passed, he had given away to the family's next youngest son, Benjamin, the best parcel of his land, the piece that had been destined to belong to the eldest son.

"Goodness. Isn't it a big deal to give away your son's inheritance?" Cheryl said as she slowed to turn into the driveway Naomi indicated.

"It is significant." Naomi nodded. "Joanna is the sweetest, most hardworking woman you will ever meet. I know she wouldn't have done it if it were up to her. But Saul is ... " She shifted in her seat, pulling the seat belt away from her. "Saul can come across as a bit harsh sometimes. He likes to follow the rules precisely. And if he really thought Mark had turned his back on them and run off to the Englisch, I could see how he might have done it."

"If that's the case, they must have been pretty upset about him leaving and pretty certain he'd done it on purpose," Cheryl said, trying to read Naomi's face.

Naomi hesitated. "Or pretty certain he wasn't coming back," she finally said.

Cheryl pulled up in front of a white clapboard farmhouse with a tall maple tree in the yard, though its limbs were now bare.

They climbed out of the car, and Naomi led the way to the house. The yard was neat and well kept, and the house looked large enough to hold eight children comfortably. Rows of black pants and dark-hued dresses hung on the clothesline strung up next to the house.

By the time Cheryl and Naomi reached the front door, a teenage girl in a dark purple dress was opening it.

"Good afternoon, Matilda," Naomi said. She introduced Cheryl, and the girl nodded, greeted them, and turned, gesturing for them to follow her into the hallway. She adjusted her glasses and eyed Cheryl, like she was uncertain what to make of her.

"Mother is just finishing up in the kitchen," she said. "But she will be out in just a moment. You may sit in the front room."

Matilda gestured to the high-backed chairs on one side of the front room with a large picture window, and Cheryl settled gently into one while Naomi took a seat in the one across from her. Matilda nodded and then turned and stepped out of the room without a word.

Naomi gave Cheryl an encouraging smile. "Matilda is very studious," she said. Cheryl gathered this was her way of excusing the girl's manners.

Cheryl looked around the room, which was clean and spare, with wide-pine floors and sturdy wooden furniture. The only decorations were a few wooden figurines carved to look like farm animals and a wooden box made of smoothly polished rosewood.

A moment later a woman walked into the room, and Naomi stood and introduced Joanna, Mark's mother. She had brown hair threaded with gray tucked up neatly under her kapp, and she wore a deep navy dress, but she had pink cheeks and a sweet smile.

"Welcome," Joanna said, wiping her hands on her apron. Cheryl could tell immediately that Joanna had all the warmth her daughter lacked. She was cheerful and made Cheryl feel at ease right away, gesturing for them to sit down. "It is good of you to stop by. Would you like *kaffee*? And we have some excellent mince pie that Matilda made."

Cheryl never ceased to be amazed at how there seemed to be pie on offer at every Amish house she visited. She supposed they must burn plenty of calories doing so much labor by hand.

"Just kaffee for me, please," Naomi said, and Cheryl asked for the same. Joanna gestured for them to sit in the chairs in the front room and returned a moment later carrying cups of coffee for each of them as well as little bowls of milk and sugar on a metal tray.

"It is so nice of you to visit," Joanna said, settling down on a stiff chair across from them. She set the tray down and handed a cup of coffee to each woman.

"Thank you for seeing us," Naomi started. "I wanted to bring Cheryl by to meet you. She's taken over the Swiss Miss now that Mitzi has gone off to Papua New Guinea."

"Oh, I love that store. There are always so many interesting things to see inside."

"Thank you. It's been fun running it so far."

"I believe my niece Lydia works there sometimes, doesn't she?" Joanna said.

"She does, actually." Cheryl took a quick gulp of the coffee to steady herself. "In fact, that's sort of what I was hoping to talk to you about. Lydia was in the shop today when she got some interesting news."

Joanna tilted her head, waiting for Cheryl to go on.

"Lydia got a text"—she looked to make sure Joanna had followed, and Joanna nodded—"from a number she didn't recognize. Whoever sent the text said they know what happened to Mark."

Joanna gasped and her face paled, but then her eyes widened and a look of hopefulness crossed her face.

"What does it mean?" she said, looking from Cheryl to Naomi.

"We are not sure," Naomi said. "But Cheryl is looking into it for Lydia. If there is any way to find out who sent that message, Cheryl will figure it out."

"And do you think..." Joanna hesitated. "If you find who sent it..."

"We are hoping it will lead to answers," Naomi said.

Joanna clasped her hands. "Oh, Naomi, is it really possible?" She pressed her lips together, and her eyes began to water. "It would mean so much to know where he is, if he's..."

Just then a door at the rear of the house slammed shut, and heavy footsteps started across the wooden floor.

"That's Saul," Joanna said, standing up quickly. "Saul, come here," she called, and a moment later a tall man with a long brown beard stepped into the room. "Saul, this is Cheryl. She's a friend of Naomi's, and guess what? She has seen a message from someone who knows what happened to Mark."

"What?" Saul stopped short. He was a large, imposing man with broad shoulders and a chiseled face topped by heavy dark eyebrows. The hours he spent working on the fields showed on his muscled frame. He said something to Joanna in Pennsylvania Dutch, and she answered in the same language then gestured to Cheryl. "What do you mean?" he said to her in English.

Cheryl explained about Lydia and the text, and he listened, his face hard.

"Can you believe it?" Joanna said. Cheryl couldn't understand how a woman as slight as Joanna was married to a hulking man like Saul. "After all this time, someone might really know what happened."

"I do not believe it." Saul crossed his arms over his chest. "I do not think it is likely that this mysterious message from an unknown sender will suddenly tell us where our son ran off to. And I'll thank you not to raise false hope in his maam. It was very hard on us all when Mark left, and my wife will believe anything if it means getting word from him. But I will not have it."

Cheryl looked from Joanna—who looked crushed—to Naomi, whose hand shook as she lowered her coffee cup.

"I do not know who you are, but please do not come in here and raise my wife's hopes. If Mark wants to get in contact with us, he knows where we are. Until that day, we do not speak of him."

With that, Saul turned and strode out of the room.

As Cheryl pulled out on to Sunset Road to drive Naomi home, she tried to figure out how to make sense of what had happened at the Troyers'.

"You have to understand," Naomi started before Cheryl could say anything. "Saul loved Mark. *Loves* him. He thought the world of him, his first son."

Cheryl tapped her hands on the steering wheel. "It sure doesn't seem like that." Barren fields flew by as she drove back toward the Millers' farm.

"I know—from the outside, it doesn't. That is what I am trying to say. But he only acts that way because he loved Mark so much and felt so betrayed when he left. He doesn't want to talk about him, not because he doesn't love his son, but because he loves him so much it is hard to not be upset when his name comes up."

Cheryl thought about this. She had a hard time believing it, especially after Naomi had told her that they'd given Mark's land away to his brother. Weren't those the actions of a parent who *didn't* care about his son? She had no doubt Joanna loved Mark. That was clear from the way she talked about him. But was Saul too worried about feeling betrayed by his son and not worried enough about what had happened to him?

Cheryl tried to remind herself that she wasn't a parent and had no idea what kinds of emotions a father would be feeling in this situation. Still, it didn't sit right. And there was one other thing she had noticed.

"They both talked about it like they were sure Mark left on purpose."

Naomi was quiet for a moment, and the only sound was the hum of the car engine. "Perhaps it is easier to accept that than think about the alternative," she finally said.

Cheryl supposed that might be true. Surely it would be easier for a mother to imagine her son was still out there somewhere—but she still wondered if there was more to it than that.

"Naomi, you don't think…" She tried to figure out how to phrase this. "Saul couldn't have…"

Naomi hesitated. Then, after a few beats, she said, "No." She took a deep breath. "No, I do not think Saul had anything to do with it." But the way she said it, a little too quickly after that pause, made Cheryl wonder if she was telling the whole truth.

"I know it doesn't seem to make sense, Cheryl, but believe me when I say that what looks like harshness to you is rooted in love."

Cheryl nodded. She believed that this was what her friend wanted to be true. But that didn't mean she wasn't going to see what more she could find out about Saul Troyer.

CHAPTER FOUR

Lydia was ringing up a group of women who were buying the last of Naomi's spiced cranberry jam when Cheryl got back to the store. Cheryl chatted with them for a few moments, and then, still ooahing and aahing over how much they loved the shop, they headed out the door.

"Thank you for keeping an eye on things this afternoon," Cheryl said, tucking her purse behind the counter.

"It was not a problem. I'm happy to have the hours."

"Well, I appreciate it. And it was a productive day. I talked to several people about Mark." Cheryl filled Lydia in on her conversations with Chief Twitchell, with Naomi, and with Saul and Joanna Troyer.

"You met my aunt and uncle?" Lydia said. "What did you think of Uncle Saul?"

"I'm not really sure," Cheryl admitted. "Why?"

"Well, a lot of people see him and assume Mark must have run away. He's known to be pretty harsh. But I don't believe that is what happened."

"Did Mark have any particular reason to want to get away from his father?" she probed.

"Not that I know of," Lydia said.

Cheryl nodded and started cashing out the antique register. Judging by the stack of bills in the drawer, it had been a very good afternoon indeed.

"Tell me more about the rest of the family," Cheryl said, counting out the bills quickly.

"Matilda is the oldest daughter," Lydia said, rolling her eyes.

"I met her. Why the eye roll?"

"She is...well." Lydia laughed. "For her, everything is black and white. She takes the rules very seriously. We call her the Bishop."

"The Bishop?"

"She thinks we do it because she is so pious. But it is really because she would very much like to be in charge. She likes to tell people what do."

"Ah."

"So first was Mark, then Matilda and after them, Benjamin. He just built a house on the land on the far corner of the property."

"He inherited Mark's land."

"Yes." She nodded. "He's nice enough. Quiet, polite, that kind of thing. And then there's Ruth, Mary, Elias, Sarah, and the baby Samuel."

"Is there any chance any of them might know about where Mark went?"

"If they do, they have kept it quiet so far." She considered this for a moment. "Matilda and Benjamin are baptized, so the text could not have come from them. Ruth is the only one old enough to be in her running-around time, but I do not believe she has a cell phone."

"Could you find out?"

"I will ask."

Cheryl placed the stacks of cash into an envelope. She would deposit it at the bank on her way home tonight.

"Elizabeth Miller heard that he might have been taking art classes," Cheryl ventured. "Do you know anything about that?"

"Oh yes, he was," Lydia said. "Over at the community college by Canton. He was very interested in art, sculpture especially. He was always carving things and making puzzle boxes and that sort of thing. He made one for me not long before he left, in fact."

Cheryl thought back to the few wooden decorations she'd seen in Saul's and Joanna's home. It sounded likely Mark had made those.

"Do you think it's at all possible Mark might have left to pursue his interest in art?" Cheryl asked.

Lydia shook her head. "No way. He *had* been looking into ways to pursue art, but again, Mark would never have left without saying good-bye. Even if he had decided to become an artist, which isn't exactly a career choice you can make when you're Amish"— she gave Cheryl a significant look—"he would have told us he was leaving. I'm sure of that."

Lydia was so certain about this point, but that didn't leave a great alternative. In any case, Cheryl would try to find out more about his interest in art and whether it might have played into his disappearance. For now, she had other questions for Lydia.

"Do you know of anyone who might have wanted to hurt Mark?"

Lydia looked startled.

"If he didn't run away, then something bad probably happened to him, right? I'm trying to find out who might have wanted Mark out of the picture."

"Goodness." Lydia thought for a moment. Her face was sober. "I guess I never thought of it quite like that. It's hard to imagine anyone hurting my cousin on purpose. But now that you bring it up, there were a few people who were upset at Mark...but I just don't know. It's hard to imagine anyone I know getting mad enough at Mark to...well, to hurt him."

Cheryl found it hard to believe as well, but she'd promised she'd help Lydia, and that meant looking into all possible options. Any of the people who were mad at Mark might have a cell phone or know something about what went on the night he disappeared. "Can you tell me who those people were?"

Lydia looked uncomfortable, but then nodded, like she'd made a decision.

"Mark was...attractive," she said, her cheeks flushing a bit. "A lot of the girls in the church had crushes on him. And he—well, he did like to flirt."

Cheryl had guessed as much, based on the way Esther and Elizabeth seemed to know all about him. She knew better than to ask for a photo though. The Amish did not take photographs, believing them to be graven images forbidden in the Bible.

"There were sometimes people who took his flirting a little more seriously than he intended," Lydia said carefully. "There is one girl, Sarah Yutzy—who was spending time with Henry

Detweiler. But then Mark flirted with her at a singing, and she wasn't interested in Henry anymore. Sarah seemed really shattered when Mark disappeared." Lydia rolled her eyes. "And Henry was pretty upset too. Sarah might not be the sharpest tack, but she is pretty. But was Henry mad enough about it to do anything to Mark?" She shook her head. "There was some old tension there, I guess. Maybe..." But she looked dubious.

Cheryl reached for the scrap of paper where she'd been recording notes and wrote down the names Henry Detweiler and Sarah Yutzy.

"Could Sarah have done anything to hurt Mark?" Cheryl asked.

Lydia laughed at that. "No. Sarah is so meek and mild she couldn't muster the imagination to do something as original as that."

Cheryl stifled a smile. Teenage girls were pretty much the same everywhere, Amish or not. Still, she thought Sarah might be worth talking to, in case she remembered anything about Mark's final days in Sugarcreek. Maybe she had a cell phone. And there was that as-yet unidentified girl who had been in the car with Mark the night he left. Was there any chance it could have been Sarah?

"Were there other girls who might have been brokenhearted about Mark?"

Lydia thought for a moment. "There was Hannah Hilty. He flirted with her a lot. She liked to dress Englisch, so they had that in common."

Cheryl added the name to her list.

"Was there anyone special in his life? Any girl he paid more attention to than others?"

Lydia paused. "No. He never seemed to settle on a girl he liked best."

Cheryl nodded. "Who were his friends?"

"Like I said, Mark and I were close."

Cheryl nodded again to acknowledge this.

"He was also very good friends with my brother Elam. Elam is married now and all wrapped up in his new baby, but before Mark disappeared I would say Elam was probably his closest male friend."

"Would it be possible for me to talk to Elam?"

"Sure. He doesn't know anything about Mark, but I'll check with him and let you know what he says. And I will pray that you find answers about Mark," Lydia said as she slipped her phone back into her pocket and untied the strings of her apron.

Cheryl felt the weight of the girl's expectations heavy on her shoulders.

"I'll do my best," Cheryl said. "But you know that I'm not a detective or the police, right? I don't have any special skills that will allow me to figure it out when the police couldn't."

"The police did not try," Lydia said. She lifted her apron off over her neck and folded it neatly in her hands. "You will be able to because you care, and they did not."

Cheryl did care; that was true. After seeing how deeply Mark's disappearance had affected so many people in the community, especially Lydia and Mark's mother, she did want to find answers if she could.

"I will do my best," Cheryl said again.

"Thank you." She turned toward the back of the store. "I have to go now," Lydia said. "I am supposed to help my maam with dinner."

Cheryl looked up at the clock and realized they had been talking for nearly half an hour.

"Goodness. I hadn't realized it was so late," she said. She thanked Lydia for monitoring the store so much of the day, and then as Lydia left, she finished tidying up and got her things together. She slipped the envelope of cash into her purse, along with the scrap of paper where she'd taken notes, grabbed her coat, and turned out the lights.

Cheryl walked to the bank and made her deposit, and then she walked back to the parking lot behind the shop and climbed into her car. She pulled the list of people to talk to out to study it one more time. Most of the people named on her list were Amish, and she wasn't going to be able to talk to them tonight, but she could try to get ahold of Jessica Stockton, the Englisch driver who had seen Mark at the side of the road the night he disappeared. She slipped on her headset and looked up Jessica's number, and then she dialed and backed out of her parking space.

She could see the church's argument for keeping technology out of Amish homes, but she certainly did appreciate the convenience of being able to make a simple phone call. Jessica's voice mail picked up, so Cheryl left a message, asking Jessica to call her back.

As Cheryl drove, she thought through the names of the girls Lydia had told her about. Was one of them the mysterious girl who had been in the car with Mark the night he disappeared? She hoped Jessica would be able to shed some light on that. She had a feeling that finding that girl would be the key to this whole mystery.

Chapter Five

The next morning Cheryl was stoking the fire in the potbellied stove in the corner of the store, hoping to take the edge off the early winter chill, when the door of the Swiss Miss opened. Cheryl turned around to tell the visitor that the store wouldn't open for a few more minutes, but then she saw that it was Jessica Stockton.

"Hello, Jessica," Cheryl said, setting down the strips of newspaper she'd been using to get the fire going. "Thanks so much for coming. I guess you got my message?"

"I did, and since I had to come down this way this morning anyway, I figured I'd just stop in. I hope that's okay. I'm taking a vanload of women to Target in Canton in a bit."

"Of course it's okay. Please, come in." Cheryl looked out the shop's front window and saw Jessica's fifteen-passenger van in the parking lot. She gestured for her to step farther into the shop, where it was a little warmer, and Jessica followed Cheryl's lead. Jessica was about fifteen years older than Cheryl, with graying blonde hair she wore curled around her face and big blue eyes. Today she wore baggy blue jeans and sneakers with a fleece vest under her heavy corduroy jacket.

Cheryl had brought her cat Beau into the shop today, and he got up from his perch over the heater vent to come sniff at the new person.

"So you're interested in Mark Troyer," Jessica said, stopping in front of a display of handmade soaps. She held out a finger for Beau to sniff, and he took a whiff and then turned and walked back to his post, tail swishing. Jessica laughed.

"I guess he's not feeling friendly this morning," Cheryl said.

"What cat ever does?" Jessica said, shrugging.

"Good point." Cheryl smiled. "Anyway, yes, I'm looking for information about Mark. And I heard you saw him the night he disappeared."

"Sure did," Jessica said. Cheryl liked Jessica's direct, easy manner. "It was the strangest thing. I was coming home after driving Rueben Vogel to a doctor's appointment. I live out on Cherry Ridge Road, way out by 164, so I pass by those fields just about every day. Well, that evening, I saw a car pulled over on the shoulder with its hazards on, so I pulled over to see if they needed help." Jessica picked up a bar of lavender-scented soap and sniffed it. "When I got there, I saw Mark Troyer—he'd been part of a group that came over to put up a shed in my backyard a few months before, so I knew who he was—looking under the hood. It was raining and dark, and I asked if he needed help, but he said it was under control. I started to go back to my car when I noticed there was someone sitting inside his car, so I got closer to make sure everything was okay. There was a girl sitting in the passenger seat."

"Did you recognize her?"

"No, I didn't know her." She set down the lavender soap and picked up a bar scented with real rose petals. "She was Englisch, I do remember that, because I thought it was odd to see an Amish kid driving around an Englisch girl. But she said everything was okay, so I got back in my car and left."

Jessica sniffed the bar of rose soap, made a sour face, and set the bar down again. Cheryl smiled. She thought the rose soap was a bit too sweet herself, but it was one of her top sellers.

"I suppose you didn't get a good look at her?"

"I'm afraid not," Jessica said. "Once I realized I might have been the last person around here to see Mark, I was kicking myself, but at the time, I didn't realize." She shrugged and picked up a bar scented with sage leaves. "I do remember the girl had glasses on, but that's it. Her hair must have been pulled back or something because no matter how much the cops asked me, I couldn't remember what color it was. Just that she had glasses, I'm pretty sure. I know it's not much to go on." She sniffed the sage soap, and her eyebrows went up. She took another whiff. "This one is nice."

"That is one of my favorites," Cheryl agreed. "Those are all hand-made by local women. They are made from all-natural ingredients."

"You can stop the sales pitch," Jessica said, but a smile on her face tempered her words. "I'll take this one. I'll put it in my sister's Christmas stocking." She looked around the shop. "I haven't been in here since Mitzi left. It looks great." Jessica started toward the counter, and Cheryl followed a step behind to ring her up. "How's your aunt doing?"

"She's doing fine," Cheryl said, sliding in behind the register. "I'm putting together a care package for her with some of her favorite things. If you have anything you'd like to include, feel free to bring it to me."

"That's really nice," Jessica said. "I'll think about it and try to bring you something later this week."

"That would be perfect. Thank you so much." Cheryl rang up the soap, and Jessica handed her a bill.

"Thanks for doing that. She'll be so pleased." Jessica put the change in her purse while Cheryl slipped the bar of soap into a bag.

"Thank you for answering my questions about Mark," Cheryl said.

"Hey, I'm happy to help. I know the family would love to have answers," Jessica said, tucking the bag into her purse. Cheryl nodded, though as she thought back to Saul's face yesterday when he'd told her to stay out of it, she wasn't so sure.

"Well, I should get going. I'm supposed to meet my group at Yoder's Corner in a few."

Cheryl waved and watched Jessica walk out the door. The girl in the car with Mark that night had been Englisch, Jessica said. That was interesting. And it seemed even more likely, she supposed, that the girl in the car would have a cell phone, and therefore might be the texter. That made it even more important that Cheryl find her.

But if the girl was not Amish, it did mean that Hannah Hilty and Sarah Yutzy were probably not the people in the car with Mark. Although Lydia had said Hannah liked to dress Englisch, so maybe it could have been Hannah after all? In any case, Cheryl would still try to talk with both of the Amish girls anyway. They might know something, even if they hadn't been there themselves. Maybe one of them could help her figure out who the Englisch girl had been. Would it have been someone from the local community, someone Mark had met at work or in town somehow? Or might she have been someone Mark had gotten to know in his art classes?

Cheryl needed to find out more about these classes. Lydia said he had taken art classes at the community college near Canton. Cheryl sat down at the computer in the back room and did a quick search. There were several community colleges in the Canton area, but a little research told her that only two of them offered art courses. Cheryl located phone numbers for the art department of the first school and dialed.

"Hello," said a woman. She sounded bored. Cheryl could hear her typing.

"Hi, I was wondering if you could help me. I'm trying to locate someone I think might be a former student," Cheryl said.

"Can't give out information about our students," she said, still typing.

"Yes, of course," Cheryl said. "Mostly I just wanted to know if he was ever enrolled there."

"Can't tell you," she said.

"Is there anyone who might be able to?" Cheryl asked. "Maybe one of the teachers?"

"Sorry, can't. Have a nice day."

Cheryl stared at the phone a few moments before setting it down again. Well, there was no need to be rude. She had just been asking a simple question. She felt her anger start to rise and reminded herself that getting upset was not going to help anything. The woman had been rude and unhelpful, but that didn't mean Cheryl could allow herself to be distracted. She simply needed to keep searching.

Cheryl called and left a message at the office of the other college's art department. She sat back, her frustration rising. She was no closer to finding out whether Mark might have met the Englisch girl in his art classes. If only she could talk to whoever taught the classes he had taken. Surely his teachers would know something. But try as she might, she couldn't figure out how to find the teachers who might have taught Mark three years ago, so she gave up.

She moved back to the front of the shop and checked to make sure no one needed help. There were a few people browsing, but so far everyone seemed to be content. She sat down at the stool behind the counter and thought.

Had the girl in the car gone to the bus station with Mark? That was what she really needed to know. Whoever she was, had she left town with him? Or helped him get there but stayed behind? Or had she done something to—well, Cheryl didn't want to think about the alternative. In any case, she needed to find out who the girl was and whether she'd gone to the bus station with him.

Was there any chance anyone at the bus station would know if Mark had gotten on the bus with a girl? Did they keep records of their passengers? Cheryl thought it was unlikely, but the only way to know for sure would be to ask. She pulled down the phone book and found the number for the bus station in Columbus.

As the phone rang, Cheryl tried to think through what she would say when someone picked up: She was trying to track down an Amish boy who may or may not have taken a bus from the station more than three years ago. Did anyone know if there had been an Englisch girl with him? It seemed hopeless, and she was almost relieved when the call went straight to a menu of options for finding bus schedules and fares. There didn't seem to be any way to talk to an actual person at this number. Cheryl hung up. This was starting to feel hopeless.

The door of the shop opened, and two women in their thirties entered. Cheryl asked if they needed help, but they were content to browse, so her mind drifted back to the night Mark disappeared. How could she find out if the Englisch girl had left with Mark or not? Everyone around here seemed to know that Mark had vanished, but had any Englisch girls gone missing around the same time? She hadn't heard anything about that, but was that simply because the Amish in the community didn't know about it?

She supposed she could look up missing persons reports. Those would tell her, wouldn't they? How would she find them? Then she realized what would be even better. She should look up old issues of the local paper. Surely if an Englisch girl had disappeared with Mark, it would have made the papers.

A few customers were ready to check out now, so she spent the next few minutes ringing up purchases. She was grateful for the sales but anxious to get back to her search. Finally, when the shop cleared out, she went back to the office in the rear of the store and sat at the computer. Beau followed her.

She opened up a browser window and pulled up the page for the *Times-Reporter*. She was pleased to see that back issues of the paper, at least for the last twenty years or so, were digitized and fully searchable.

Cheryl's fingers hovered over the keyboard. Lydia had said that Mark had disappeared in late September three years ago, so she narrowed the filters to look at articles from around that time and hit Search. She scrolled through the pages of headlines the search engine returned. The top hit turned out to be a small article from the first week in October about how the police were looking for information on the whereabouts of Amish teenager Mark Troyer, believed to have run away more than a week prior.

Cheryl skimmed the article. It was clear the reporter had spoken to the police and believed, like Chief Twitchell did, that Mark had simply left home. It was not very informative and didn't tell her anything she didn't already know. The reporter seemed to have simply talked to the police and not done much of anything else. There was no mention of the Englisch girl.

Well, that wasn't especially helpful, but at least she knew she had the right time frame, and she knew that if Mark had made the paper, the disappearance of an Englisch girl would certainly have hit the news. She continued to scroll through the headlines, and partway down the page she saw something interesting.

Runaway's car found outside bus station; raises questions.
Cheryl clicked on the article.

A car registered to Mark Troyer, an Amish teen from Sugarcreek who has been missing since September 25, was found parked a block from the Columbus bus station, police reported Monday. Security footage from nearby cameras is being reviewed to see if they can determine when the car was left and by whom. "We do not have any indication that there was foul play involved in his disappearance," Chief Twitchell, of the Sugarcreek Police Force, said. "There is no reason to assume this finding contradicts this."

Inside the car, the police also found half a dozen CDs, an illustrated book about the artist Martin Puryear, two empty canisters of motor oil, and a receipt from Wooded Hills racetrack from September 24. The number 87 was handwritten on the back of the receipt. The police are looking into whether any of these objects might be clues about Troyer's whereabouts.

This is the fifteenth car this year found outside the bus station that has been tied to a missing person's case. In ten of those cases, the owner has been found dead.

Troyer's family and friends are eager for word from him. He has not been heard from since he disappeared, but the Amish family declined to comment.

Well, that was interesting. Cheryl read through the article again and then wrote the list of objects found in his car onto her piece of paper. Hadn't one of Naomi's girls said something about Mark being into gambling? Was this proof that he had, indeed, been to the track the day before he vanished? Could that lend credence to the theory that he had gotten into gambling debt and been forced to disappear?

Or, Cheryl realized, her heart sinking, *could that whole rumor have been started because of the receipt found in his car?* She couldn't see that there was any way to know. She'd have to look into that more.

And she'd never heard of this artist Martin Puryear. She typed his name into a search engine and saw that he was a sculptor who often incorporated wood into his art. She read a bit more about him and discovered that his work often had religious imagery and redemptive themes. It wasn't Cheryl's favorite style of art—it looked like the kind of thing people in big-city galleries would appreciate—but she could see why someone like Mark might have been interested in his work. But did the fact that a book about the artist had been in his car mean anything? Cheryl had no idea.

She reread the article again and then scanned through the rest of the headlines her search had turned up, but that was all that was relevant. Beau settled into her lap, and she patted him absently.

She returned to the search page and ran searches to find out if an Englisch girl had been reported missing around the same time as Mark, but nothing turned up. Still, that didn't mean much. If Mark *had* left with the Englisch girl, she might very well have simply told her family where they were headed. They might have had no idea she was connected to the Amish boy who barely made the papers. It didn't mean she hadn't left with him.

Cheryl also looked out for any reports of—it was gruesome to even think it—bodies that might have turned up, but, thankfully, there was nothing of that sort either.

Cheryl went back and started looking through the headlines of the paper in the weeks before Mark's disappearance, not really sure what she was searching for, just anything that might shed light on what Mark could have been thinking. Her eye caught on a feature piece on a local artist named Scott Stearman. Stearman, it said, was a sculptor who worked out of a studio on his property in Walnut Creek. Stearman made large bronze and stainless steel sculptures, mostly in the shape of people or animals.

Cheryl was really impressed with Stearman's talent. But what caught Cheryl's eye was a line in the story, buried several paragraphs into the article, that alluded to the fact that Stearman often had several people working for him in his studio.

Cheryl had taken an art class in college, and she had heard that some artists used interns and helpers. Would this have been something Mark might have looked into? Mark had wanted to study art, Lydia said. Even if he had been taking art classes at a community college, with no more than an eighth grade education, it was unlikely he would have gotten into a program to study art at a more advanced level. But apprenticing with an established artist would have been the perfect opportunity for a young Amish boy looking to learn more.

Cheryl pulled up a new window and searched for the name Scott Stearman and was brought to the artist's Web site. The site featured a bit more information on the man and his work, and Cheryl was pleased to see that he had made a number of religious-themed sculptures and that he attended a church in his area. Cheryl clicked on a tab marked Contact and was led to a form she could fill out to send him an e-mail. Cheryl quickly composed an e-mail, explaining who she was and how she'd found him and that she was interested in finding out if he'd ever hired an Amish apprentice. She hit Send and sat back. Hopefully he'd reply soon. In the meantime, there had to be other artists in the area who might also take on apprentices and might possibly know something about Mark. How could she figure out who they were? Then she had an idea.

Cheryl heard someone clear their throat out in the main area of the shop, and she hopped up and went to the front. Beau shook himself, disgruntled at being disturbed. A couple customers were hovering around the register.

"Oh my goodness, I'm so sorry," Cheryl said. She'd gotten so distracted by her research that she'd totally been neglecting her customers. She quickly rang up purchases for the women who'd been waiting—throwing in a few pieces of penny candy each to make up for her inattentiveness—and then moved away from the counter to see if any other customers needed help. A tour bus pulled in not long after that, and she spent the next hour or so busily ringing up soaps, cheeses, and hand-carved wooden toys. By the time Esther arrived at noon, the crowd had thinned, but she had sold through a good amount of merchandise.

"How is it going?" Esther asked as she pulled on her apron and started straightening the display of jars of local honey.

"The shop has been busy," Cheryl said.

"That is good," Esther said with a shy smile. "But I meant the search for the person who sent the text."

"Ah. Well, mostly I've encountered more questions so far," Cheryl said. "Actually, there are a few people I'd like to talk to, to see what they can tell me. Would you mind watching the shop for a bit while I run out?"

"Of course not," Esther said. "I will handle things here." Cheryl knew the store was in good hands, and she grabbed her coat and purse and headed out the door.

She walked quickly across the street and climbed up the wooden steps of the covered porch of the Honey Bee Café, a charming restaurant and coffee shop that Cheryl frequented. It shared a building with the Artistic License, a new art gallery that had opened when Bye Bye Blue studio had closed earlier in the year. She intended to stop at the art gallery after she'd enjoyed one of the best sandwiches in Sugarcreek. She closed the glass door against the chilly wind and stepped inside the café, breathing in the delicious scents of fresh-baked bread and comforting coffee. She walked past the comfortable couches and charming bistro tables toward the counter at the back. The menu was printed on a chalkboard hung high on the wall, but Cheryl didn't need to read it to know what she wanted.

"Hey there, Cheryl," Kathy Snyder said from behind the counter. "What can I get you today?"

"How about turkey with cheese," Cheryl said. "And a small latte, please."

"Coming right up." Kathy smiled and took one of the pre-made sandwiches from the display case. It looked delicious, made with crusty bread and fresh lettuce and a hint of tangy mustard. Cheryl looked around the restaurant while Kathy worked on the latte. Though there were a handful of people here, chatting or staring at laptop screens, there was no one close enough to overhear.

When Kathy turned back, setting her drink in a paper cup on the smooth countertop, Cheryl leaned in.

"I was actually wondering if I could ask you a quick question," Cheryl said. Kathy rang up the purchase on the touch screen in front of her.

"Of course."

"I've been looking into the disappearance of the Amish teenager Mark Troyer," Cheryl started, and Kathy nodded.

"Oh, that was so terrible." Kathy told her the total, and Cheryl handed over her credit card. "To just vanish like that..." She shook her head. "I can't even imagine."

Cheryl nodded. "Mark's cousin Lydia works at my shop part-time, and she told me about him, and I'm trying to help her out. I hear that you found one of his shirts right around the time he disappeared?"

"That's right. Goodness, it was so shocking. I was just taking the trash out, right down to the trash cans at the back of the shop"—Kathy gestured out the window at the left side of the store—"and as I was tossing a bag in, I noticed something odd. It was dark red on a white background. I'm not even sure why I glanced into the trash bin instead of simply tossing the bags in like I normally do, but I'm glad I did." She handed the credit card back to Cheryl and kept talking. "I reached in and pulled it out, and let me tell you, I nearly lost my lunch when I saw what it was."

Chapter Six

"Was it a white, long-sleeved shirt," Cheryl asked, studying Kathy's pained expression, "like most of the Amish men around here wear?"

"Yes, except there was blood all over one of the sleeves and down the front."

"How much blood was there?" Cheryl asked. It was a gruesome question, but she was trying to picture it.

Kathy shrugged. "I'm not really sure how to measure that. Enough that I was concerned, I guess." She handed Cheryl a copy of her receipt.

"What did you do after you pulled it out?"

"Well, first I dropped it on the ground." She laughed. "And then after I stopped freaking out, I picked it up and looked it over a little more carefully. That's when I realized it was Amish, because of the collar. Before that I thought it might have been just a regular man's shirt."

Cheryl nodded. She knew that each district in the area had its own rules about the specifics for clothing, and if you knew what you were looking for, you could tell what district a person belonged to by the shape of their bonnet or the buttons and collar of their shirt.

"I retrieved it, obviously, because I thought it was strange, but this was the same night he disappeared, and no one had any idea he was missing yet, so I didn't realize what a big deal it was at the time. It was only after I heard that an Amish boy named Mark had gone missing that I put it together. I called the police right away, of course."

Cheryl thought through all of this. One question was niggling at her. "How did you know the shirt belonged to Mark?"

Kathy laughed. "His name was written right there inside the collar. I thought it was strange at first, but then I remembered how the Amish hang the whole family's clothes on a clothesline to dry and realized that if you've got several men in the family, it makes good sense to label each garment."

"Ah." That did make sense, now that she thought about it. "What did the police do when you called them?"

"Not much." Kathy rested her hands on the wooden counter. "They took the shirt and said they'd look into it. I just assumed it proved to be a dead end in connection with Mark's disappearance." She shook her head and leaned in toward Cheryl. "But between you and me, I'm not sure how much digging they really did."

Based on her interactions with Chief Twitchell so far in this matter, Cheryl wondered the same thing. "So you think the shirt means he didn't just run away?"

"I don't know for sure, but come on. You've got a missing boy and one of his shirts turns up in a trash can covered with blood?

Wouldn't you assume that's at least worth looking into? A sign that there might have been foul play?"

Kathy's voice was getting louder and rising in pitch. Cheryl felt her blood pressure rising as well. The police had ignored a key piece of evidence here. How could they just write off a young man like that?

"Do you know what happened to the shirt?" Cheryl asked, trying to keep her voice level.

"I would guess the police still have it," Kathy said. "I haven't seen it since I turned it in."

"And you never heard anything more about how it ended up in your trash can?"

"Nope, though obviously I've wondered. I did make a list of the people who had been in the café that evening to show to the police, not that they ever followed up on it."

Cheryl dug into her purse and pulled out a pen and her scrap of paper. "Can you tell me who they were?"

"There was Ben Vogel. He comes in here a lot and always gets the ham and cheese, hot." Kathy ticked off the name on her fingers.

Cheryl nodded. Ben came into her shop fairly regularly as well, and he played checkers with his brother Rueben.

"Henry Detweiler came in to get some cookies. He works across the street at Hoffman's Furniture, and he comes in here sometimes. He'd had a fight with the girl he was seeing and was trying to win her back, and she's a big fan of my cookies." Kathy grinned and held up another finger.

Henry Detweiler. Cheryl had heard that name before. He was one of the people Lydia had listed as having a reason to be angry with Mark. She would definitely be trying to talk with Henry.

"Let's see. There was an Amish boy—Moses something or other. His mother was sick, so she asked him to pick up dinner for the father and brothers. There are no girls in that family, and I suppose when the mother is sick the men are helpless when it comes to food." She held up another finger. "And Roger Rowell. Roger lives over in Cincinnati but used to come through this way a lot for business. He would stop by whenever he was passing through." She held up another finger. "Come to think of it, I haven't seen him in a while. I hope he's doing okay."

She looked down at the four fingers she now held up. "I think that was it. That was the list I gave to the police."

Cheryl quickly scrawled down the names, noticing one glaring absence. "No Mark?"

Kathy shook her head. "Nope. He had been here once or twice, but certainly not regularly, and not that day for sure. Which made it doubly strange that his shirt turned up here."

Cheryl thought about this. Mark may not have come in to the Honey Bee, but was it possible he'd stopped in to the art gallery that shared the building with the café? If he was interested in art, it didn't seem out of the question that he would have gone there.

"Kathy, are your trash bins anywhere near where the trash cans for Artistic License are?"

Kathy nodded. "Oh yeah. It would have been Bye Bye Blue back then, but we both put the trash out in the same area, down at the bottom of the steps in the back."

Cheryl thought about this. "Did the police ever talk to anyone there about it?"

Kathy shrugged. "I'm not sure." She cocked her head. "I guess it's possible someone might have meant to throw the shirt in the bin for Bye Bye Blue, but I'm not sure that makes me feel any better. In either case, you've still got a bloody shirt and a missing boy."

"I totally agree," Cheryl said. After her lunch, maybe she would head down there. The new gallery had been opened by Roxanna Velandria, an artist who had worked at Bye Bye Blue part-time for many years. It was possible she remembered something about that night. Cheryl picked up the plate her sandwich was resting on and thanked Kathy for the information, then she remembered something.

"By the way, I'm putting together a care package for Aunt Mitzi. I wanted to send her some of her favorite things from Sugarcreek to remind her of home. Is there anything you'd like to put into it?"

"That's a wonderful idea," Kathy said and turned to grab a bag of freshly roasted coffee beans from the shelf behind the counter. "This is her favorite blend. Can I put this into the care package?"

"That would be wonderful. Thank you so much." Cheryl set her sandwich down and tucked the beans into her purse and then took her sandwich and coffee and ate quickly at one of the small bistro tables. Then she waved good-bye to Kathy and headed down the stairs at the side of the café and into Artistic License Gallery.

Cheryl always loved coming to Artistic License. The exposed stone wall and heavy, rough-hewn beams that held up the ceiling were a stark contrast to the smooth, cream-colored walls and high-end lighting that focused your attention on the beautiful paintings displayed throughout the gallery.

"Hello, Cheryl," Roxanna called, stepping out from the area she'd marked off for art classes and demonstrations. A long table ran down the center of the space surrounded by chairs, and the walls were hung with samples of work from Roxanna's students. Some of it was quite impressive. Roxanna was laying out jars of water and tubes of acrylic paints in front of each chair. "It's good to see you."

Cheryl had gotten to know her some since they were around the same age and both ran businesses downtown, and Cheryl was always impressed by her common sense and warm, friendly demeanor.

"It's good to see you too. These paintings are beautiful." Cheryl gestured toward the main room of the gallery, where a series of landscapes filled the walls. The way the light hit the mist that appeared in each picture gave the whole series an ethereal, almost spiritual quality. They were stunning. "These are beautiful."

"Aren't they? An elderly woman out in Charm made them all. She learned to paint to help her process her grief after her husband passed away." Roxanna pulled a handful of paint tubes out of a plastic bin she held and distributed them at each place, laying the tubes just so.

"Wow. That's amazing." She had a gift, that was for sure, and it was wonderful that it had helped her through a tough time. Had art helped Mark Troyer process his feelings in a similar way? "Do you know a lot of the artists in the area?"

"A good number of them." Roxanna set a cerulean blue tube down next to a cadmium red and lined them up precisely. "Why?"

"Did you know an Amish kid named Mark Troyer?"

"Oh yeah. Tall, blond, cheekbones to die for?"

"I guess so. I've just heard he's good-looking." She shrugged. "Did he ever take any classes here?"

"Not that I know of." Roxanna set tubes of paint in front of the final chair and then set the box back into a low cabinet against one wall. "I can't say for sure, since I was only here part-time back when he disappeared, but I handled most of the paperwork, and I know I never saw his name on the registration forms. I know he was into art, but from what I understand, he was more interested in sculpture, and we've never taught that here."

"I read about a local sculpture artist who sometimes takes on apprentices. I wondered if Mark might have done something like that—apprenticing with a sculptor."

"Could have." Roxanna pulled another plastic box out of the cabinet, and Cheryl saw that it was filled with brushes of all shapes and sizes. "Who did you read about?"

"A guy named Scott Stearman."

"Oh yeah, Scott. He's a good guy, and a great artist."

"I sent him an e-mail to ask if Mark interned with him, but I haven't heard back. But I wondered if you might be able to give me the names of other artists in the area so I could ask them about Mark."

"Sure thing." She set the plastic box down on the table. "Let's see. There's Max Wiley. He makes these big iron sculptures. He lives up near Toledo, but I know he takes on interns. And you should talk to Megan Reid. She makes large glass pieces, and she sometimes has people help her." She paused and looked up. "And you should probably talk to Lester Coblentz too." She paused. "His art is a little different in that he makes guitars, not sculptures, but they're these beautiful handmade things. I don't know for sure if he takes on help or not, but he grew up Amish. I wouldn't be surprised to hear he had found a way to help an Amish kid looking for a way out." She fanned the brushes out and spread them around the table, putting a few near to each place.

Cheryl wrote down all three names and put a star next to the name Lester Coblentz. Guitar-making may be different than what Mark was interested in, but the Amish connection sounded promising. Roxanna led her to the sleek laptop set up on the counter at the front of the gallery, and she looked up phone numbers and e-mail addresses for the three artists she'd mentioned, and Cheryl recorded those on her paper too.

"Can I ask you another question?" Cheryl asked.

"Of course." Roxanna stayed behind the counter and typed something on her computer. "I'm happy to help if I can."

"From what I understand, the day Mark was last seen one of his shirts was found in the trash can outside of here."

"That's right." Roxanna nodded and started copying a name from her screen onto a folded white place card. "Kathy Snyder found it right out there in the trash bins."

"Had Mark been here that day, by any chance?"

Roxanna shook her head. "I know the police asked that too." Cheryl noted this. That meant they had investigated the bloody shirt, at least a little, despite Kathy's insistence they hadn't. "They talked to everyone who worked here, and like I told them, he didn't come in here much. This stuff isn't really his style; he was more into sculpture. They asked me to try to remember everyone who'd been in here in the past few days, and I'm afraid I didn't have much luck then." She shook her head apologetically. "I'm sorry, but it's been, what, three years?" She shrugged. "I'm afraid I don't really have any idea what to tell you."

"That's all right." Cheryl was disappointed that Roxanna couldn't give her any more leads as far as the shirt, but she was grateful for the names of the local artists. "Thank you so much for your help."

"I'll let you know if I remember anything else," Roxanna said and waved as Cheryl headed toward the front door. A moment later, Cheryl stepped out into the bright sunshine. There were cars parked in front of most of the shops in the little shopping area, as well as buggies and bicycles tied up here and there. She might never get used to how strange it was to see that, but it made her heart glad. She cast a quick glance back at the Swiss Miss. There were a few cars parked out front, but it didn't look swamped. She was sure Esther could handle the store for a little while longer, and she walked the short distance to Hoffman's Furniture. While she walked, she called the number the texts had come from, but the phone call went unanswered. Her call was dumped into the same anonymous voice mail. She left another message, but was starting to doubt anyone would ever return them.

Hoffman's Furniture had been started by Jacob Hoffman's father decades ago and was housed in a spacious, low-slung building with big plate glass windows that displayed the fine, hand-crafted merchandise. Cheryl stepped into the store.

"Cheryl! So good to see you!" Jacob called in his booming voice, coming out of the back room of the shop. "How is that bedside table working?"

When Cheryl had moved to Sugarcreek, she had come here to buy a few pieces to round out the furniture Aunt Mitzi already had in her home and had fallen in love with the well-crafted, hand-hewn pieces that filled the display floor. Jacob and his team put a lot of care and skill into each piece they made, and it showed. She'd purchased a mission-style red oak nightstand.

"It's beautiful. Thank you so much."

"I am glad you like it. Now, have you come for a dresser to go with it? I can get you a good deal." He cocked a crooked smile and laughed, a warm, heartfelt laugh. "We have a matching piece here"—he indicated a tall dresser with four deep drawers—"or we can make you one that's a bit smaller, if you'd prefer." He gestured toward the back of the shop where there was a door to the workshop where his team of employees made the furniture by hand.

"Not today," Cheryl said, though she did eye the handsome piece Jacob's hand rested on. It was beautifully crafted, and it *would* mean that she would have space to store her summer clothes—she stopped herself. She had a perfectly good dresser at the house and didn't need a new one. She supposed this was how Jacob had managed to stay in business for so long. "I'm actually here looking for a Henry Detweiler. I was told he works here, or used to at least."

"Ah, yes. Henry is in the back. Come this way." Jacob led her toward the back of the store, threading past handcrafted tables and chairs, rockers, and beds. "Are you sure you don't need a bench?" He laughed, knowing that the hard, backless benches were primarily used by the Amish in their church services.

"Not today, thank you."

"All right. I'll be right back." Jacob opened the door that led to the workshop and stepped into the back. Through the open door, Cheryl could see a large, high-ceilinged room filled with half a dozen Amish men bent over wooden workbenches. The clean scent of sawdust filled the air.

"Henry," Jacob called, and a man on the far side of the room looked up. "Miss Cooper would like to speak with you."

Henry was young, probably not more than his early twenties, and he wore a plain white shirt and suspenders, but his face was clean-shaven, which Cheryl understood to mean he was not married. His eyes widened, and she saw confusion pass over his face, so she smiled and tried to look as friendly as possible. She knew Amish men and Englisch women didn't often have much interaction, and she was thankful Jacob was here to make Henry feel more at ease. He set down the piece of wood he'd been sanding and stood. His boots clomped across the worn wooden floor as he walked toward them.

"Hello, Henry. My name is Cheryl Cooper."

He eyed her warily. She realized that all the other men in the room were watching them.

"Could I talk to you for a moment, maybe back in the showroom?"

He didn't respond, but when she turned to move, he followed, and Jacob came a few steps behind. "I know you have to get back to work, but I'd like to ask you some questions about Mark Troyer," she said.

He froze. "I do not know anything about Mark Troyer." Henry had red hair and a sprinkling of acne on his chin.

"I believe you," she said, trying to keep her voice soothing. "I'm simply trying to talk to people who knew him"—it was the truth, if not the whole truth—"and I wondered if you could tell me about your last interaction with him before he disappeared."

Henry looked over at Jacob, who was watching and listening carefully. Jacob nodded, and Henry, somewhat reluctantly, proceeded.

"I did not know him well," he said stiffly.

"I was told that you had a disagreement with him over a girl."

Henry shifted his weight and glanced at Jacob again. Jacob took a few steps back to give him a little more privacy, but stayed close enough to see what was going on.

"I had been taking Sarah Yutzy home from singings, and he knew it," Henry said simply.

"Do you mean he shouldn't have gotten between you and Sarah?" Cheryl asked.

"I mean he had no business turning her head if he wasn't serious. He flirted with her one night, and I was going to take her home, but suddenly she wasn't interested." He shook his head. "Mark flirted with everyone. I do not know why she thought he was serious about her, but then she was always a bit silly. It was for the best that things ended between us."

Cheryl tried to make sense of this. "So you're saying that you're glad Mark flirted with Sarah because it ended something that wouldn't have worked out?"

"Yes." He avoided looking her in the eye, but she couldn't tell if that was because he had something to hide or because that was how many Amish men interacted with women.

"Did you feel that way at the time?"

He shifted his weight again. "Probably not. But I can see now how badly it would have gone."

Cheryl nodded. She was only a few months out from a breakup with the man she'd thought she'd marry, and as much as it still hurt, she could already see that they would have been poorly matched.

"Did you say anything to Mark about it at the time?"

Henry didn't answer for a moment. Then, quietly, "I did ask him to stay away from Sarah." His cheeks were turning a bit pink.

"What did Mark say?"

"He laughed and said she was a great girl."

"He didn't agree to stay away from her?"

"No, but he didn't have to. Everyone knew he flirted with every girl and was serious about no one. Everyone except Sarah, obviously."

Cheryl could see that despite his protestations to the contrary, Henry was still affected by Sarah's rejection. He might not be still pining for her, but her choosing Mark over him still stung.

"When was the last time you saw Mark?"

Henry shrugged. "That conversation was a few weeks before he disappeared. I probably saw him around after that, but I did not talk with him."

Cheryl suspected that he'd been acutely aware of whether Mark had been around Sarah in those weeks, but didn't know whether to believe him about not talking to him. Most Amish were truthful as much as possible, but that didn't mean someone wasn't hiding something.

"Do you know anything about what happened to Mark Troyer?" she asked.

Henry shook his head. "I was as surprised as everyone else. I do not know anything about it."

"I hear you stopped in at the Honey Bee Café the night he disappeared."

He eyed her. "Yes. Sarah liked the cookies there. I bought some to bring to her."

"That was sweet."

"It did not help. She was no longer interested in me."

It was clear that Sarah's betrayal still stung. She felt for him. "Did you see anything strange while you were there?"

"If you're asking about the shirt that was found in the trash can, I do not know anything about that."

Cheryl watched him. He still wasn't meeting her eye, and he was shifting awkwardly. But did that mean he wasn't telling the truth? She couldn't tell.

"Thank you very much for your time," she said, adjusting the strap of her purse on her shoulder. "I appreciate it."

Henry made a noise that sounded like a grunt and then turned to go back to work when one more thought popped into her head.

"Henry, do you have a cell phone by any chance?"

He looked confused and shook his head. "No. They are not allowed."

He seemed so bewildered by the question that she believed him on this point.

"Thank you, Henry. I appreciate it."

Henry turned and walked back through the doorway into the shop, and when he'd disappeared, Jacob volunteered, "He is a good kid. A hard worker."

Cheryl nodded. "I'm sure he is." He may be a good person and a hard worker, but could he have been upset enough about Mark driving his sweetheart away that he had done something drastic?

It seemed unlikely. Henry didn't seem to be the excitable type. But then again, he hadn't married yet. Did he still have feelings for Sarah after all? Had he simply not found the right girl? Was it possible he'd seen Sarah as his best chance?

Cheryl didn't know what to think, but she knew Jacob was waiting for her to leave before he went to help the Amish couple who had just come into the shop, so she thanked him and headed out on to the street again.

Cheryl checked her phone to see the time and was startled to see that it was almost time for Esther's shift to be over. Had she really been away from the shop for that long? She hurried back to the store. The wood-burning stove felt wonderful and smelled even better, and pale winter light streamed in through the latticed front window. Esther was ringing up a few customers. Cheryl rushed to help her, and when they left, Cheryl thanked Esther again.

"It is all right. I do not mind," Esther said. She slid a piece of paper across the counter. "By the way, Lydia called. She said her brother Elam can meet with you tomorrow around six. Here are the directions to his house. It is not far from Lydia's house, on the back of the property."

CHAPTER SEVEN

Cheryl read the directions to Elam's quickly. It looked simple enough.

"Thank you." Maybe now she'd finally get some answers.

Esther left, and Cheryl spent the next couple hours taking care of a wave of tourists. When the shop finally cleared out just before closing time, Cheryl surveyed the damage.

It was pretty tidy, and Esther had done a good job restocking the shelves while she'd been out, but...she noticed the supply of jams and jellies was still very low. There must be no more in the back. She knew Naomi had to make a fresh batch of the spiced cranberry, but she was pretty sure she had more of other varieties stocked in her basement. If she wanted jam to be on the shelves in time for tomorrow's customers, she would have to drive out to the Miller farm again tonight.

Which wasn't such a bad thing, she acknowledged as she slipped her coat on. It had been a long, confusing day, and she would welcome a visit with her friend. And she knew Naomi wouldn't mind her dropping in. Naomi seemed to always be genuinely glad to see her, no matter what time of day it was. Back in Columbus, an unexpected visitor would have sent Cheryl's world into chaos—her apartment wouldn't have been clean, she wouldn't have had food prepared, she would have been in the middle of something—but around here, it seemed to be perfectly acceptable. Welcome, even.

She packed up Beau and dropped him off at her house, and a few minutes later Esther was ushering her into the Millers' warm, comforting kitchen. Naomi looked up from the pot of soup she was stirring and smiled as Cheryl walked in.

"Hello, Cheryl. Two visits in two days. We are blessed." Behind Naomi, Elizabeth was washing dishes in the deep porcelain sink, and Esther had returned to the living room where she was rolling silverware in napkins for the upcoming fund-raiser. Naomi gestured for Cheryl to sit down in one of the kitchen chairs.

"I'm sorry to drop in"—she couldn't stop herself from saying it, even though she knew her friend didn't mind; old habits die hard—"I was hoping I could trouble you for some more jam." Evening had fallen, and the kitchen, lit only by kerosene lamps, was dim, but it felt soothing. Maybe she should get rid of the harsh fluorescent lights in her own kitchen...

"Jam?" Naomi nodded. "I have not had a chance to do that cranberry yet..."

"Oh, I know. But I was hoping you had a reserve of some of the other flavors. We're nearly out."

"That is good news." She set down the spoon she'd been using and turned to Elizabeth. "Could you run down to the basement and bring up what we've got?"

Without a word, the teen turned off the water and wiped her hands on her apron and then headed to the stairs that led to the basement. Cheryl knew that while Esther worked at her store,

Elizabeth brought in money for the family by assisting mothers after the birth of a new baby. Cheryl imagined her quiet, efficient grace was exactly what new mothers needed. But she must not be working with a new baby at the moment since she was around a lot this week.

"I am sorry I have not had time to make more. This fund-raiser is taking so much time. We have all been working hard. What do you think of Elizabeth's plans for flowers?"

Cheryl looked at pencil sketches that were lying on the table. They showed bunches of some kind of flower with big leaves in what looked like crude buckets. The drawings were beautifully done—Elizabeth was quite skilled—but it was hard to see how they would translate into floral centerpieces.

"They're very nice," Cheryl said. "You mentioned the fund-raiser yesterday. For the boy in your church, right?"

Naomi took a pinch of salt from the jar on the counter and tossed it into the soup. Cheryl didn't know what kind of soup it was, but it smelled delicious.

"Exactly. He was getting very thin and was tired all the time, so his parents, my cousin and her husband, took him to a doctor. They did a number of tests and were told he had diabetes." She took a taste of the soup and made a face.

"Goodness." One of Cheryl's friends growing up had had type 1, or childhood onset, diabetes, and she knew it was a serious medical condition that required a lot of monitoring and regular insulin. "I'm sorry to hear that."

"It is hard news, though the doctors say that as long as he is treated, he should have a normal life. The family will need to buy him an insulin pump, as well as a monitor and testing meter. It is all very expensive to buy and maintain, so the community is trying to help." Naomi picked up her spoon and dipped it into the soup and then took a taste.

"But their medical insurance will cover the costs for that, right?"

Naomi shook her head. "The Amish do not have medical insurance."

"What?" Cheryl twisted so she could see Naomi better. "Why in the world not?" When she'd left her corporate job, Cheryl had lost her top-tier insurance plan as well, but she'd still signed up for an individual plan when she moved to Sugarcreek. She was young and healthy, but you just never knew what might happen.

"We take care of each other," Naomi said simply.

"Yes, but what about when something like this happens? Insurance would cover most of the costs. And this is something he'll be dealing with the rest of his life. How will that work?"

"We will take care of him," Naomi said simply. "There is a fund that we give money to when we can to cover things like unexpected medical emergencies. And what that won't cover, we will help the family pay."

"For the rest of his life?"

"As long as he remains part of our community."

Cheryl tried to wrap her mind around this. "But what if the costs are too great? What if something horrible happens, and there's just not enough money to cover it?"

"Then we pray."

It was so simple, and yet so foreign. A community that took care of its own, no matter what. A community whose faith under-girded everything they did. Cheryl didn't understand why they did everything they did, but she could definitely see the appeal of the Amish way of life.

"Well, in that case, we'd better make sure this event raises a ton of money for this family."

Naomi nodded. "Oh yes. The Esches can use all the help they can get."

"Where is the fund-raiser being held?" There were some meet-ing rooms at hotels not too far out of town, and her own Silo Church had a very nice auditorium that could be dressed up for events.

"It will be in the Esches' barn," Naomi said.

"A barn?" Cheryl tried to imagine a black-tie gathering among pig stalls and wandering chickens.

"We clean it out first, of course, like we would do for hosting church," Naomi said.

Cheryl knew that the Amish did not use a church building and rotated homes for their services, but since she had never attended an Amish church service, she couldn't picture what that would look like. Surely they wouldn't be setting up tables in dirty stalls, like she was imagining.

"Okay. Well, are you doing an auction? Or a silent auction?" Cheryl had been to many of these sorts of events in her banking career, and she knew the auctions were what brought in the serious cash if you could get the right prizes donated. "And how much will it cost to buy a table?"

Naomi wrinkled her brow. "We will use the card tables we'll borrow from neighbors. We will not need to buy any."

Cheryl saw that her friend didn't understand what she was saying. "At the fund-raisers I've been to, most people pay to reserve a whole table, and then they invite people to fill the seats. You don't do that?"

Naomi shook her head. She was looking at Cheryl like she was speaking a foreign language.

"But you are having a silent auction, right? What sorts of things have been donated?"

"I do not understand what a silent auction is. I have been to livestock auctions, but they are very noisy."

Cheryl could see that her idea of a fund-raiser was very different from her friend's. "What about tickets? You must sell those, right?"

"Oh yes." Naomi nodded, and her face relaxed. "We sell tickets at the door. Everyone brings a dish, and then we all eat together. It is a wonderful time."

"Wait." Cheryl couldn't believe what she was hearing. "You all make the food, and then you pay to eat it?"

"Of course." Naomi looked at her like *she* was the one who wasn't making sense.

"And that works? People do it?"

"Of course. We eat very well." A smile passed over Naomi's face. "You should come. You will see. It is a wonderful way for the community to support the family."

"I would be allowed?"

"Of course. It is open to anyone. You could come with my family if it would make you feel better."

"That would be great. I'll do it." She cut a glance at Naomi. "Your whole family will be going?"

If Naomi understood what she was getting at, she didn't let on. "Anyone who doesn't will have to fend for themselves for dinner that night." She tossed another pinch of salt into the soup and stirred again.

"I'd love to join you." Cheryl leaned back, pressing her lower back against the hard chair. "And I think you could raise even more money if you do a few simple things. Would it be okay if I thought about what would make sense and gave you a list of ideas?"

Naomi looked dubious, but she nodded. "All right."

The sound of footsteps pounding up the wooden basement steps announced that Elizabeth was returning, and a moment later she eased a large cardboard box onto the counter.

"This is everything we have left," she said, using her apron to brush perspiration off her forehead. "There's some peach, apricot, and blueberry, as well as a batch of rose hip jelly that none of us were too crazy about."

"It was just fine," Naomi said, playfully swatting at her daughter with her spoon. "They just don't know good jelly when they see it. Your customers will enjoy it."

"I am sure they will," Elizabeth said, but Cheryl saw relief on her face as she went back to washing the dishes.

"Thank you so much," Cheryl said. "I'd hate to miss out on the chance to sell it because we're out of stock."

"I'd hate for you to miss that chance as well." Naomi laughed. "I will make more next week. Hopefully this will tide you over until then." She tasted the soup again, nodded, and set the spoon down. "Now tell me what else is going on. How is the search for information about Mark Troyer?"

Cheryl told her about her conversations with Jessica Stockton, Kathy Snyder, Roxanna Velandria, and Henry Detweiler, as well as what she had read in the newspaper about the artists and about the things that had been found in Mark's car.

"What is your next step?" Naomi asked as she pulled a loaf of freshly baked bread from the oven.

"I'm supposed to talk with Elam Troyer tomorrow. Lydia tells me he was very close to Mark," Cheryl said, holding up one finger. "And I'm hoping I'll hear back from the other community college and see if I can talk to his teachers. I'm trying to track down the Englisch girl who was in the car with Mark the night he disappeared, and I wonder if it might have been someone from one of his classes." A second finger went up. "And I guess I need to talk to Hannah Hilty." She put up another finger.

"Why Hannah?" Naomi said, tapping the pan to loosen the bread.

"Lydia mentioned her. Mark flirted with her, and she liked to dress Englisch, so I wanted to see if it might be her by some chance."

"She is a server at Yoder's Corner," Elizabeth said. Goodness. That girl was so quiet Cheryl had almost forgotten she was there. "You can no doubt find her there."

"That's helpful. Thanks. I'm still hoping to talk to anyone who might have had a reason to be upset at him, so I'd like to track down the girl Sarah Yutzy. I'm not sure how to get in touch with her, but I'll find her."

"She's Sarah Schwartz now. I know her maam well. I can introduce you," Naomi said. "What else?"

"And I need to look into the artists that Roxanna Velandria told me about to see if any of them took Mark on as an apprentice." Her thumb went up.

Naomi's bread dropped out of the pan onto the counter, sending up puffs of steam.

"I also need to talk to the rest of the people Kathy Snyder mentioned were around the Honey Bee the day the shirt was found." She lifted a sixth finger. "I'm hoping to hear back from the police about whose cell phone the number is registered to." Seven. "I want to talk to someone at the bus station in Columbus to see if he went there, and I'd like to see what I can find out about the Wooded Hills racetrack because of that receipt." Two more fingers.

She glanced over at Elizabeth, who was still washing dishes with her back to them. "And I want to find out more about Saul Troyer." She was now holding up all ten fingers.

Naomi didn't say anything for a moment, and she seemed to be thinking. She pulled a serrated knife out of a wooden block.

"Goodness. You will be busy. And you will run your store during the Christmas shopping season?" Naomi finally said. She began slicing the bread. "Are you sure you have time to assist with the fund-raiser?"

"Absolutely. I want to help that little boy and his family."

Naomi nodded silently. "Please let me know what I can do to help you solve this mystery. Maybe we can go meet Sarah Schwartz tomorrow."

"That would be great," Cheryl said.

Naomi hesitated for a moment, like she was trying to decide whether to say something or not. Her hands worked steadily, cutting the bread into pieces. Tiny wisps of steam curled up from each slice. Cheryl's instinct was always to rush to fill the silence, but she knew from experience to wait for her friend to speak.

"I know you must look into every lead," Naomi finally said, placing the slices into a basket lined with a clean tea towel. "But I do not think Saul..."

Just then the back door slammed, and Cheryl heard the sound of heavy boots on the scrubbed pine floor.

"It sounds like the men are done," Naomi said, referring to her husband, her son Eli, and her stepsons Levi and Caleb. She hesitated and then sighed and covered the bread with the towel. "Cheryl, would you like to stay for supper?"

Whatever Naomi had been about to say about Saul, it seemed to have been swallowed up by the moment. Cheryl wanted to ask her to go on, but knew that her friend would speak her mind in her own time.

Cheryl looked around the warm, cheery kitchen filled with the most delicious smells and thought about all the people who would be sitting around this wide table shortly.

Cheryl's heart did a little leap thinking of Levi just in the other room, but she squashed the feeling. There was nothing she would enjoy more than staying for dinner, but she knew she had already imposed on Naomi enough. Besides, she wanted to work on her list of ideas for the fund-raiser, and she could reach out to the artists Roxanna had told her about tonight as well.

"I should get going," she said, though she lingered a moment longer as she heard footsteps coming through the living room toward the kitchen.

"Hello, Cheryl," Levi said as he stepped into the room. "I did not know we had a visitor." He held up his hands apologetically, which were covered in grease, but his smile was warm. He moved to the sink, and Elizabeth stepped out of the way to let him use the faucet. Levi's blond hair fell in his eyes, and it hung there while he washed his hands.

"Oh, hello, Levi," Cheryl said as if she were surprised to see him. "How are you?"

"I am much better now that I have fixed the broken wheel on the winter buggy," he said, turning his head so he could talk to her while he rubbed a bar of soap over his knuckles. "Are you staying for supper?"

Cheryl felt the tug of longing even more strongly now, but she shook her head. "I'll get out of your hair. I have some things I need to do."

Was she imagining it, or was there a hint of disappointment on Levi's face? Usually when she felt the sense of attraction between her and Levi rising to the surface, she tried to quash it. She knew that romance was impossible, that a relationship with them could never go anywhere unless he left the Amish—which would break Naomi's heart—or she joined the church, which she just could not imagine. But still, it hung there sometimes, like warm breath on a winter's day, just visible for a moment before it disappeared.

"It was wonderful to see you," Naomi said, breaking into the moment. Was that on purpose? Cheryl could never be sure. "I will come by the shop tomorrow, and we can go visit Sarah."

"That would be great." Cheryl stood and moved toward the box of jams on the counter.

"Levi, maybe you could help Cheryl carry this box to her car," Naomi said, carefully avoiding eye contact with both of them.

"Of course." Levi dried his hands on a dish towel and picked up the box.

Elizabeth led them to the door, holding it open so Cheryl and then Levi could go out, and Cheryl stepped down the porch steps onto the hard-packed dirt of the yard. As they walked together toward her car, Cheryl tried to think of something to say, something to ask him, but suddenly her mind had gone blank. Levi didn't seem to know what to say either, and they walked in awkward silence.

"Thank you for your help," Cheryl finally said as she opened the trunk of her small car.

"Of course," Levi said simply. He set the box down and straightened up and then gave the smallest hint of a smile. He looked like he was about to say something, but then he turned quickly and headed back toward the house without another word.

Cheryl sighed as she settled into the driver's seat. It was probably for the best anyway. Cheryl backed her little car up and turned it around and then headed down the gravel driveway toward the road. As she drove, she tried not to think about Levi, about how his face had lit up, just a bit, when he'd seen her sitting in the kitchen. She knew nothing could ever come of it. Naomi was a good friend, but even she wouldn't be able to support anything developing between Cheryl and Levi that could only lead to heartbreak.

CHAPTER EIGHT

Cheryl got a busload of customers almost as soon she opened the store Wednesday morning. She quickly sold through a bunch of Christmas ornaments, most of her holiday-scented candles, and a large percentage of the jams Naomi had given her last night. She was so busy she'd barely had time to say hello to Ben and Rueben Vogel, who had come in to play checkers at the small table in the front window of the shop.

Ben and Rueben were brothers, but Ben had left his church to become Englisch while Rueben remained Amish. Cheryl was pleased to see them, not only because she found it charming that they used the Swiss Miss as a place to connect, but also because Ben was one of the people Kathy Snyder had placed at the Honey Bee the night before Mark's shirt had appeared in the trash can. Cheryl wanted to talk with him, and here he was in her shop. For now, though, the tourists seemed to think the sight of a wizened old Amish man playing checkers with a man in jeans and orange sneakers was thrilling, and they tittered and laughed and even, Cheryl was pretty sure, took a few surreptitious photos with their phones. The brothers seemed to tune out all the activity around them, and Cheryl left them alone to play quietly together while she rang up her customers' purchases, one after the other.

By the time the crowd had thinned, the brothers had put away the game pieces neatly and Rueben was already gone while Ben was pulling on his coat. Cheryl was glad she hadn't missed him, and she called out to him now.

"Ben, do you have a moment?" Cheryl stepped out from behind the counter and started walking toward the front of the shop.

He stopped and nodded. "Of course. What's going on?"

Cheryl stopped in front of him, trying to figure out how to phrase this. "I know this is kind of a strange question, but have you ever heard the name Mark Troyer?"

Ben paused for a moment, and then his blue eyes widened. "Is that that kid who disappeared a while back?"

"Exactly."

"That was such a sad story. Did they ever find out what happened to him?"

"No. But I've been looking into it a bit, as a favor to his cousin Lydia who works here. I learned that one of his shirts was found in the trash can behind the Honey Bee the day he disappeared, and Kathy Snyder mentioned that you'd been in that day. I wondered if there's any chance you might have seen anything strange that day."

It was quiet for a moment. Ben had left the Amish community over fifty years ago, but he still often paused for a beat before he spoke, a habit shared by so many of the Amish Cheryl knew.

"Oh, that's right," he finally said. "The police asked me about that too." He shook his head. "I'm sorry, Cheryl, but I don't remember seeing anything strange that day."

Cheryl nodded. She supposed it was possible he had missed something, but it was hard to imagine Ben trying to mislead her. She believed him. So that was one name scratched off her list. But there was still a way he might be able to help.

"I've talked to a lot of people who think Mark might have left. Just ran away and left the church."

"I see." Ben sighed. "I suppose it is possible. It would certainly be a happier conclusion than, well, the alternative."

Cheryl nodded. "So you think it's possible?"

Ben laughed. "I'm living proof that it's possible. But I'll be honest, it's not easy. As hard as it is to be Amish sometimes, it's even harder to leave behind everything you've ever known and start a new life on your own. The challenges really are stacked against you."

"What do you mean?"

"Well, you only have an eighth grade education, for one thing," Ben said. "That's just fine as long as you stay in the church, but it doesn't get you very far in the outside world. Then there's the trouble of not having documents. Birth certificate, social security number, that sort of thing."

"Mark had a driver's license, so it seems he had gotten that piece of it taken care of, anyway."

Ben nodded. "That is helpful, then. But money is a challenge as well."

"He had a job. He worked at Weaver Lumber."

"But in most Amish families, most of the money children make at their jobs is turned over to the parents. The teen may be allowed to keep a small percentage of it for pocket change, but usually the bulk of it goes to the parents to help pay for food and other expenses."

Cheryl thought about this. She knew Mark must have saved up some money, if he'd managed to buy a car and pay for a cell phone, but if Ben was right, it would have been difficult for him to save up enough to make a fresh start. Things like a deposit on an apartment seemed out of reach.

"But I think the biggest challenge is often how limited our experience in the outside world is. When you grow up in a place where everyone believes the same things, where family and faith are woven into everything you do, it can be hard to comprehend a world where that isn't the case. And it can be quite a shock when you get out there and discover what the rest of the world is like."

Cheryl processed this. "So you *don't* think he just left, then?"

Again, there was a pause before he spoke. "I didn't say that. It does happen, more than you might think. I'm just saying that given all the challenges, there has to be a pretty strong reason for a young person to attempt it."

Could pursuing art have been a strong enough motivator for Mark to leave it all behind? What about the Englisch girl?

"When I left, it was the hardest thing I'd ever done," Ben said quietly.

"But you thought it was worth it," Cheryl said.

Ben nodded. "It was. I wasn't content with stopping school at eighth grade. I was so curious about the world, I wanted to learn more. I wish I had figured out that I had to go before I made a commitment to the church. That would have saved many broken hearts. But once I realized that I wanted to be a doctor, there was no way I could stay."

Cheryl had been told that Ben's mother had passed away when he was quite young from an infection that would have been easy to treat with the right medication.

"I figured I could do more good in the world by healing people than by staying here, so I left. And then I met my Nelda, and that was that."

"You've been married a long time, haven't you?"

"Almost forty-five years."

"Do you ever regret leaving?"

Ben paused. "Leaving was hard, but it was what I needed to do."

"So maybe he did leave."

Ben shrugged. "I don't know enough to say. I do know that it's very difficult, but it is not impossible. If he wanted it badly enough, sure, he could definitely have gone." Ben thought for a moment, running his hand through his white hair. "The strange part is if he left without telling anyone. Maybe he thought it would be easier to leave without facing a terrible conversation with his parents, and he would be right, it would be easier. But it would also be cowardly. I don't know much of anything about this boy, but I don't know too many Amish who are cowardly. We're descended from martyrs, and proud of it. I don't know anyone who has left without at least saying good-bye." He was quiet for a moment. "So I don't know what to think."

"I don't either." Cheryl sighed. This conversation with Ben had been very helpful, but somehow only left her more confused. "But thank you for your help. I really appreciate it."

"Please let me know if there's anything else I can do," Ben said.

Cheryl nodded, and Ben stepped toward the door. "Actually, I have one more question," Cheryl said. Ben stopped. "Do you have a cell phone?"

She felt ridiculous even as she said the words. It was very hard to imagine the white-haired, formerly Amish Ben Vogel sending that strange text to Lydia Troyer—did he even know Lydia Troyer?—but Cheryl was trying to remember to ask everyone.

"Sure." Ben pulled a flip phone out of his pocket. "Why?"

"Do you mind telling me your number?"

"Not at all." Ben told her the phone number, and Cheryl realized that it didn't match the phone that had texted Lydia.

"Thank you so much," Cheryl said, and Ben waved, pulled on his Windbreaker, and headed out the door.

Cheryl saw that the remaining few customers were moving toward the register, so she went to the back of the shop to ring them up, and then the store was empty. Cheryl decided to take advantage of the quiet and use the time to find out what she could about the other people Kathy mentioned who had been at the Honey Bee the day Mark disappeared. One of them had to know something about how his shirt ended up covered in blood and discarded in the trash. At least she hoped one of them did. She pulled the list of names out of her purse and studied it.

Ben Vogel, ham and cheese, hot

Henry Detweiler, buying cookies for girl

Amish Boy Moses Something or Other with no sisters
Roger Rowell, Englisch, stopped by when driving through

Well, she'd already talked to Ben and Henry, and she was going to need help tracking down this Moses fellow. Maybe Esther or Lydia could help her when they came in. But in the meantime, maybe she could find out something about Roger. Cheryl looked around the shop one last time and then stepped into the small office at the back and jiggled the mouse to wake up the computer. She typed the words *Roger Rowell* into a browser window and gasped when she saw what came up.

CHAPTER NINE

Cheryl stared at the computer screen and read quickly, trying to take in what she saw. When she had Googled the name Roger Rowell, looking for info on the man Kathy Snyder said had been in the Honey Bee the night Mark disappeared, the first thing that had come up had been an obituary. Roger Rowell was dead.

Cheryl clicked on the obituary and read it. Roger had been young, only in his midfifties when he'd died of a heart attack last year. He'd sold educational textbooks throughout central Ohio, it said. That explained why he stopped in when he was passing through Sugarcreek, she realized. She also read that he had left behind a wife and two college-aged children. The obituary contained a picture of what looked like a jolly, smiling man.

It was always sad to read of someone's passing, and Cheryl said a quick prayer for Roger's wife and kids, who were no doubt still mourning his loss. But this also meant that anything Roger had seen that day at the Honey Bee was lost forever now. Cheryl sighed. Well, there was always this Moses boy. If she could figure out who he was, maybe he would be able to tell her something useful.

Cheryl heard the door of the shop open, and she pushed back from the computer and headed out into the main part of the store.

Cheryl stopped short. Mark's mother Joanna was walking across the store toward her.

"Hello, Joanna," Cheryl said, trying to mask her surprise. "It's nice to see you."

"Hello, Cheryl," the woman said, looking around the shop like she was checking to see who was around. "I hope you do not mind me stopping in like this. I wanted to talk to you."

"It's a store," Cheryl said, smiling. "We like it when people come in."

Joanna didn't seem to understand that she was joking. Her movements were jerky and rushed.

"I told Saul I was going to Hoffman's Furniture, so I only have a few minutes," Joanna said. That explained the furtive glances around. She didn't want her husband to know she was talking to Cheryl.

"I am sorry about, well, about how my husband was the other day," she said. "He is—" She broke off, looking around the store as if looking for the right word to materialize in front of her. "He can seem harsh. I know that. He is an upright man, and he expects others to be the same. And he was very hurt about Mark."

Looking at Joanna now, she could see that she wasn't actually a small woman. It must have been only in contrast to her husband that she had seemed slight.

"He seemed pretty insistent that Mark left," she said.

"Yes." She paused. "I think it is easier for him to believe that than to think about the alternative. Even being angry is better than believing..." Her voice trailed off.

"But Mark will never stop being my son. And no matter what he says, that's true for Saul too. You know the story of the prodigal son?"

Cheryl nodded. She knew the verses from Luke about the son who had run off and squandered his inheritance, but came home repentant and was welcomed home by his father with open arms anyway. They were some of her favorite verses in the Bible: "But the father said to his servants, 'Quick! Bring the best robe and put it on him. Put a ring on his finger and sandals on his feet. Bring the fattened calf and kill it. Let's have a feast and celebrate. For this son of mine was dead and is alive again; he was lost and is found.'"

"I think about that story a lot," Joanna said. "Saul talks as if Mark is no longer his son, but if he were to show up on our doorstep, I know he would welcome him home. And I wanted to ask you"—again she looked around like she didn't want to be overheard—"to please, don't stop looking for Mark." The plea was so honest, so plaintive, that Cheryl wouldn't have been able to say no even if she'd wanted to.

"I won't," she told Joanna. "I am trying to find out everything I can about who might have sent the text. But I do have some questions."

"Of course. Anything." She was playing with a button on her heavy, handmade coat.

Cheryl tried to think about how to phrase this. "Tell me more about your family."

"Saul and I have eight children," Joanna said.

Cheryl nodded. "And Matilda and Benjamin are the only ones who have joined the church, right?"

"So far."

"And Ruth is the only one on rumspringa, right?"

Joanna nodded.

"Do you know if she has a cell phone?"

"Ruth just got one." She shook her head and narrowed her eyes. This was interesting. Lydia hadn't known about that; then again, it sounded like it was a recent development.

"You're not happy about that," Cheryl said.

"No." Joanna toyed with the metal button of her coat. "Ever since she got it, she seems to spend most of her time sending messages to her friends instead of talking to her family. I would not be sad if they were verboten, even for the teens."

"Do you happen to know what Ruth's cell phone number is?"

"Yes. I have it written down," she said. She reached into the pocket of her coat and withdrew a small black bag, and she poked around inside until she pulled out a tiny black book. Inside was a list of phone numbers and addresses in precise handwriting. Cheryl almost laughed when she realized what it was—an old-fashioned address book. She hadn't seen one of those in years. She kept everyone's contact information in her phone.

Joanna flipped a couple of tiny white pages and then pointed to a number and read it out loud. It was not the number that the text had come from.

"Is there anyone else?" Cheryl asked.

Joanna shook her head.

"Did you ever hear anything about Mark being into gambling?"

Joanna sighed. "People said that after . . . after, well, you know." Joanna had set her bag down on the counter and was back to worrying the button on her coat. "Many of our boys do go to the track at some point, just to see it. They grow up around horses, you see?"

Cheryl nodded. She could understand how growing up around horses could make them interested in seeing the horse races.

"But I do not believe Mark was involved. Mark was a good boy."

Cheryl hesitated. Was it worth pointing out that even good boys sometimes experimented with things like gambling?

But Joanna continued, "Besides, he put all of the money he made into his car and his art classes. I can't see how he would have had the time or money to spend at the racetrack."

Cheryl could see Joanna spoke from her heart, but she couldn't ignore the receipt from the racetrack that had been found in his car. She knew every mother wanted to believe the best about their child, sometimes at the expense of seeing the truth. Was Joanna right that it was all rumors, that he hadn't wasted his time and money on horses, or was she deluding herself, refusing to see what Mark had been like? Cheryl couldn't tell, but she had picked up on something else to ask Joanna about.

"So you knew he was taking art classes."

"Yes."

"How did you feel about that?"

"I did not mind so much. It seemed to me that of all the things he could have gotten into in his running around years, art classes were not such a big deal." Joanna paused. "Saul did not support it, though."

"What do you mean?"

She hesitated again. "He forbade Mark from going to classes. He said he would not allow it."

"Why was that?" Cheryl sort of agreed with Joanna on this one. Of all the things Mark could have gotten in to—drinking, drugs, all kinds of things—art classes didn't seem like such a big deal.

"It was not the art that bothered him so much," Joanna said carefully, no doubt realizing how this all made her husband look. "Though art, like the kind you find in museums, is not a realistic profession in our community. It was the fact that the classes were at the college that worried Saul."

"Why is that?" Cheryl had her guesses, but she wanted to hear what Joanna had to say.

Joanna pushed a button of her coat through the fabric, opening the coat a little. "Just because we do not have formal education past eighth grade, it does not mean we stop learning," Joanna said carefully. "But still, we worry..." She paused. "Not all of what is taught at Englisch schools matches our thinking," she finally said. "And we do not want our children to be led astray."

Cheryl imagined that was probably exactly what drew some Amish to long for the education you'd find in classrooms outside of the Amish schools, but in this case she wasn't sure formal education was what Mark was looking for. She got the impression he was simply looking to learn more about his interest in sculpture.

"Did Mark listen? When his father forbade him from going to art classes?"

"No." She paused. "And that is why I am so sure he ran away and is still out there somewhere." For a moment the only sound was the crackling of the fire from the wood-burning stove. "Saul forbade him to go to classes, and they argued. I have never seen my husband so angry. I do not think..."

Again, she hesitated, turning to look around the shop to make sure no one could overhear.

"Saul is not a violent man. Our people believe in peace. But Mark was arguing with him, and he was so angry, and...well, Saul hit him. With his palm open, but right across the face. And I have always wondered if that was what made Mark leave like he did."

Cheryl knew Joanna was trying to make a case for why she was sure Mark had left and was out there somewhere, but Cheryl remembered the hesitation in Naomi's voice before she insisted that Saul would never hurt his son.

"Was that the first time Saul had ever hit Mark?" She tried to phrase her question carefully. Not only was this a delicate topic in general, it would be especially so in this case.

"*Ja,*" Joanna said, but there was an edge in her voice and a hardness in her face that Cheryl wasn't sure how to read. Did Joanna really believe everything she was saying? Or was there a smidgen of doubt somewhere in there that she was trying to ignore?

There was a moment of quiet, and then, suddenly, Joanna tucked her bag back into her pocket. "I need to be going."

Joanna seemed afraid of what would happen if Saul found out she had been talking with Cheryl. Was there a reason—she hated to think this, but couldn't ignore the thought—that Saul didn't want Cheryl to find out what had really happened to Mark?

"But I wanted to ask you to please, do not stop looking." Joanna's voice was pleading. "Please find out what happened to Mark."

Again, there was just the sound of the fire crackling.

"I promise I will do everything I can to get answers," Cheryl said, and Joanna nodded, her lips pressed together.

"Thank you," Joanna said and turned to go. Cheryl watched as she threaded her way through the shop and disappeared out the door. She would keep her promise to Joanna. She would do everything she could to find out what had happened to Mark.

She just hoped that Joanna wouldn't be disappointed—or in danger—because of what she found.

CHAPTER TEN

Cheryl spent a little while tidying up the store, but then Lydia Troyer came in for her shift. Cheryl spent the next few minutes catching Lydia up on who she'd talked to and what she'd learned—which wasn't much, she had to admit—and then while Lydia went to restock the shelves, Cheryl went to the back room to see if she had any new e-mails. Her heartbeat sped up when she saw that Scott Stearman, the artist featured in the newspaper article, had written back to her. But as she read his message, she learned he'd never heard of Mark Troyer.

Well, Cheryl thought, *that was another door closed*. But at least there was one more name she could cross off her list. She'd e-mailed the other artist before bed last night; hopefully she'd hear back from the other artists quickly.

She turned her attention to the work-related e-mails and updated the store's Facebook page. Before she knew it, Esther Miller was walking through the door for her shift. Cheryl was thrilled to see that Naomi came in behind her. Through the front window, she could just see Levi driving the family's buggy out on to the street.

"I found some more jam," Naomi said, holding up a dusty cardboard box. "It is a bit old, but it doesn't go bad."

"Wonderful." Cheryl gestured to the shelf where the once-again-depleted jam display sat. "I can definitely use it." Esther took off her coat and hung it by the door, waved hello, and headed to the small office at the back of the shop to put down her things.

"I am glad." Naomi set the box down on the shelf and looked around the shop. "It is cheerful in here. I like the Christmas tree."

"Thank you," Cheryl said. "I tried not to go overboard, but it's nice to have some holiday decorations."

"Of course." Naomi nodded. "Would now be a good time to go visit with Sarah Schwartz?"

It took a moment for Cheryl's brain to catch up with the change of topic, but this was one of the things she loved about Naomi. She was always direct and to the point.

"Now would be perfect, as long as Esther and Lydia are okay holding down the fort here for a while."

"That is fine," Esther called. She was standing by Lydia, talking excitedly in Pennsylvania Dutch.

"All right then. I'll grab my purse," Cheryl said.

Naomi directed Cheryl down a series of country roads and eventually told her to stop in front of a small wooden house at the edge of a big piece of property. The main farmhouse sat a few hundred yards away, and Cheryl assumed that Sarah's husband, whoever he was, had inherited a piece of his family's property and built his own home right here. That happened a lot in these parts.

Naomi had brought along an apple pie—there was always pie—and a small gift in a brown paper bag, and she carried them both as she led Cheryl up the walkway to the covered porch of the small, snug home.

Naomi knocked on the door, and a moment later it opened to reveal a heavily pregnant young woman.

"Hello, Sarah," Naomi said, holding up the pie. "I brought a visitor who wanted to meet you."

"Hello, Mrs. Miller," Sarah said, opening the door so they could step in. "This is a pleasant surprise. Please come in." She looked at Cheryl quizzically. Cheryl knew that the Amish were sometimes skeptical of outsiders, and Naomi quickly explained.

"This is my friend Cheryl," she said. "She took over for Mitzi at the Swiss Miss. We were hoping you had a few moments for a visit."

"Of course." She gave Cheryl a slight smile. "I am Sarah." Dark curly hair spilled out from under her kapp.

"I'm pleased to meet you," Cheryl said.

Naomi handed the girl the pie. "For the baby," she said, winking.

"The baby does seem to like pie." Sarah laughed. "That is why I've eaten so much of it lately."

Sarah set the pie down on the counter, and Naomi handed over the bag. Sarah thanked her and giggled when she pulled out a pair of yellow knitted booties. "These are very cute," Sarah said, holding them up. "Thank you. It is hard to believe it won't be long until I need them."

"It will be here sooner than you think. Your mother said January?"

Sarah nodded. "Early January." She set the booties gently down on the counter and gestured for them to follow her. Sarah led them slowly down the hallway, waddling a bit with each step. The house was small, but snug and warm.

"I am sorry. I am just finishing up folding the laundry," Sarah said as she led them into the living room where dark dresses and pants were stacked in neat piles. "It takes me longer to do just about everything these days."

"Oh yes, I remember how that is," Naomi said, smiling. "Please do not worry about us. You sit," she said, gesturing toward a rocking chair in the corner of the room next to the fireplace. Sarah gratefully lowered herself into the chair, and Naomi moved a pile of shirts so Cheryl could sit down on the sofa. Then Naomi reached for the next dress in the basket and started to fold. "Cheryl would like to ask you some questions."

"All right." The girl smiled at Cheryl, though she looked a bit wary.

"I'm trying to find some information about Mark Troyer," Cheryl said. "And I understand you knew him."

Sarah's face blanched, and her mouth opened a little, but she nodded. "Ja, I knew him. Not well, but I did know him." She looked down at her swollen belly. "It all feels like such a long time ago now."

It had been about three years, but given the changes that had obviously happened in the girl's life since then, Cheryl had no doubt that it felt longer.

"Can you tell me how you knew him?" Cheryl asked.

"I always knew *of* him, of course," Sarah said. "But he was a few years older, and there were always lots of girls hanging around him. I had never really talked with him until we were at a singing and were paired together for Please or Displease."

At Cheryl's quizzical look, Naomi quickly explained, "It's a game played at singings."

Cheryl was interested to find out more—didn't they just, well, sing at singings?—but she didn't want to distract from the purpose of her questions, so she let Sarah continue.

"We started talking after the game. Mark was...well, all the girls wanted to get his attention, so of course I was flattered that he was paying attention to me."

"You were being courted by Henry Detweiler at the time, weren't you?" Cheryl said.

Sarah's eyes widened, and then she nodded. "Ja, Henry had driven me home a few times, and he had invited me for dinner with his family."

"Did things change when you talked to Mark?" Cheryl had heard Henry's side of the story, but was interested to hear Sarah's take on it.

Sarah ducked her head. "I told you, I was flattered. And I guess I did hope for a while that maybe he liked me as more than a friend." She paused, and her cheeks flushed again. "I told Henry I couldn't get a ride home with him that night after all because I was hoping Mark would ask me. Now I can see that was silly. Mark flirted with everybody, but he never seemed to be serious about anybody." She shrugged. "But I suppose every girl thought she might be the one to change that."

Cheryl knew that narrative. She'd seen it in dozens of romantic comedies and romance novels. It was comforting somehow to hear that Amish girls struggled with the same feelings that everyone else did, even if they hadn't grown up watching the movies and reading the books.

"How did Henry react to that?" Cheryl asked.

"He was not pleased. He was angry. His reaction..." She thought for a moment before continuing. "It made me realize that he was not the man I wanted to marry." She rubbed a hand across her belly absently. "My *daed* is a kind, patient man, and I wanted to be with someone like him. This showed me that Henry was not that man."

Cheryl couldn't help but be reminded of her ex-fiancé, Lance, as she listened to Sarah talk. Had there been signs all along that he was not the man Cheryl should be with?

"So things with Henry ended after that?" Naomi said, bringing her back to the present.

"Yes. He tried to convince me to go with him again, and he brought me cookies he knew I liked from the Honey Bee once. But I had seen who he really was and was not interested."

"Were you still hoping things might work out with Mark?" Cheryl asked.

Sarah was quiet for a moment. "Maybe in the back of my mind," she admitted. "But then, after what happened to him, I was so thankful I was not connected to him." She shrugged. "And soon after that I met Matthew. I knew right away he was the kind of man I wanted to marry. He is kind and generous, and he has never lost his temper around me. It worked out for the best."

"Matthew is a good man," Naomi said. Cheryl looked up and realized that Naomi had finished folding the laundry and was now tidying the books on the bookshelf.

"You said 'after what happened to him,'" Cheryl said. "What do you think happened to Mark?"

Sarah's eyes widened, and she stroked her belly. "I do not like to think about it. But he must have—I mean, they never found his body, but..."

"You think he was killed."

Sarah winced at the words, but nodded.

"What makes you think that?"

"We'd all heard he was mixed up in gambling," Sarah said carefully. "I suppose that was part of the appeal for me, that he was a little bit dangerous. But then when he—" She broke off.

"What made you think that?"

"He was always going off in that car of his at night and wouldn't talk about where he went. And he had money for his car and his phone and all that. It had to come from somewhere." She shrugged. "When he went missing, it seemed pretty clear that the people he was involved with had caught up with him."

"Do you know anything about these people he was involved with?"

"Oh no." She shook her head.

"Or what sort of gambling he was involved in?"

"I do not know. I stayed away from all that."

"That is wise," Naomi said, and Sarah smiled at her.

"Do you have any idea where we might look for answers about all this?"

"No, I am afraid not."

Sarah's answers raised as many questions as they answered, and Cheryl knew she would be looking into the gambling possibility a bit more. But for now, she had another question for Sarah. "You said Henry was very upset after Mark, well, talked with you. Do you think there's any chance Henry might have done anything that would make Mark want to leave?"

She hesitated and then finally answered, "No, I do not believe he would." She grimaced and rubbed her belly again. "I do not think he would have the courage to stand up to Mark or to threaten him," she said. "And certainly not to do anything worse. Besides, he is not a bad man. He was not the man for me, but he is not evil."

Cheryl looked at Naomi who nodded, as if approving her story.

"Okay." Cheryl thought for a moment. "Just one more question then. Do you have a cell phone?"

"Oh no." She looked at Naomi and laughed. "Sometimes I wish I did. Things would be easier. It would be nice to simply call the midwife when my time comes, in case the baby comes quickly. She has a phone, but I do not. I gave it up when I joined the church."

Naomi smiled. "Do not worry. It is your first child. Your labor will last a long time. You will have plenty of time for Matthew to summon the midwife."

Sarah laughed. "I am not sure that makes me feel better."

"It will be wonderful. Hard, but wonderful." Naomi looked to Cheryl. "Do you have other questions for Sarah?"

"No, I guess not. Thank you so much for taking the time to talk with me."

"I hope you find the answers you are looking for. It would be so wonderful to find..." She hesitated. "To find answers."

"I will do my best." Cheryl and Naomi stepped out into the cold November day.

"I think she was telling the truth," Cheryl said as she opened the car door.

"Ja, I believe she was." Naomi sat down on the passenger seat.

"And she thinks something bad happened to Mark," Cheryl said. She turned on the engine and cranked up the heat. "I wish she'd had more information about that, though, aside from assuming it had to do with gambling."

Naomi put her hands to the vents where warm air blew out. "I think there is a real possibility Mark was mixed up in gambling and someone came after him," Naomi said slowly. She looked like she was going to say more, so Cheryl held her tongue and backed the car out of the short driveway. "But you should keep in mind that Sarah has not seen much of the world."

Cheryl turned this over in her mind, trying to make sense of it, and then finally turned to Naomi. "What do you mean?"

"We try to protect our children," Naomi said. "We do not want them to be exposed to bad influences. And though we give them freedom to explore as they become teenagers, we also try to caution them against the dangers to be found in the world."

Cheryl started to understand what Naomi was saying. "You think Sarah was taught that gambling always leads to bad consequences."

It often did, Cheryl knew, and she did not partake of it herself, but she didn't believe that anyone who casually played a hand of poker and visited a racetrack would necessarily be hunted down by a gang of mafia-types, which is what Sarah had seemed to indicate.

"I do not know," Naomi said carefully. "I always prayed that my children would stay away from it. And Seth as well. As far as I know, they have. But it is possible that they have visited a race-track, and nothing bad has happened to them." Naomi moved in her seat and adjusted her seat belt. "I do not know if Sarah realizes that possibility."

Cheryl wondered the same thing. Still, there was evidence of his gambling—the betting slip—and that something bad had befallen him—the bloody shirt—so Cheryl was not going to discount the possibility.

As Cheryl drove back toward the road, she thought about Sarah. She was so young; she couldn't possibly be older than her early twenties. And she seemed so naïve. And yet she already had a husband and a home and a baby on the way. Cheryl had thought she'd have those things by this point in her life as well. If things had gone differently with Lance…

She shook her head. She needed to stop thinking about him.

"Could we make a quick stop before you take me home?" Naomi asked. Cheryl nodded, grateful for the chance to abandon that train of thought. "I need to check in with my cousin about the fund-raiser for her boy Jonas. It is on the way."

"Of course."

Naomi nodded. "Thank you. I will tell you where to turn."

"Actually, I wanted to talk to you about the fund-raiser," Cheryl said. "I spent some time thinking about it last night, and I came up with some ideas for how to make the fund-raiser better."

"Oh?" Naomi sounded hesitant, but she waited for Cheryl to go on.

"The first thing I think you should do is get the word out about the event. Right now, how is anyone supposed to know about it? The obvious things to do are put up flyers around town and post information online—I could post something about it on the shop's Facebook page, for starters—but I think we could do even more than that. An ad in the paper wouldn't cost that much, and it would spread the word all around the area."

"I do not know...," Naomi started, but Cheryl gestured for her to let her finish. This was Cheryl's world. She was good at this stuff. She'd attended and helped organize enough events at her bank that she knew she could pull this off.

"Media attention will help too. I can call the paper and pitch them. This is a human interest story. Readers love this kind of thing. I bet they'll send a photographer and a reporter to the fund-raiser, and you'll get donations coming in even after the fact that way."

Naomi's hands clutched her purse on her lap.

"We could also reach out to more Englisch people in the area. I don't have a list of high net-worth individuals, but there must be plenty who regularly make large charitable donations. This isn't an approved five-oh-one C three obviously, so they wouldn't be able to write it off on their taxes, but I bet for a cause like this we could still pull in a sizeable donation base with the right outreach."

"What is a 'high net-worth individual?'" Naomi's knuckles were white.

"Basically, it just means rich people," she said as she turned the car. She could hear the hesitation in Naomi's voice, but Cheryl knew that if she could get at least some of her suggestions implemented in time, they would be able to make many times what they otherwise would have. She just needed to get Naomi to give it a shot. "Of course, to bring in more of the rich people, we'll probably need to have the event catered, and it may be tricky finding someone at this point, but I can look into which local caterers can pull it off by Saturday."

Cheryl had interviewed several caterers as she planned her wedding, and she was familiar with the sorts of packages most of them offered. If they stuck to standard foods they could make in bulk, it was possible.

"There's not much we can do about the location at this point probably, but maybe with some nice flowers we can make it feel less like an old barn and more like a rustic chalet."

Naomi silently indicated that Cheryl should turn right on to a narrow dirt road. Cheryl slowed the car and flipped on her blinker.

"We'll probably need to raise the ticket price to cover that cost, but if people don't have to supply all the food, they'll probably be willing to pay more anyway."

"We already have much of the food prepared," Naomi said quietly.

"Of course. We can probably use that as well and cut down the caterer's costs or something. We can work that out."

Naomi didn't say anything, but indicated that she should slow down for a driveway just up ahead.

"I'll need to get started today to be able to pull it off in time, but I think we can do it."

Naomi was still quiet, but she nodded, and Cheryl took that as permission to move ahead. She turned off the car, and Naomi stepped out and led Cheryl toward the large white farmhouse.

A girl was hanging laundry on a clothing line by the side of the house, and she called out something in Pennsylvania Dutch.

Chapter Eleven

That's Elizabeth," Naomi said, responding to the girl in the yard with a wave. "She said her maam is in the barn." She led Cheryl around the house and across a wide lawn to a stately red barn.

Cheryl always thought it must be very confusing to keep everyone straight when so many members of a family shared the same name, like this cousin did with Naomi's elder daughter, but she had never seen it cause any real confusion in Amish homes. As with most things, they seemed to be able to figure it all out somehow.

"Sylvia?" Naomi called out, stepping inside the open sliding door. An answer came in Pennsylvania Dutch from the far side of the barn, and Naomi led her past stalls with a few sleek brown horses and a dappled dairy cow and into a wide open area rimmed on three sides by a hayloft. The wide-plank floor had been carefully swept, and it smelled fresh and sweet, like newly cut hay. Dust motes caught in the sunlight that streamed in through the small cracks between boards on the far end of the barn.

A woman in Amish dress was bent over a mop bucket, wrangling the handle into a large tub of steamy water. She straightened up and greeted them in their language, and then Naomi introduced Cheryl and they switched to English.

"I have heard much about Naomi's Englisch friend Cheryl," Sylvia said. "I am so glad to finally meet you." She was very thin and had dark hair and startlingly blue eyes as well as a sweet smile. "Please excuse me for not greeting you more properly. I am trying to get this floor clean before Millie wakes up from her nap."

"Millie is six months old and giving Sylvia quite a test of patience," Naomi said, smiling knowingly.

"My other children were all good sleepers," Sylvia said, flopping the dripping mop onto the wooden floorboards. "This one is contrary in just about every way."

"Your other children were too easy. It is good for you to see how the rest of us have it," Naomi said, smiling lovingly. "Let me help with that." She reached out for the mop.

"No, thank you. It is good for me to have something to do to keep me active. Otherwise I get antsy, and I just worry." She swiped the mop across the floor, and the boards turned a darker shade of brown. Cheryl had never seen a barn with such a nice, clean open area, but then she wasn't exactly an expert when it came to barns. It made sense that it was pretty nice if this was where the family hosted church a couple times a year. A good florist could turn this into a beautiful space, Cheryl decided. It would be rustic and simple, but charming, with some swags of evergreen around the hayloft and bunches of fresh holly at each table. And maybe some roses and fresh lilies for the centerpieces.

"How is Jonas doing?"

"He is all right. He is getting used to giving himself shots, though I am not. It is difficult for me to give it to him because I know he doesn't like it, even though I know it helps him. I will be thankful when we get the insulin pump."

"I am sure it will all get easier as time passes," Naomi said, and Sylvia nodded and moved to a different part of the floor. "I wanted to let you know that we are expecting between seventy-five and a hundred people based on what we have heard so far. I wanted to make sure we would have enough tables."

"That many? That is wonderful."

Cheryl wondered how many of those would be children who wouldn't be contributing to the total amount raised. She was sure she could double that number—and with adults likely to give at least modest donations.

Sylvia stopped and surveyed the room. "I will ask Enoch to check with his brothers. I am sure we can find some more tables."

A good caterer could also provide them, Cheryl silently added.

"Good then. Are you sure you do not need help with the floor?"

"Oh no. Thank you for all you are doing. We cannot express how thankful we are."

"I am glad to do it." She looked at Cheryl. "And Cheryl has some ideas for how we might be able to make it even better."

"Wonderful. Thank you, Cheryl." Sylvia plopped the mop back into the bucket and swiped a hand across her forehead.

"I am glad to help."

A door banged shut back by the animals, and a young boy yelled something in Pennsylvania Dutch.

"That is Jonas," Sylvia said. "He must be home from school for his lunch. I will finish this later." She leaned the mop against the side of the bucket, and the handle rested on the wall.

"Come meet Jonas," Naomi said, following behind Sylvia back toward the door. "He is a good boy."

The boards sank gently beneath them as they walked back into the section of the barn where the animals stood. Cheryl let her fingers trail along the soft muzzle of one of the horses as they walked past. A moment later they stood in the bright sunlight, and she saw a small boy, probably seven or eight, washing his hands in the water from a hand pump. He had a shock of carrot-colored hair and big brown eyes, and he wore a miniature version of the overalls and white shirt the men wore. As a ginger herself, Cheryl had a soft spot for kids with red hair. Sylvia said something to him in their language, and he greeted Cheryl and Naomi with a shy smile.

"Hello, Jonas," Cheryl said.

He ducked his head, and his cheeks turned a bright pink. He said something in Pennsylvania Dutch, and then ran off toward the house.

Cheryl and Naomi thanked Sylvia again, and then they headed back to the car. As Cheryl drove down the rutted dirt driveway, she felt even more strongly that she needed to start making plans to make this fund-raiser even more successful. Jonas and his mother deserved that.

Cheryl dropped Naomi back at her house and then continued on back into town. She parked the car behind the shop, but before she headed inside, she decided to make a quick stop at Yoder's Corner to see if Hannah Hilty was in. Lydia said that Hannah had been interested in Mark, and they had related well because Hannah was also interested in the Englisch world. Maybe Hannah could tell her more about Mark's final days.

Cheryl stepped inside the familiar restaurant, which was busy with the lunch crowd. "Hello, welcome to Yoder's Corner." Cheryl didn't recognize the girl who spoke, but she was Amish, like all the servers here. She wore a long dark dress with an apron that had Yoder's Corner embroidered on it and stood behind a wooden hostess stand.

"Hi there. I was hoping to talk with Hannah Hilty. Is she here today?"

"Ja, would you like me to see if I can get her for you?"

"That would be wonderful. I'd like to talk to her if she has a moment," Cheryl said.

The girl nodded. "I will see."

Cheryl watched as she walked toward the rear of the restaurant and leaned in to say something over the noise to a girl with dark-framed glasses. They both looked at Cheryl, and then the girl—Hannah—shrugged, set down a tray of empty dishes in a window that led to the kitchen, and followed her to the front of the restaurant.

"Hello, Hannah, I'm Cheryl Cooper. I run the Swiss Miss," she said. She'd discovered it often helped strangers feel more comfortable when they realized she wasn't an outsider to Sugarcreek. "I was wondering if I could talk to you." Up close, Cheryl could see that the girl had a light sprinkling of freckles across her nose and that she was wearing mascara and a thin line of eyeliner.

Hannah studied her. The makeup was evidence of the Englisch influence. And Jessica had said that the girl in the car with Mark had had glasses . . . was there any chance?

"I have a few questions about Mark Troyer."

The girl wrinkled her brow. "I don't know anything about Mark Troyer."

"I'm just trying to talk to anyone who was friendly with him," Cheryl said. She hesitated. How could she convince this teen to open up? "There aren't very many people who really knew him, it seems, and I'm told you had a special connection with him."

Hannah hesitated, and then she nodded. Cheryl could see that had done it. All she needed to do was make the girl feel special. The Amish really weren't so different from everyone else.

"I have my break in about five minutes," Hannah said. "Can you wait?"

"Of course."

"I'll come back in a little while." She headed back to the kitchen while the hostess, who was obviously pretending not to listen, looked down at some papers on her stand.

Cheryl watched the servers walking back and forth, their long skirts swishing. She could go for one of Greta Yoder's cinnamon rolls right now, but she had her lunch waiting at the shop, so instead she just watched.

Greta Yoder spotted her as she walked out from the kitchen, and she smiled, held up one finger, and then turned and went back into the kitchen. A moment later, she returned, carrying a sausage. She was a large woman, tall and wide, and she always seemed to have a smile on her face.

"I heard you are sending a package to your aunt," she said, holding out the sausage. "Please send this from me. I wish I could send a cinnamon roll, but I do not think it would still be fresh by the time it gets there."

"Thank you," Cheryl said, taking the smoked meat from the older Amish woman. Cheryl wasn't sure what the rules about shipping meat internationally were, but she would look into that. It was cured—right here in the back of the restaurant, if Cheryl had to guess—so there was no chance of it going bad on the way. "She will really appreciate this."

"Mitzi always loved my sausage," Greta said and then, as if realizing that she had come a little too close to boasting, ducked her head.

"I am grateful for this," Cheryl said, and Greta nodded, excused herself, and headed back to the kitchen.

A few minutes later, Hannah walked back to the front of the restaurant wearing her coat, and Cheryl followed her out the front.

"I figured it would be better to talk outside," Hannah said. Cheryl didn't relish the thought of standing out in the cold, but she followed Hannah to the bench that sat in front of the restaurant. Hannah pulled her coat around her tightly and then sat down, and Cheryl sat next to her. The cold of the bench seeped into her legs. "So you want to know about Mark Troyer."

"Yes. I'm trying to talk to everyone who knew him well. Can you tell me how you knew Mark?"

"I wouldn't say I knew him well, but, as you said inside, we had a special connection," Hannah said. Her hair was mostly tucked up under her kapp, but Cheryl could see it was long and sandy blonde, and she was very thin. She couldn't partake of the food they served at Yoder's Corner often, Cheryl thought wryly.

"And what was that?"

"We both wanted to leave," Hannah said simply. Now that they were sitting, Cheryl noticed jeans poking out from under Hannah's skirt.

"Did you have..." Cheryl tried to figure out how to phrase this. "Feelings for Mark?"

"We flirted some, and for a while I thought he might have been interested in me."

Cheryl wondered how many girls in Sugarcreek had felt that same way.

"But then I realized that he was like that with everyone. But still, we talked sometimes about what we were going to do when we got away from here."

"What did you want to do?" Cheryl asked.

"To be an actress. Still do," the girl said. "As soon as I save up for my bus ticket to California, I'm out of here."

Listening to the passion in her voice, Cheryl thought there was a good chance this girl would leave. It wasn't just the jeans under the dress or the makeup, it was also the way she spoke, with Englisch colloquialisms. She had studied the outside world.

"It must be hard working here." Cheryl used her thumb to indicate the restaurant that catered to tourists and perpetuated every stereotype of the Amish.

"Ehh." She picked at a hangnail, and Cheryl noticed she had a coat of clear polish on her nails. "I know how to put on the good Amish girl act, and the tips are good."

She was savvy, or at least pretending to be.

"Do you have any idea what happened to Mark?" Cheryl asked, pulling her coat tighter around her as a gust of winter wind whipped past.

"I assumed he left, just like he always wanted to." She shrugged. "I was pretty jealous, actually. He was always talking about it, but I didn't realize he was that close to being able to make it on his own."

"Did you ever talk about going with him?"

Hannah gave her a strange look. Cheryl tried to read it but couldn't be sure if it was confusion or if she was trying to hide something. "No."

"Did you see him at all in the days before he left?" Cheryl was trying to figure out if Hannah could have been the one in the car that night.

"No."

Was she avoiding the subject? Or was she just direct? Cheryl didn't know.

"Where do you think he went?"

Hannah continued to pick at the nail polish that flaked off her index finger. "Dunno. I guess to study art. That's what he wanted. We had that in common too, me with acting and him with sculpting." She brought her hand to her mouth and bit at a hangnail. "He was always going on about this one sculptor he liked. Martin something or other."

Martin Puryear. They'd found that book about him in his car.

"Do you know if he'd ever been in touch with his favorite artist?"

"I don't know." She shrugged.

"Just one more question. Do you have a cell phone?" Cheryl asked.

"Sure." Hannah reached through a fold in her dress and pulled a cell phone out. It was a sleek new touch-screen model in a pink case studded with rhinestones. "Why?"

"Could you call this number?" Cheryl listed off her own cell phone number, and Hannah typed it in and hit Call. A moment later, Cheryl's phone rang, and Hannah's number popped up on her screen. It was not the number the text had come from.

"I should probably get back. My break is almost over," Hannah said.

"Of course. Thank you so much for taking the time to talk with me," Cheryl said.

"I hope you find him," Hannah said, pushing herself up. "It would be nice to hear from someone who has made it out."

"I'll let you know," Cheryl said and headed across Route 39 back toward her shop. So far, Hannah seemed the most likely candidate for the Englisch girl in the car, but that didn't necessarily mean it had been her. Cheryl would keep looking.

When Cheryl got back to the shop, there were a few customers browsing, but Esther and Lydia were on top of things, and after giving Lydia a quick update on who she'd talked to and what she'd learned—not much, was the upshot—she stepped into the office at the back of the shop and pulled her sandwich out of the small fridge. She unwrapped it and logged into her e-mail account, where there was one message from an e-mail she didn't recognize. She clicked on it and was delighted to see that it was from Megan Reid, one of the artists Roxanna had told her about. She skimmed the e-mail quickly and felt her hopes deflate as she read that Megan had never heard of Mark Troyer. Well, at least she could cross one name off her list, she thought, and pulled the list of names out of her purse and did just that. She was still waiting to hear from Max Wiley, who made iron sculptures, and from Lester Coblentz, the guy who had grown up Amish. Hopefully one of them would respond soon with information.

Cheryl took another bite of her sandwich and scanned through the rest of her e-mail, but there wasn't anything interesting. Her fingers hovered over the keyboard, and she thought back to Joanna's visit this morning, about how she had seemed to keep looking over her shoulder, like she was afraid of her husband finding out where she really was. Could Saul know more about Mark's whereabouts than he let on?

She wasn't even sure where to start looking for answers. If she'd been looking for information about an Englisch man, she would start with an Internet search, but the Amish lived off the grid, and a quick search for the name Saul Troyer did not turn up any information on the Amish man she was looking for.

Cheryl sat back, the chair creaking beneath her. Normally if she had a question about an Amish person, she'd ask Naomi about them. But she'd already asked Naomi about Saul, and she seemed to think Saul wouldn't have hurt his son. Cheryl wanted to believe her friend, but... well, there were too many other signs that something was not quite right. And Naomi always did see only the best in people. Still, Cheryl wasn't sure where else to turn.

"Cheryl?" She looked and saw that Lydia was poking her head into the office. "Someone is asking for you."

Cheryl set down her sandwich, brushed off her hands, pushed herself up, and then, casting one last glance at her computer, walked into the main part of the shop. Cheryl braced herself for a customer wanting a refund or some vendor looking for distribution but she was pleased to see Jessica Stockton waiting by the Christmas tree near the front of the store, browsing the ornaments on display.

"Hello, Jessica." Cheryl smiled. "Come back for more soap?"

Jessica laughed. "No, though I'll probably walk out of here with some of these cute little ornaments for my nieces." She picked up a hand-carved teddy bear and held it up to the light. "I actually came to see you." She lowered the ornament and hung it back on the tree.

"For one thing, I brought this." She reached into her pocket and pulled out a paper bag. "It's some of the cinnamon hot chocolate mix I give out every year for Christmas. Your aunt was always asking me for the recipe, and I never gave it to her." She grinned.

"Thank you," Cheryl said, taking the bag. "I know Aunt Mitzi will appreciate this."

"The other reason I came back is that I've been thinking about seeing that car at the side of the road since we talked, and something's been bugging me."

"Oh?"

Jessica nodded. "I didn't get a good look at the girl in the car with Mark that night—didn't know it would matter—but I know she was wearing Englisch clothes. But when I picture her there in the front seat, something is off. It wasn't anything I can put my finger on, but..." Her voice trailed off, and she lowered the cat ornament and set it into one of the small shopping baskets Cheryl had stacked by the door. "I know this sounds crazy, which is why I haven't said anything before. But it was like her clothes were too big somehow."

"Her clothes were too big?"

"They didn't fit right. And I don't remember seeing any jewelry, but I can't be sure if that was because she wasn't wearing any or if I just looked too quickly. But something about her"—she shook her head—"something about her was off."

Cheryl tried to figure out what to make of this.

"I knew it sounded crazy," Jessica said. "I probably shouldn't have said anything." She reached for another ornament, this one a hand-whittled horse. "But I thought, well, better to look like a fool than to keep something quiet that might help."

"You don't look like a fool at all. I'm grateful. I'm just trying to figure out what to do with that information."

Jessica shrugged. "I don't know. I was hoping it might spark something for you."

"It might. I appreciate you telling me." She thought for a moment. "But you're sure she had glasses?"

"I am pretty certain she did have those." Jessica laid the horse ornament in her basket. Cheryl tried to picture the scene. Had it been Hannah, there in the passenger seat? Or was it some girl from his classes? How would she ever figure it out?

"Well, this probably didn't help you, but I did find some stocking stuffers, so at least there's that," Jessica said, smiling.

"I'd be happy to ring you up." Cheryl led her to the counter at the back of the shop, and they chatted about Jessica's plans to travel to Texas to visit family for the holidays. Jessica waved good-bye and headed out, and Cheryl returned to the back room to finish her sandwich and think about what Jessica had told her. What were Mark and the girl doing in the car that night? Did she leave town with him? Did she help him get away? Or had she—Cheryl hated to even think about it—could this girl lead them to a more grisly discovery?

Cheryl realized she needed to find out whether Mark had left on purpose or vanished against his will. That was what this whole thing came down to, at its heart. Had Mark's car ended up at the bus station because he'd gotten on a bus and gone away, or had it been abandoned there to get rid of some kind of evidence? Cheryl needed to find out. And one of the things she'd told Naomi she wanted to do was check with the people at the bus station to see if they kept passenger lists.

She dialed the number for the bus station in Columbus again. No one picked up, but she heard the same message she'd heard before. She couldn't find another number for the station. She checked the clock in the corner of her screen.

Well, she'd probably have better luck getting a straight answer in person anyway. And it was still early. It took nearly two hours to get to Columbus from here, but if she hurried, she might have just enough time. She had several hours before she was supposed to meet with Elam. Lydia's shift would be over in an hour or so, so she'd need to see if Esther could stay a bit late today... She might just have enough time to make a quick trip to Columbus. Surely she'd find some answers there.

Chapter Twelve

A few minutes later, it was all sorted out and Cheryl was in her car heading down Route 39 away from Sugarcreek. Esther was glad to earn a little extra money and stay for a few more hours, and Cheryl would give her a ride home after she got back from Columbus. As she drove, the small settlements and villages gave way to wide-open farmland. Even stripped bare for the winter, the fields were lined with long, straight furrows that played funny tricks on your eyes, but it all felt wholesome and comforting. She listened to Christmas music as she drove, and the familiar songs and uplifting lyrics were a balm to her spirit.

When the towns started getting closer together again, she knew she was approaching the outskirts of Columbus, and things started to look familiar. The highways that threaded through the city got grittier, and the buildings were closer together, and soon she was following the directions on her GPS to navigate to the bus station downtown. She hadn't spent much time in this part of town when she'd lived here, and as she climbed out of her car at the municipal lot across from the station, she took in the broken windows in the empty warehouses that surrounded the bus station. You didn't come this way without good reason. How had Mark's car ended up here?

Cheryl took a deep breath, pulled her hat down against the winter wind, which seemed even more bitter here, and trudged through the lot and across the street to the main entrance of the bus station. It was a squat building with a flat roofline and a big neon sign in front. Cheryl pulled open the heavy glass doors, fighting against the wind, and stepped inside.

Cheryl looked around, and then she made her way to the ticket counter at the far side of the room.

"Hello, I'm trying to find out about a passenger who may have taken a bus from this station a while back." Even as she spoke the words, Cheryl felt the futility of this mission. The man on the other side of the glass stared at her blankly.

"I was wondering if you kept passenger lists," Cheryl added to clarify her goal. He didn't respond.

"Do you?" she said. Was he hard of hearing? She spoke louder. "Keep passenger lists for your bus rides?"

"No, ma'am," the man finally said. "Are you here to buy a bus ticket?"

"No, I'm not." Cheryl tried to keep the frustration out of her voice. "I'm trying to find out whether a boy named Mark Troyer took a bus from this station. His car was found nearby, but we're not sure whether he got on a bus or not. Is there any way to tell?"

The man shrugged. "Not likely," he said, shaking his head.

Okay, so this was going to be harder than she thought.

"Are there credit card records that could be checked?"

The man sighed. Under his maroon sweater vest, his belly jiggled. "That would take a long time, even if I could get permission for that, which I doubt. Do you know that he paid with a credit card?"

"No, I was just hoping you could check."

"When was this?" The man raised an eyebrow. "That your friend may or may not have taken a bus?"

"Three years ago in September." She felt all hope go out of her as she said the words. The woman in line behind her cleared her throat.

"I'm afraid our records don't go back that far," he said simply. Cheryl didn't know whether or not that was true, but she was sure she wasn't going to get him to check in any case. She tried one last thing.

"He was Amish. Would anyone remember seeing an Amish boy in here?"

The man blew out a breath. "We get Amish in here all the time. They're all the same. No way to know if your friend was here or not." He leaned over to look around Cheryl. "Next customer."

Cheryl stepped aside, deflated. She had known it was a long shot, but she hadn't expected to be dismissed so quickly. And she hated to hear her friends insulted like that—Cheryl shook her head. A few months ago, she might have assumed all Amish were alike as well, but since moving to Sugarcreek, she'd come to know that the Amish were as diverse and unique as everyone else, even if they did dress alike. After spending so much time in her new warm, welcoming home, it was hard to adjust to the way people sometimes treated you in the big city.

Cheryl turned and headed back out to her car. Well, this was a waste of a trip. She dug into her purse and pulled out her car keys.

But not everyone in Columbus was like that, she reminded herself. There were plenty of good people here. She'd loved living here for most of her adult life.

Before she got back on the road to head back, she swung by Short North, an upscale neighborhood with lots of new restaurants and shops not far from Ohio State University. Wreaths were hung on the light poles and lighted garlands were strung up over the main shopping strip in this part of town. Cheryl drove to a little French chocolate shop she loved that had wonderful truffles. She used to bring some for Aunt Mitzi when she went out to Sugarcreek to visit, and Mitzi had loved them. She bought a small assorted box to tuck into Mitzi's care package. Then she got back on the highway and headed toward home.

By the time Cheryl got back to Sugarcreek, twilight was settling over the cornfields, and she had just enough time to run in and relieve Esther, check her e-mail, and close up the shop before she had to drive out to meet with Lydia's brother Elam. Cheryl saw that she had a message from Max Wiley, one of the artists she was still waiting to hear from. His message was short and terse, but his point came through—he had not heard of a Mark Troyer. Cheryl crossed another name off her list.

Cheryl's headlights illuminated the darkening dirt road as she pulled up in front of Elam's house. Kerosene lamps cast a soft glow in the windows. She knocked on the door and was greeted by a heavy-set woman who introduced herself as Miriam, Elam's wife, and led her into the kitchen. A tall man with the same dark hair and long face as Lydia's was washing his hands at the sink. He had the standard Amish beard and suspenders, but somehow they didn't give him the dour appearance they lent so many Amish men.

"Elam? Lydia's friend Cheryl is here." Miriam seemed to be in the middle of preparing dinner, as piles of chopped vegetables littered the counter.

The man looked up and nodded. "Hello." He was quick to smile, and she could see that despite the responsibilities that he shouldered, he was cheerful and friendly. Or as friendly as he was allowed to be with a strange Englisch woman.

"I'm Cheryl Cooper. Lydia told me you would have some time to talk?"

He nodded and gestured toward the table. "I will be right there."

"Can I get you something to drink?" Miriam asked, but before she had a chance to answer, a baby cried at the far end of the house, and Miriam quickly excused herself and hurried off to soothe the child.

"You want to know about Mark." Elam wiped his hands on a dish towel and turned to her.

"Yes. I'm sure Lydia told you about the text she received"—he nodded and stepped around the counter—"and I told her I would try to see if I could find out who sent it."

"So you came to talk to the Amish man," he said, cracking a smile. He sat down in a chair at the far end of the table.

Cheryl laughed. "I didn't think you sent it yourself. I know that once you join the church, you don't use them anymore. I came to ask more about what Mark was like in the days before he disappeared. Lydia tells me you were one of his closest friends."

"Oh yes, we were very close. At least, I thought we were." He scratched his beard. "But truth be told, I was as surprised as anyone when he turned up missing." His face, so quick to smile before, turned serious. "It made me—well, I was worried, of course. I would have thought..." He scratched at his beard again. "If he'd planned to leave on purpose, I am sure he would have told me."

"So you think..." She tried to phrase this carefully. "You don't think he ran away."

"I do not." He clamped his hands together. "But I do not know what did happen to him. I wish I did. I have prayed all this time for answers, but so far there is nothing."

Cheryl tried to think of things that a best friend would be able to tell her that no one else would.

"I've been told that there was an Englisch girl seen in Mark's car the night he disappeared. Do you have any idea who that might have been?"

He shook his head. "I wish I did. I have often wondered who it might have been. But Mark was... well, we were all jealous of his success with the ladies." He gave her a grin. "He never mentioned any girl being special, and certainly not any Englisch girl."

"Do you think it could have been someone from his art classes?"

"Could be." Elam shrugged. "I do not know. I tried to figure it out at the time, but I did not get anywhere. But even if I did know who it was, I am not sure if it would lead us to him. Could a girl have—" He stopped talking, but Cheryl's brain filled in the rest. He believed Mark was dead and wondered whether a girl would have killed him. The look on his face showed that he doubted that outcome.

Cheryl changed the direction of her questions. "I have heard that Mark was involved in gambling. Do you know anything about that?"

Elam shifted in his seat and looked around the room. Then he spoke. "We all went to the racetrack sometimes. Not a lot, just"— he looked around again—"sometimes."

"What did you do at the racetrack?"

He cocked an eyebrow. "What does anyone do at the race-track? We bet on horses."

She suppressed a smile. It was funny to hear those words from the staid Amish man in front of her.

"We were young," Elam added, as if reading her thoughts.

"Do you know if Mark got into debt from gambling?"

"I doubt it." He looked uncertain. "Unless he went when I didn't know about it. There was a lot of time where he was off, and nobody knew quite where. After everything happened, I know we all wondered what he'd been up to, but at the time, we just did not ask."

"A receipt from the racetrack was found in Mark's car. It was from the day before he disappeared. Do you know if Mark went to the racetrack then?"

"I am sorry. I do not know."

Cheryl sensed he was holding something back. Was he telling her everything he knew? How would she be able to tell?

"Did you notice Mark acting strangely in the days leading up to his disappearance?"

"Not really." He looked down at his hands. "I thought about it a lot, after. Should I have seen something? Should I have known? But I just don't know. He just seemed like Mark. That is part of why I am so sure he did not leave by his own choice. There was no indication that he was planning to go."

Miriam came back into the room, a baby held to her shoulder. "Could you hold him?" she asked her husband, and Elam reached out his arms and took the infant from his mother's arms and settled him on his lap. Miriam went back around the counter and started peeling a carrot.

"Mark was last seen on September 25, three years ago. Did you see him that day?"

Elam hesitated and glanced up at Miriam and quickly away. It was so quick, such a slight motion, that Cheryl wouldn't have seen it if she hadn't been watching him carefully. But it was there.

"No, I did not," he said. Cheryl tried to understand what that look meant. Was he trying to communicate something to his wife? Or to see if she was listening?

"When was the last time you saw him?"

"At church on that Sunday." He bounced his knee, and the little boy smiled and cooed. "We chatted afterward, and when it was time to go, we said good-bye. That was the last I heard of him."

Cheryl couldn't put her finger on what it was—the way he studiously avoided looking toward his wife, or the way his voice caught just a little on the last few words—but something didn't feel right. She got the sense Elam wasn't telling her the truth about something. But how could she find out what was the truth? All she could think to do was keep asking questions.

She thought for a moment. "If he didn't run away, do you have any idea what might have happened to him?"

"I have lain awake in bed so many nights wondering that," he said, shaking his head. "At first I thought his car might have gone off the road. It was raining that night, and it can be hard to see out here on these roads. But then they found the car at that bus station." The baby in his lap leaned forward and gnawed on Elam's hand. "I am sure you heard that his shirt was found in the trash can outside the Honey Bee." Cheryl nodded. "I don't want to assume the worst, but—I do not know."

"Did he have any enemies?"

Elam laughed. "Plenty of guys hated him for catching the eye of their girls. But enemies? No. Nothing like that."

Cheryl tried to think of what more to ask, but she wasn't seeming to get anywhere. Reluctantly, she pushed herself up.

Cheryl still sensed there was more going on than he was willing to share, but she could see she wasn't going to get any more information from him right now.

"Thank you so much for taking the time to talk with me."

"You are welcome. There are many people who will be happy if you can find what happened to Mark."

He didn't say that he was one of those people, Cheryl mused as Miriam led her to the door. She would need to see what more she could find out about Elam and what he knew about Mark's last days.

Cheryl climbed into her car and turned the engine on, but before she could put on her seat belt, she heard her name being called. She opened the door and stepped out and saw a figure running through the empty meadow beside the house toward her. It took just a moment for it to register as Lydia. She must have run over from her own house on the far side of the property.

"I saw your car and knew it was you," Lydia said breathlessly. "I'm so glad I caught you."

"Lydia, what's going on?" The girl was out of breath, and in the dim light Cheryl's headlights cast over the yard, she could see that her eyes were wide with—excitement? Fright? Cheryl couldn't tell.

"You have to see this," Lydia said and held something out. It took a moment for Cheryl's eyes to register it as her cell phone. "I got another text."

Chapter Thirteen

Cheryl took the phone and looked down at the screen, which glowed in the darkness of dusk that surrounded them.

You're on the right track. Open the box.

"When did you get this?"

"About ten minutes ago."

Cheryl took the phone and pulled up the number it had been sent from. It was the same number as the previous text. "Oh my."

"But what does it mean?" Lydia asked.

Cheryl read the words again, trying to force them into some sort of order in her mind. "I don't know." They were on the right track. Track. Could it have something to do with the racetrack? Was there some connection to gambling after all?

"Could it be a reference to the racetrack?" Cheryl said. Lydia shrugged. Cheryl read it again. "Do you know what box this is referring to?" Cheryl asked.

"No. I have no—" She stopped suddenly and narrowed her eyes. "Wait. It couldn't mean..."

"What?" Cheryl was jumpy with anticipation as she waited for Lydia to finish a thought.

"I may know what the box is," Lydia said. She held a hand to her chest.

"What?"

Lydia looked around the dark fields surrounding the driveway. "Could you give me a ride back to my house? I need to show you something."

They piled into Cheryl's car, and a few minutes later Lydia was leading her into her house. Like most Amish homes she'd seen so far, Lydia's home was neat and felt serene, even though this one was filled with children of varying ages getting ready for dinner. Lydia introduced Cheryl to her mother Almina and some of her siblings, including the adorable wide-eyed baby Beatrice, and then led her into the large living room. Lydia left the room and returned a moment later with a small wooden box, about the size of a shoe box.

The top section of the box was made of cherry, but alternating strips of pine and mahogany created a striped pattern around the bottom edges of the box. On the front was a keyhole. "I think maybe it's this. I need to get this box open."

"Okay. Where is the key?" Cheryl asked.

"Hidden inside somewhere, I assume," Lydia said. "It's a puzzle box. Mark loved to make them."

Cheryl remembered Lydia saying something about a puzzle box earlier in the week. She had heard of puzzle boxes. Usually, you had to slide a series of panels or unlock a series of locks to get to something that was locked inside.

Lydia handed it to Cheryl, and she took it and examined it in the dim light from the kerosene lamps. It was heavier than she'd expected, and up close she could see that the top panel was decorated with finely crafted wood inlaid in a sunset design. Cheryl remembered seeing similar boxes at Mark's parents' house.

"Mark made this?" Cheryl examined the box from every angle, looking for a line or seam that would indicate a piece to move.

Lydia nodded. "He had made a number of them, hiding small things inside, and he just got better every time. He gave this to me for my birthday a few days before he disappeared."

"Was there anything inside?" Cheryl shook the box, but nothing rattled or moved. If there was anything inside, it was well protected.

"I do not know. The day he gave it to me, I was sitting at the outdoor picnic table trying to figure out how to open it. I had gotten as far as finding the first panel." She gently took the box from Cheryl, flipped it upside down, and pointed to a line so fine and on the grain that she wouldn't have seen it if Lydia hadn't pointed it out. "This used to slide open." She gestured toward herself, indicating the way the piece of wood would have moved. "And then this"—she indicated a piece of the dark mahogany wood at the bottom—"slid this way. I think that would have allowed this piece to slide over"—she indicated a strip of pine that met it at the corner—"but this is as far as I got before Mother asked me to help take down the laundry because a storm was coming in. While I was busy, Homer took the box and tried to open it himself," she said.

Cheryl remembered Homer as one of the brothers she'd been introduced to a few minutes ago. He was probably eleven or twelve and a bit on the chubby side.

"But when the rain started, he ran in and forgot about it. He left it under a tree. It got soaked, and the wood warped. I could never get it open after that."

Cheryl's heart sank. It was such a beautiful piece, and if it was indicative of Mark's talent with woodworking, he really was very skilled. It was an easy leap from this to sculpture—this box was a work of art.

"I am sure that if I had been able to get the right pieces moved, I would have found a key hidden somewhere that would have opened the box. I was going to ask Mark for help, but then he disappeared just a few days later, and in the craziness after that, I forgot all about it." She held it up toward the light and examined the design on the top panel. It was worked in different colors of wood. "I have kept it because it is beautiful and it reminds me of Mark, but I gave up trying to get it open a long time ago."

Cheryl reached for the box again, and she tried to slide open the panel Lydia had indicated, but it was jammed, the wood warped, just like she had said. She turned the box over, looking for any other lines or anything to indicate a way in, but she didn't see anything.

"What sorts of things did he usually hide inside?"

"Just little things. Candy or a small toy for a child. That is why I didn't try harder to get it open. It didn't seem worth ruining the beautiful box for a piece of candy."

Cheryl appreciated her impulse to protect this gorgeous piece. But she also felt her curiosity growing every moment. What could possibly be inside that was so important?

"Is there any other box you can think of that the text might have been referring to?" Cheryl held out only vague hope that this might be the case.

"No." Lydia shook her head. "I don't know of any other boxes that need to be opened."

Cheryl had to admit the timing was too perfect. If he'd given it to her just before he disappeared, there had to be a reason.

Cheryl gave the box another gentle shake, but again heard nothing inside. "It doesn't sound like there's anything in here."

Lydia shrugged. "Maybe it's something very light. I do not know. But I do know that we need to find a way to get it open."

Cheryl agreed. "And there is no other way to get inside? No backup mechanism?"

"Not that I have found." Lydia pressed her lips together. "We could always cut it open."

Cheryl examined the beautifully chosen and carefully hand-in-laid design on the top of the box. It would be a shame to cut into this piece and destroy it if there was any way to avoid it. And what if cutting into it damaged whatever was inside?

"Let's try to find another way in before we do that," Cheryl said, and Lydia agreed. Lydia promised to keep trying, and she would keep Cheryl posted.

As Lydia walked Cheryl back to her car, Cheryl told her about her trip to the bus station, as well as her conversations with Elam, Hannah, and Sarah. Lydia hesitated as they approached the car, and Cheryl looked back and noticed that she seemed downcast.

"What is it?" Cheryl said. It was dark out here in front of the house. Sometimes she thought she'd never get used to living out here without streetlights.

"You have already spoken to so many people about this. You will soon run out of people to ask, and we are no closer to finding out who sent the texts or what happened to Mark."

Cheryl felt torn. On the one hand, Lydia was voicing her own frustrations and fears. On the other hand, she couldn't lose hope now, not when they had just gotten a nudge in the right direction. Whoever had sent the texts was out there somewhere; Cheryl would find them and they would lead to answers about Mark.

"I'm still waiting to hear back from several of the artists I contacted," Cheryl said. "None of them are Amish, so they probably have a cell phone. Any of them could have sent it." She hitched her purse up on her shoulder. "And I want to go to the racetrack, especially after that new text, and see if anyone there knows anything about Mark. And I'm still trying to find out who the Englisch girl in the car was." Lydia's face was beginning to perk up, so Cheryl continued.

"And I still need to track down one person who was seen at the Honey Bee the same day as his shirt was found." Cheryl tried to think of who else she needed to find.

"Who is the person from the Honey Bee?" Lydia asked.

"Moses somebody?"

"Ach. Moses Schrock." Lydia nodded. "He's Old-Order Swartzentruber Amish. You'll find him at Weaver Lumber."

Cheryl recognized the name of the most conservative of all Amish sects, but that's not what caught her attention. Weaver Lumber. That was where Mark had worked.

"He worked with Mark?"

Lydia shrugged. "I am not sure if they worked there at the same time or not. But Moses works there now."

"I'll try to stop by tomorrow then," Cheryl said, and Lydia gave her a weak smile. "I'm not giving up," Cheryl said. "And neither should you. I'll see what I can find out. In the meantime, you work on getting that puzzle box open."

"I will," Lydia said, but she cast her eyes downward a touch too quickly. "Thank you."

"Of course." Cheryl stood still and watched Lydia for a moment, but it was so dark out that she couldn't tell if Lydia was avoiding her gaze or if Cheryl was just imagining it.

"I will see you tomorrow," Lydia said and then turned and headed back inside.

As she drove home, she couldn't stop thinking about the look on Lydia's face. Was there something Lydia wasn't telling her? Lydia couldn't be keeping anything from her, could she? Why would she, when she was the one who had asked Cheryl to look for answers in the first place?

Cheryl kept her eyes trained on the dark road and tried to focus. There was no reason to suspect Lydia of anything. Cheryl was getting so turned around she didn't know who she could believe anymore.

Chapter Fourteen

Thursday morning, the Swiss Miss seemed warm and cheerful, and she lit the wood-burning stove and set up the register feeling grateful for her life. Lydia came in just as she was turning the sign to Open, and they chatted for a few minutes. Lydia had tried all evening to get the puzzle box to open, but had had no luck, and neither had her father or her brothers.

"I think we may need to cut it," she said.

"That would be such a shame," Cheryl said, thinking about the beautiful inlaid wood and the skilled craftsmanship. "Let's keep trying to get it open another way, and if we can't, then we'll cut it open."

Lydia agreed, and then when Cheryl mentioned running out for a while, Lydia promised to take good care of the shop. Cheryl grabbed her coat and purse and climbed into her car.

She'd found the address for Weaver Lumber in the phone book last night, and she punched it into her phone's GPS now. It wasn't far away, just a few miles out on a back road a bit off the main highway. She didn't know if Moses Schrock would be working today, but she figured it was best to just go on out and see.

Weaver Lumber was housed in a small wooden building in front of a large covered lumberyard, with stacks of wood piled higher than her head in many places. Cheryl assumed from the thick tree trunks piled on their sides at the far end that much of the lumber was milled here on-site. Cheryl pulled up next to a buggy and went inside the main building. The interior of the store, like the exterior, was plain, but the walls were lined with samples of different kinds of wooden planks, siding, and flooring. An Amish man stood behind the counter writing on a carbon-copy receipt and looked up when Cheryl stepped inside. Behind the counter was a hand-lettered sign that read We Cut to Size.

"Hello," she said, stepping up to the counter. The sound of a power saw biting through wood floated out from the behind the shop. Cheryl was surprised to hear that, as well as to see a desktop computer sitting on the counter, but she had heard that sometimes the Amish were allowed to use tools at work that they couldn't use in their personal lives. "I'm looking for Moses Schrock. Is he working today?"

"He is in the back," the man said. He eyed her skeptically. She assumed not too many Englisch women came here asking for Moses. "I am Larry Weaver. Who can I tell him is here to see him?"

"My name is Cheryl Cooper." She hesitated. That name would mean nothing to Moses. How could she make sure he would be willing to talk with her? "I wanted to ask him about Mark Troyer."

That name got his attention. His eyes widened, and he paused and stared at her for a moment. "Mark Troyer?"

"Yes, please."

He set his pen down. He watched her a minute longer, hesitating, considering, and then he nodded. "Wait, please."

He stepped through a door that led, Cheryl assumed, to the back. With the door open, the sound of saws whining and the smell of sawdust was even more pronounced. While she waited, she flipped through a rack of flooring samples. The Brazilian cherry was beautiful, but—goodness, could that really be the price?

She looked up as a boy stepped into the showroom. He was thin and mousy, and he was trying, Cheryl could see, to grow a beard, though it was patchy and very thin. She assumed that meant he was married and had committed to his church and therefore would not be allowed to own a cell phone, but she would check.

"Moses?"

The boy nodded, but—like many of the Amish men she'd talked to—didn't meet her eye.

Another customer came in the door of the small shop, and the man behind the desk reluctantly stopped listening to their conversation and went to greet the customer.

"My name is Cheryl Cooper," she said to Moses. "I run the Swiss Miss. Do you know the store downtown?"

He nodded again.

"I'm trying to find out more about Mark Troyer. Did you know Mark?"

"Yes. He worked here."

"And you worked here with him?"

He shifted his weight from one foot to the other. "I had just started when he . . . when he disappeared." He glanced at his boss, who was busy showing flooring samples to the Amish man who came in behind Cheryl.

"Did you know him well?"

"No." He kept his eyes pointed downward. "He was older. He helped me learn how things work around here. But we were not close."

It was hard to tell with the way he was avoiding her eye, but she got the sense he was telling the truth.

"I wanted to talk with you because Kathy Snyder remembers seeing you at the Honey Bee the day Mark disappeared."

He tilted his head, like he was confused, but nodded.

"Yes. I went there to buy food for my family for dinner. My maam was sick, and there was nothing to eat."

That lined up with what Kathy had told her.

"Do you remember about what time you were there?"

"After work. So around five thirty, I guess. I rode my bike over and it was still light out, but starting to get dark by the time I got home."

Cheryl considered how best to phrase her next question. "Did you see anything unusual while you were there?"

He thought for a moment and then shook his head. "No. Like what?"

He seemed sincere. But he had to have at least heard about the shirt in the trash can; it seemed like everybody around here was familiar with the details surrounding Mark's disappearance.

"You know about the shirt that was found in the garbage can behind the café, right?"

Moses glanced at her, his brow wrinkled. "What?"

"You don't know about that?"

He shook his head. She would think he was lying except that he seemed so earnest.

"One of Mark's shirts was found in the garbage can behind the Honey Bee. The night Mark disappeared." She watched him to see how this news hit him.

"What?" Again, it was hard to believe this was news to him, but he seemed genuinely surprised. "What about his shirt?"

"It had blood on it. A lot of people assumed it meant something bad had happened to him. That he was..." She faltered. "That he was hurt. They think the bloody shirt was a clue about what might have happened."

Moses shook his head, and his eyes widened. "I did not know people thought that."

Now it was Cheryl's turn to be confused.

"What do you mean?"

Moses swallowed, and then he looked up and met Cheryl's gaze. "I know how the shirt got in the trash can."

CHAPTER FIFTEEN

Cheryl tried to take in what Moses Schrock had just told her. "You know how Mark's bloody shirt got in the trash can behind the Honey Bee?"

"Yes." Moses nodded. "I put it there."

"What?"

"I did not know anyone would find it and think..." Moses was mumbling. "I did not know. People must have been so worried... Oh, I did not mean to make them think..."

Cheryl tried to follow his thoughts, but he was not making sense.

"Moses," Cheryl said. His head snapped up. "Can you tell me how the shirt ended up there?"

Moses looked around. "I had just started working here when Mark disappeared."

Cheryl nodded. He had said that before.

"I did not know how to use much of the equipment, but I was excited to learn. My family is Swartzentruber." He looked at her to see if she understood. She nodded. She knew the Swartzentruber Amish were the most conservative branch of the Amish around here, and they did not approve of many "conveniences" the Amish like Naomi used, such as propane-powered appliances, indoor plumbing, outdoor phone shanties, and padded furniture. They did not even hang the orange reflective safety triangle on their buggies, worried that it could be seen as decoration. They were hard core.

"I had never seen a power saw before I started working here," Moses said. "I was excited about it, and Mark was patient with me, helping me learn how to use some of the saws. But one time I tried to cut a piece without help, and I cut my finger deeply on the blade."

Cheryl recoiled. She quickly glanced down at his hands and saw that he still had all his fingers.

"It was not turned on, thank goodness," Moses said quickly. "I was just positioning the blade. But it was a deep cut nonetheless. The blades are very sharp. It bled a lot. I tried to stop it, but I quickly bled all over my shirt. I knew that my maam would be very upset, not to mention Mr. Weaver." He looked around again, making sure his boss was not in the room. "I was not really supposed to be using that saw. Or any saw, actually." He took a deep breath. "I did not want to lose my job. I did not know what to tell him to explain why I had blood all over. But Mark said he had an extra shirt in his car."

Cheryl could see where this was going now. "He let you borrow his shirt so you wouldn't get in trouble."

"Yes. I was going to bring it home and wash my own shirt before my maam saw it and then bring it back. But then I knocked my hand while I was piling a stack of lumber, and the cut opened up again. It bled much more than I thought it would. It got all over Mark's shirt. I told him I was so sorry, and I promised I would clean it, but Mark did not seem concerned at all. He said not to worry about it. He did not need it anymore and to just take it.'"

She could picture it. But that didn't explain one thing. "But how did it end up in the trash can?"

Moses ducked his head, like he felt a bit ashamed. "I stopped by the Honey Bee on the way home, since my maam was sick, like I said. And I realized I now had two bloody shirts to hide from her. I realized it was going to be easier to deal with one than two, and since Mark had told me to just get rid of it, I did. I tossed it in the trash can and did not think twice about it."

The explanation made sense, and Cheryl couldn't decide if she felt relief or frustration at hearing it. It was so simple, and so believable. And yet…

"But why didn't you tell anyone about this before? You must have heard what people were saying after Mark vanished."

Moses shook his head. "I did not. I never…"

She waited for him to go on.

He took a deep breath. "I told you my maam was sick. She…well, she passed a few days after that."

Cheryl gasped. The poor boy. That was horrible.

"I did not come in to work for a while, so I did not even know that he was gone at first." He shrugged. "Of course, when I came back, I learned he was gone. But after what he'd said about not needing the shirt anymore, I assumed he had simply left. A lot of people seemed to think that. After all, he had a car. He took classes at the community college. He wore jeans and used his cell phone constantly. He was practically Englisch already."

"And you never heard about the shirt in the trash can?"

"No. No one ever told me that. I would have told someone what had happened if I knew."

After all, Cheryl thought, why would anyone mention it to him? No one would have any reason to assume he had anything to do with it. She reasoned through what he'd said. In the wake of a death, especially the death of a mother, it did make sense that he would be out of touch with what was going on with the rest of the world. Something like a coworker leaving to join the Englisch—especially one who, as he'd pointed out, had one foot there anyway—would not seem extraordinary. And if he was Swartzentruber, he would not be part of the same church as Mark's family and community. They would not necessarily interact outside of work. She could see how it was possible.

"I have just one more question," she said. Moses nodded, waiting for her to go on. "Do you have a cell phone?"

"I do not." His cheeks pinked, and he glanced around quickly again. "I would love to. But it is not allowed."

Cheryl nodded. It was what she had expected to hear. "Thank you for your help, Moses," Cheryl said. She pulled a business card for the Swiss Miss out of her purse. "If you think of anything else that might be relevant, please stop by or give me a call."

Moses promised he would, and she thanked him and headed out the door. She stopped just outside of the shop and thought about what Moses had said. She knew many people kept all kinds of things in their cars—some things they wanted to have on hand and other things that got left behind and never cleaned out. Maybe Mark really just happened to have a spare. But was it more plausible that he had a shirt in his car because he had other clothing there as well? That he had a suitcase packed? That he was not sad to part with a shirt that would mark him as Amish, a shirt from the life he was anxious to leave behind? He'd said he didn't need it anymore. Could that be because he wasn't intending to be Amish anymore?

In either case, the bloody shirt was explained. It was one of the factors that had made it look like Mark had been hurt, or worse. With that clue no longer relevant, there was less to believe that someone had hurt Mark. She was hopeful that meant he was still out there somewhere.

She felt her heartbeat speed up. She hadn't realized how much she'd been hoping to find a reason to believe he was still out there. She had never met Mark, but she had come to care about him. Talking to so many people who knew him and cared about him, she had started to feel like she knew him too. But even if he was still alive, she still wasn't any closer to figuring out where he was.

Well, she had one non-mystery-related chore to do, and now was as good a time as any to tackle that. She had all the treats different people had given her for Aunt Mitzi in her trunk. If she was hoping to get it to Aunt Mitzi before Christmas, she had better get it shipped out soon. Cheryl drove to a pack-and-ship place out in the strip mall a little ways outside of town and carried the goodies inside. While she boxed up and addressed the package, she kept sneaking glances at the girl behind the counter. She was wearing jeans and a red U-Pack-It polo shirt, and she had thick-framed glasses.

Cheryl watched her as she helped the customer at the front of the line. She seemed friendly and outgoing. Cheryl could see the outline of a cell phone in the pocket of her jeans. And she was Englisch and wore glasses and looked to be about the right age...

Cheryl shook her head. She was being crazy. She couldn't go around suspecting every girl with glasses of being the girl in the car with Mark that night. But still, she couldn't stop herself. When it was her turn, Cheryl chatted with the girl a bit, and then, while she was entering Mitzi's address into the store's computer, Cheryl ventured, "Do you by any chance happen to know anything about a boy named Mark Troyer?"

The girl narrowed her eyes and shook her head. "I don't think so." She continued to type on the computer. "Why? Who is he?"

Cheryl felt ridiculous. "Never mind."

The girl shrugged and went back to entering the information into the computer. Cheryl paid and thanked the girl and then headed outside.

She was losing it. She was doubting everyone now. She couldn't go around asking everyone she met whether they were behind Mark's disappearance. She was starting to believe everyone was hiding something...

But then she thought about the texts she'd received. Someone out there *was* hiding something. Someone knew where he was. And that someone wanted them to know it too.

You're on the right track, the last text had said.

She would find him. She wouldn't stop until she'd figured it out.

Cheryl stepped out into the parking lot and strode toward her car. She knew just where she had to go next.

CHAPTER SIXTEEN

Cheryl called the shop as she drove, and Lydia reassured her that she could manage things while Cheryl made a quick trip to Wooded Hills Racetrack. The track was about a half-hour drive from Sugarcreek, but she found it easily and parked in the wide lot, which was not very full on a Thursday morning in early December.

The gray sky hung low and heavy as she walked inside the gates and up the steps to the concourse. In front of her there were high metal tables covered in chipped paint in a sad grayish blue and screwed to the cement floor. Bins attached to the tables held slips of paper and pens attached to the table with metal cords. A few men hunched over scraps of paper, filling out their wagers for an upcoming race, Cheryl assumed. Beyond that, rows and rows of metal bleachers sat under a high metal roof. A small crowd was gathered in the first rows. In front of the bleachers was the race-track—a dull green infield surrounded by a red-brown dirt track. A race was in process, and Cheryl watched as half a dozen horses sprinted around the final curve toward the finish line. The con-course was fairly empty, save for a few men holding paper slips and a few with plastic cups. The whole place gave off an air of desperation.

A few cheers went up as the horses crossed the finish line. She turned and took in the windows that lined the back side of the concourse. People were already making their way toward the windows, ready to collect their winnings, she assumed.

You're on the right track, the text had said. Was it a reference to something here she was meant to find? Did it have anything to do with this racetrack at all? *Please, Lord*, she prayed as she looked around. *If there's something I'm supposed to discover here, please make it clear*. Because if it was up to her, she'd be out of here as quickly as possible.

Cheryl wasn't sure what else to do, so she approached one of the windows. "Hello," she said to the man behind a screen of bulletproof glass. She felt the futility of this mission before she even opened her mouth. "I'm trying to find out about a friend of mine. He...well, he disappeared a few years back. And he had a betting slip from this racetrack in his car." The man narrowed his eyes and crinkled his eyebrows. "He was Amish," she added as an afterthought. She felt ridiculous.

The man behind the glass didn't answer for a moment. He was an older man with a gray mustache and wire-rimmed glasses.

"I don't know what you...," he started, but then his eyes widened and he sat up a bit straighter. "Wait, I remember this," he said, his eyes lighting up. "It was in the papers, wasn't it?"

Cheryl nodded, relief flooding through her. He might not know how to help her, but he had heard about this at least.

"This Amish kid disappeared, and he had a betting slip from this place in his car."

"Exactly." She was nodding so much she felt like a bobblehead. "It was dated the day before he disappeared. And I'm trying to find out if anyone here saw him or might remember him."

The man behind the window was nodding slowly. "That's right. I read about that. I remember, because I thought it was strange. They were trying to make it out like maybe he'd got into trouble with gambling and someone had come after him or whatever."

"That's what I'm trying to find out," Cheryl said. "If he was into gambling. If he came here." She leaned in a bit more so she could see the man better through the smudged glass. "If he had, he would have been allowed to place bets?"

"As long as he was eighteen and had money, sure."

Cheryl knew that both of these were true, so that didn't help. "Do you think anyone here might remember seeing him?"

"I doubt it. We see a lot of people in here. You got a picture?"

She shook her head.

"Well, I can't say if he came here or not then." He shrugged. "We get some Amish in here sometimes, but he was doing his ramspringy or whatever, right? Where he could dress normal and stuff?" She nodded again. "I probably wouldn't have noticed him then, even if he did come here. But I remember reading about what they were saying and thinking it sounded strange. If he had gotten in trouble with gambling, it would have been hard to do it here."

"Why is that?"

"Because we don't extend credit. You can't bet what you don't have. With us anyway. If he'd been working with an outside individual"—Cheryl assumed this was his code for bookie—"then all bets are off, so to speak. But if he had a slip from here, then that seems unlikely." Cheryl had thought the same thing herself.

"They tried to pin it on us. That's why I remember it."

Cheryl thought the criminal accusation wasn't exactly fair, but he looked like he was going to say more so she let him continue.

"But I also thought it was weird because if you want to make a lot of money gambling, there are easier ways to do it than coming here." He gestured toward the sad men shuffling toward the other windows. None of them looked thrilled to be here. "It made me think they were just grasping at straws, trying to come up with any reason at all to explain what happened, when it seemed obvious he just left the Amish and became normal."

Cheryl would have phrased it differently, but she was starting to agree with his point.

"Is there anything at all you can think of that might explain why he would have a betting slip from this racetrack in his car?"

The man shrugged. "Aside from coming here, not really. But that doesn't mean much. I don't think you're going to have much luck finding him looking around here."

Cheryl was only too glad to hear that. She thanked him and made her way back out to her car as quickly as she could. She hadn't learned anything certain, but the man had echoed what she'd started to suspect—that the whole gambling idea was just a distraction, a rabbit trail that would only lead her further away from the answers she sought.

Cheryl got back in her car and gratefully pointed it toward home.

Chapter Seventeen

As Cheryl got closer to Sugarcreek, she decided to make a quick stop before she went back into the shop. She hadn't talked to Naomi since their visit to Sylvia Esch's barn yesterday, and she wanted to run the ads she'd designed by her friend, as well as get her permission to go ahead and book a caterer for the event. She'd also come up with a list of vendors to approach about silent auction items, and she had a list of florists she could call and examples of rustic-chic centerpieces she'd found on Pinterest. If she was going to pull this all together by Saturday, she needed some answers, so she turned on to the old country road that led to her dear friend's house.

When she knocked on the door, she was startled to see Levi answer it. His sun-streaked blond hair was messy, and his blue eyes were clear and sparkling.

"Hello, Levi," Cheryl said, and he gave her a shy smile. Unlike most Amish men she'd met, Levi didn't avoid meeting her eyes, but sometimes, like now, he looked away a bit too quickly, like he was embarrassed to be caught looking at her. "Is Naomi here?"

"She's in the kitchen. We were just finishing up lunch." He was wearing a standard white shirt, but the sleeves were rolled up to his elbows, and she could see the muscles in his forearms flex as he closed the door. She took a deep breath and fought down the thrill of excitement that ran through her. Levi was her good friend's stepson. That was all he was and all he could ever be.

Levi stepped aside, and she followed him to the kitchen.

"Hello," Naomi said. She was wiping down the counter with a dishrag. She looked at Cheryl and then at Levi, who was waiting, his eyes on Cheryl. "I am just finishing up in here, and I was going to pick some winter vegetables for dinner," Naomi said. "Do you mind coming out with me?"

"Not at all." Cheryl loved visiting Naomi's vegetable garden. The idea of raising your own food was so inspiring, and the vegetables that came out of the garden tasted fresher and better than anything you could buy at the store. "That sounds great."

"Good. Levi, you will go help your father with the horses in the pasture?"

"After I finish mending the bucket for the water pump," he said, keeping his eyes on the other side of the room.

"Okay then." She hung the rag on the faucet and lifted her coat off the hook by the back door. She took a small pair of scissors from a drawer next to the sink and tucked them into a pocket of her dress. "Cheryl, could you bring that basket?" She pointed to a wicker basket on the table.

"Got it," Cheryl said and followed her friend out the back door. Naomi walked quickly across the dirt yard and through the small gate that led to the vegetable garden. This time of year much of autumn's bounty had been harvested, but there was a sheet of plastic arched over a section of ground at the far side of the garden, a homemade greenhouse of sorts, where leafy greens thrived. Naomi led her past stalks of broccoli and green shoots, which Cheryl knew marked potatoes, toward a group of vines.

"I am making butternut squash soup," Naomi said, bending down to examine a creamy beige squash. "I need two nice big ones."

Cheryl nodded and bent down to look under the large green leaves for a ripe squash.

"I wanted to show you some ads I designed for the fundraiser," Cheryl said. "And I have a couple caterers who could pull it off by Saturday, but I need to let them know today."

Naomi didn't say anything for a moment, but continued rooting around in the dirt. Cheryl lifted up a leaf and found a squash that had been nibbled by an animal of some sort.

"I do not think you need to hire a caterer," Naomi said. "We have most of the food made already."

Cheryl had been prepared for this answer. That was okay. She had a backup plan. "In that case, we'll play up the fact that there will be wholesome home-cooked Amish food," Cheryl said. "People will love that. I still think we'll be able to charge a decent price for the tickets."

Naomi pulled up a weed and set it gently on the dirt. She sat back on her heels.

"I do not know, Cheryl," she said. "I do not think we need all these people who will be lured by the promise of a home-cooked Amish meal. We've always had plenty of people come who already expect that, and we have had a good time. I do not think we need to invite a lot of these 'high net-worth individuals.'"

Cheryl paused. There was a bit of an edge in her voice. Cheryl had rarely heard that from her friend.

"But don't you want to raise as much money as possible for Jonas?"

Naomi reached for the stem of a squash and broke it with one quick motion. "I do want to raise money to help my cousin's family. But I also want them to enjoy the party."

Cheryl tried to understand what her friend was getting at. "But won't they enjoy it more the more money we raise?"

"No. They will not." Naomi brushed the dirt off the skin of the squash and set it down gently in the basket next to her. "Having wealthy Englisch people they do not know will make them feel out of place and uncomfortable, even if the people are there to help their son."

Naomi broke the stem of another squash and held it up to examine it. Then she set it in the basket, took a deep breath, and continued.

"Cheryl, I am so thankful for all that you are doing to help us, but I do not think..." Naomi hesitated and appeared to be searching for the right words. "This advertising, and the silent auction, and florists... This is not our way," she finally said.

"But that's my point. Maybe if you did things a different way, you would have a more successful fund-raiser."

Naomi was silent for a moment, and then she pushed herself up. "I suppose it depends on what you think success is."

She picked up the basket and rested the handle in the crook of her arm and then gestured for Cheryl to follow her toward the hoop house. Cheryl tried to interpret what her friend was really saying as she stood up and made her way across the carefully planted rows toward the plastic greenhouse.

"Everything that you have come up with would no doubt help to raise more money for my cousin's child. I thank you for that, for caring enough to spend so much time trying to help us." Naomi unclipped a corner of the plastic sheeting and pulled it back, and then she pulled the small pair of scissors from her pocket. "But please, let us do this our way this time. You come and see, and then maybe in the future you can help us on another fund-raiser."

Cheryl didn't know what to say. Naomi did not want her help. Cheryl knew that Naomi wasn't trying to hurt her, but it did feel like a rejection, like Cheryl's ideas weren't good enough.

"I really do appreciate your help," Naomi said, looking up at Cheryl. "And I do hope you come on Saturday."

"Of course," Cheryl said. She smiled, but it felt like the wind had been knocked out of her. Why couldn't her friend understand that the more money they made, the better off that little boy would be? She knew the Amish culture did not embrace change readily, but surely even they could see that raising more money now would lighten this family's burdens for many years to come.

"Thank you for understanding," Naomi said, straightening up. "I think I've got about enough here." She held up her basket, which had quickly been filled with the lush, plump leaves. "Will you come in for a cup of kaffee?" She brushed the dirt off of her skirt.

"Thanks, but I should probably get back to the shop," Cheryl said. It wasn't because she was hurt, it was just that she had already been gone for so long today. Cheryl brushed the dirt off her hands. They probably needed her there.

"Thank you for coming by," Naomi said. She lifted the basket and stepped over the rows toward the gate. "I really do appreciate it."

Cheryl nodded, but the words sounded hollow. She pasted a smile on her face and waved good-bye to her friend and then walked around to the front of the house.

"Cheryl."

Levi was on the front steps hunched over a metal bucket, a pair of pliers in his hand.

"Hi, Levi." Cheryl didn't like the way her heartbeat sped up just seeing him sitting there.

"Is everything all right?"

Levi now had a heavy wool coat on over his shirt, and he gazed out from under his wide-brimmed hat with a concerned look.

"It's fine." She couldn't let her disappointment show, not to Naomi's stepson. He, like Naomi, would probably think she had it all backward when it came to the fund-raiser.

"Come sit." He patted the empty space on the front step next to him. Cheryl knew she should probably just get back to the shop, but... well, she didn't want to be rude. She'd just sit for a minute. She crossed the yard and lowered herself onto the step next to him.

"Did you talk about the fund-raiser?" Levi said. He used the pliers to press the metal handle against itself.

"Yes." Cheryl pulled her legs up to the step below her and rested her elbows on her legs. "I had a lot of ideas that I thought would help bring in more money, but she doesn't want to use them," she said. Even as she said the words, she knew they hadn't come out quite right, that she wasn't being totally fair, but it felt good to say them.

"It is not that she didn't want to use them," Levi said, carefully twisting the metal. "It is that she is worried about losing what it is that makes our fund-raisers so special."

Cheryl thought about the dusty barn, the homemade food, the borrowed card tables. She knew they thought this stuff was special, but she didn't see how it could be as good as what she'd had planned.

"I thought the whole point was to raise money to help this sick kid," she said. She knew she sounded like a pouting child, but Levi didn't seem to mind. He simply kept at it, twisting the metal to repair the broken handle.

"That was your mistake then," he said. "That is part of it, but not the whole point."

"What do you mean?"

Levi clamped the pliers down, leaned in to examine his work, and then nodded and set the pliers on the step.

"I mean raising money is important, sure, but the real goal is to show the family that we support them through this trial," he said simply. He was quiet for a moment, and the only noise Cheryl could hear was the clip-clop of horse's hooves somewhere off down the road. "For us, it is always about caring for people first. The money is not nearly as important. It is the people in our lives that are the most important thing."

He looked at her as he said these last words, and for just a moment she thought he might have meant...

But then he quickly looked away, and Cheryl felt silly for thinking he was talking about anything but the fund-raiser.

"I do hope you will come," he said. "You can see what a real Amish party is like."

Cheryl didn't want to go, but she knew she was being childish and petty. She had been told once or twice in her life—often by Lance, come to think of it—that she was too quick to get upset, and she suspected now was one of those times. She had to go to the event. Especially if Levi wanted her there.

"I'll be there," Cheryl said, and if she hadn't known better, she would have sworn she saw something like a smile on Levi's face.

"She is grateful, you know. We all are." He twisted the pliers again, and then set them down on the ground. "She was worried about how to say no without hurting your feelings. That would have been the last thing my maam would have wanted to do."

Despite her bruised ego, she knew that Levi was right. Naomi was her dear friend. Cheryl knew—had seen day to day through their friendship—that people were the most important thing to Naomi. Her family and her friends were what Naomi cared deeply about.

"Thanks, Levi," she said. Cheryl sat there for a moment, rolling all that around in her mind, and, well, if she was being honest, enjoying just sitting here with Levi. She would just stay for a few more minutes, and then she would make herself get up.

A buzzing noise broke the comfortable silence. It took Cheryl a minute to realize that the noise was coming from her pocket. It was her cell phone. "I'm so sorry," she said, digging the phone out.

"It is all right," Levi said, but the sound seemed to have stirred him from his complacent reverie as well. He straightened up and reached for his pliers.

She looked at the screen, hoping it might be a call from the mysterious texter or from the artist she was still waiting to hear from, but one glance told her it was a call from her shop.

"Hello?" She held the phone to her ear.

"Cheryl?" It was Esther, Naomi's daughter. "I thought you might want to know that Chief Twitchell just called here. He says he has some news for you."

"What is it?"

"I do not know. He said to come by the station."

Cheryl looked at Levi. His eyes were wide, questioning.

"I'll be right there."

CHAPTER EIGHTEEN

A few minutes later, Cheryl parked in front of the police station and rushed in. She had to wait while he finished up a phone call, but then she was ushered inside his office.

"Hello, Cheryl. I got those phone records you were askin' about," he said without preamble.

"Yes?" Cheryl held her breath. Could she really be about to find out who owned the cell phone that sent the texts?

"First off, the number that was registered to Mark Troyer was cancelled back in October three years ago." Which meant that soon after Mark disappeared, someone closed the account his number was registered to.

"Who cancelled it?"

"It doesn't say. I only know that the account was closed and the number shut down. There is no more information about that."

"Okay." Cheryl felt some of the air go out of her lungs. That piece of information could mean anything. Had Mark cancelled his old phone contract and gotten a new number when he moved away and started a new life? Or had someone else stopped service to his number, knowing he wouldn't be needing it anymore?

Cheryl shook her head. She was being silly. What kind of murderer cared enough to tidy up his victim's financial accounts after the fact? That was crazy. But her mind went there anyway. She really needed to find out what had happened to Mark so her brain would stop making ridiculous leaps.

"Was there more?" Cheryl asked. There had to be.

"I also looked into that other number you asked about. The one you got the text from?"

"Yes?" Cheryl waited for him to go on.

"It seems that phone number is registered to an Elam Troyer."

"What?" Cheryl almost fell out of her chair.

"Does that name sound familiar to you?"

"Yes," Cheryl said. "I know Elam." But how could Lydia's brother be the one texting the messages about Mark? He wasn't allowed to use a cell phone and had said he knew nothing about the messages. "But it can't be him."

"Well, the phone is registered to him, so I'd start there. That's all I can tell you."

"Thanks so much," Cheryl said. "I appreciate your help."

"Glad to help." Without another word, the police chief looked at his computer screen, and Cheryl was dismissed.

Cheryl headed back to the shop, trying to make sense of what she'd just heard.

"What did he say?" Esther said as soon as she walked in the door.

Cheryl closed the door behind her and tugged off her coat, trying to figure out how much to share. Then, reluctantly, she repeated what she'd learned. Esther was surprised to hear the news, but agreed to keep it from Lydia until Cheryl had a chance to talk to Elam.

Soon, Esther was hopping on her bike and heading back to the farm, and Cheryl helped the customers that trickled in. When it was time to close up shop, she straightened and turned off the lights, and then she climbed back into her car and headed out to Elam's house. She had thought Elam had been hiding something when she talked to him yesterday. Could he have been hiding the fact that he had been texting his sister? Cheryl thought it through from every angle and couldn't come up with a way in which it made any sense. If he did know what happened to Mark, why not simply tell Lydia—or, better yet, tell his aunt and uncle? Why the anonymous text? Hopefully talking to Elam would answer the questions she couldn't figure out how to resolve.

She didn't know if Elam would be there, but maybe his wife would be able to tell her where to find him. When she arrived, Miriam welcomed her and directed her toward the barn, where Elam was feeding the horses. Cheryl stepped carefully across the yard and found Elam inside the barn, which was lit only by the light of a couple kerosene lanterns. He was shoveling clean hay into a trough in the stall of a beautiful dappled gray.

"Elam?" Cheryl called, trying not to startle him. "It's Cheryl Cooper."

Elam straightened up and looked toward Cheryl. He didn't look unhappy to see her, Cheryl noted. Just surprised. But Cheryl didn't think it was wise to read anything into that.

"I'm sorry to bother you. Miriam told me you were in here," she said.

He nodded but still looked at her skeptically. He tossed the rest of the hay into the trough and then brushed off his hands and stepped out of the horse's stall and closed the gate behind him.

"I was hoping to talk to you again. I just heard from Chief Twitchell." His brow wrinkled as she said the name. Out of fear and guilt, or simply because the Amish tried to avoid the police whenever possible? "He had been helping me find out who owned the cell phone number that texted Lydia. He worked with the phone company to trace the phone's owner." His expression didn't change; there was no sign of recognition. "It turns out the number is registered to you."

"To me?" Elam rested his foot on the board at the bottom of the gate, but his face didn't betray anything.

"I'm afraid so." She waited a moment, but he didn't seem to be ready to speak up, so she added, "Do you have any idea why that would be?"

Elam didn't say anything, just scraped the sole of his boot along the piece of wood. Cheryl heard the animals moving around in their stalls and a soft sigh from one of the cows. He seemed to be thinking things through, trying to figure out how to respond.

"It could be my old phone," he said.

"Your old phone?"

"From when I was on rumspringa," he said. "I bought a cell phone. Most kids do," he said. "I actually went to the store with Mark, and we got them together. Same kind and everything." He set his foot down on the ground. "But I do not have it anymore."

"What did you do with the phone at that point?" Cheryl asked.

He hesitated again. The dappled gray horse was munching on the hay in its bin.

"I gave it to Thomas," he said quietly.

"Thomas?"

"My younger brother. He's a year older than Lydia."

"Ah." Cheryl thought she might have met Thomas at Lydia's house the previous night, but she couldn't be sure. If Elam had given the phone to Thomas without changing the billing information, the phone could very well be registered to Elam but used by Thomas. All he would have to do was wipe the phone's memory, and he would be able to use it like it was brand new. Or not wipe it, and just use it with Elam's contacts on it. As long as someone prepaid for minutes, it would still work. "And he still has it?"

"I do not know." He shook his head. "It is not as if I make a habit of calling him."

Cheryl understood. "Would Thomas be at your parents' house?"

"I would guess so. He works in the back at Hoffman's Furniture, but I think he would be home by now."

Hoffman's Furniture? He would know Henry Detweiler then. Was there a connection there?

"Thank you, Elam. I appreciate your help."

Cheryl turned to go, but Elam cleared his throat. "Actually, there was one thing I wanted to tell you," he said, putting his foot back up on the gate and reaching in to the stall. The horse lifted her head, and he patted her muzzle. "Yesterday you asked me where I was the night Mark disappeared, and I did not answer you truthfully."

Cheryl remembered that she'd thought his reaction had been off. Now she waited expectantly for him to go on.

"I could not talk about where I had been that night because I do not want my wife to know I had been with Sophie Weintraub that night." Cheryl didn't know that name, but she assumed it was a local Amish girl. "She was... It was silly. But things were getting serious with Miriam, and I..." He shook his head. "I don't know. I was trying to figure out what I wanted. And Sophie's maam and my maam had always been friends and had joked about us getting married for many years. But I picked Miriam in the end. Still, Miriam would be hurt to know that I had been with Sophie. I managed to keep it from her this whole time, so I did not want to say it yesterday."

Cheryl understood his logic, but wondered if he might be underestimating his wife. Cheryl had spent enough time with a man she'd later discovered she couldn't trust; if he'd been honest about his doubts about the marriage from the beginning, he might have hurt her less in the end. Still, it wasn't her place to comment on their marriage, so Cheryl simply nodded.

"I am glad I married Miriam," Elam hastened to add. "And I have not talked to Sophie since then. She married a friend of her cousin's and moved to Michigan."

The way he was working to convince her made Cheryl feel sure he was telling the truth. In fact, her impression of him tonight was different from the previous night altogether. She had believed he'd been hiding something from her before, but now he was coming across as honest and open. Had it really just been that he'd been trying to avoid hurting his wife last night? Or had something changed?

"I should finish getting the animals fed," Elam said. Cheryl nodded and realized he was indicating that it was time for her to go.

"Thank you for your help," she replied. But he was already stepping into the stall to feed the next horse.

Cheryl found her way back out to her car and made the quick drive to Lydia's parents' house. Lydia was out, but her mother greeted Cheryl at the door, baby on her hip, and invited Cheryl in. She sent one of the younger children to fetch Thomas from the barn, where he was helping his father with chores. A few minutes later, a younger version of Elam, with the same dark hair and same thin nose, was standing in front of her. He looked to be about seventeen and was clean-shaven and wiry.

"Hello, Thomas, I'm Cheryl."

He nodded like he knew that.

"I was just talking to your brother Elam, and he told me he gave you his old cell phone when he joined the church."

Thomas nodded, but didn't show any reaction otherwise. Surely he must know about the mysterious texts. If he had been the one sending the texts, would he have made some indication?

"Ja, he gave it to me, but it's busted," Thomas said.

"What do you mean it's busted?" Cheryl asked.

"It broke, I don't know, maybe eight months ago? I will show you. It's in my room." He turned abruptly and tromped up the wooden stairs. A few minutes later, he returned holding a phone with a shattered screen. It was a very popular model of phone, but an older version than one currently available. Cheryl had a newer version of the same phone herself. But that made sense, since Elam would have bought it several years back. Cheryl took it and pushed the button at the bottom to turn the screen on. The screen remained black.

"The battery is dead," Thomas said. Cheryl tried the power button at the top, but it didn't work either.

"I got a new phone," he said, pulling out a sleek newer model from his pocket. Cheryl looked at it. Thomas could have gotten a new phone himself, but he could have kept the same phone number. All you had to do was move the SIM card—a memory card found in cell phones that was tied to the number—from the broken phone to a new one. Cheryl had done that very thing when she'd last upgraded her cell phone. So if the old SIM card was in the new phone, Thomas was her man.

"Can I see it?" she asked. He handed it over, and Cheryl navigated to the screen that told you the number of the phone in her hands. The number that showed up on Thomas's screen was a different number than the one that had sent the texts.

Just in case, she used Thomas's new phone to make a call to her own phone, but the number that showed up on her screen was not the number the texts had come from.

"You got a new number?"

He nodded. "I switched carriers, and they offered me a good deal to get a whole new setup. Plus, I kept getting calls from this girl who wanted to talk to Elam." He shrugged.

So if he had a new phone and phone number, and if the phone number that had been associated with this phone was still sending texts, then that meant…

Cheryl dug out a paper clip from the bottom of her purse and straightened one side. She found the small pinprick hole on the side of the old phone with the shattered screen and stuck the paperclip in. A tiny tray slid open. A tray where the SIM card should have been.

"Where did the SIM card go?"

Thomas's eyes widened, and his face betrayed confusion.

"What do you mean?"

"The little memory card that's supposed to be here?" Cheryl pointed to the slot. She used her fingers to show that the memory card was about the size of a postage stamp. "Where is it?"

He bent over to look where she was pointing. "I do not know. I did not realize it was gone."

Cheryl felt a wave of frustration crash over her. That SIM card could be put into the SIM card slot in just about any phone, and a text from that phone would register as a text from the number registered to Elam.

Cheryl reached for a chair to brace herself. She had just realized that she was no longer looking for a specific cell phone to find out who had sent the texts. Now she was looking for a SIM card, which could be moved around between many different phones.

Her task had just gotten infinitely harder.

Chapter Nineteen

Cheryl tried to keep calm. A SIM card was less than an inch square. It could be hidden in a pocket, a purse—anywhere. Not to mention inside just about any phone out there. But there had to be a way to find it.

"Do you have any idea who might have the SIM card?" Cheryl asked.

"No." Thomas shook his head.

"How long has the phone been in your room?"

"Since it broke. That was back in March." He reached out for the phone, and she handed it back to him.

"Has anyone been in your room since then?"

"No one except my family. I share the room with Paul, but any of the kids or my parents could have been in." He turned the phone over in his hands and looked at the back, as if searching for clues. "Except for the times we've hosted church, I guess. Then there were people all over the house. I cannot say who might have been in my room then."

Cheryl knew that church members took turns hosting the Sunday services in their homes or—in some cases, such as Jonas Esch's family, in the barn—and she knew that the house would be filled to the brim on those days. She imagined that if these were anything like the services at Silo Church, after the service while parents chatted the children would run free. There would be no way to tell who would have gone into his room.

"Did you show the phone to anyone for any reason?"

He thought for a moment. "At one point, right after it broke, I was considering giving it to whoever wanted a free phone. I brought it to a singing and showed it to a number of people, but when they saw how badly cracked the screen was, no one took it." He ran his fingers over the shattered glass screen. Cheryl had broken her share of screens through the years, and she had tried to use the phone as long as she could afterward if the crack was small or out of the way, but this screen must have been dropped from some height, and lines snaked through the glass pretty much the entire way. The phone was pretty much unusable, and she could see why no one had taken it.

"Why did you keep it after that?"

"I had been planning to try to sell it for parts, but I never got around to it."

That explanation could have sounded fishy except that Cheryl had done the exact same thing. When she'd left her apartment in Columbus, she'd found two old broken phones so outdated they weren't even worth trying to sell anymore.

"And have you been paying the bill this whole time?"

Thomas's mouth dropped open. "I do not know. We left the number in Elam's name, but I set up automatic transfers from my bank account when I took over the phone from Elam. But surely they would have cancelled that when I got the new one, right?"

"If you changed carriers, not necessarily." She shook her head. Phone and data plans were not cheap. Could he really have just not noticed? The Amish were usually so good with money. Then again, Thomas was a teenager, and teens—even Amish teens— were not known for their foresight. "You haven't noticed if the phone company is still deducting money from your account every month?"

"I have not looked."

Cheryl took that to mean that they were. So that explained how the account the SIM card was tied to was still active.

Cheryl tried to review what Thomas had just told her. "So anyone who was at the singing could have known that you had an unused cell phone, and that you had gotten a new number, mean- ing the SIM card was still in the old phone. Right?"

He nodded.

"And then, anyone in your district could have been in and out of your room in the times you've hosted church since then. How many times was that?"

"One? Maybe two? I'm not sure."

It didn't matter, Cheryl realized. In either case, the pool of people who would have known about the phone and had access to it was huge. If she couldn't find a way to narrow down the possi- bilities, this was going to be hopeless.

Who was most likely to have taken the SIM card?

She realized Lydia had access to the phone—she lived in the same house, after all—and would have known when her brother got a new model and where he kept the old one. And Cheryl still wasn't sure about the girl, but she couldn't see a reason Lydia would be making the whole thing up. Still, she wasn't going to rule her out.

But Elam would also likely have known when his younger brother broke the phone he had given him and replaced it. And Elam could come and go in the house any time he wanted. Not only had he grown up here, he now lived just across the alfalfa field. No one would question him going into Thomas's room. The thing was, she didn't know how he would have sent the texts if he wasn't allowed to use a cell phone himself. Maybe he had given it to someone? He had been Mark's best friend. If anyone knew where he was, surely it was Elam. But if he did know where Mark was, why go through this whole charade? Cheryl wasn't sure, but maybe she wouldn't cross him off her suspect list just yet.

Then she remembered something Elam had said. Thomas worked at Hoffman's Furniture. He must work there along with Henry Detweiler. Was there any chance…

"What about Henry Detweiler?"

Thomas cocked an eyebrow.

"You work with him, right?"

He nodded, a skeptical look on his face.

"Could he have known about the phone?"

"Yes. He was interested in it, so I showed it to him at work."

So he had both the knowledge of the phone and, like everyone else in their district, the opportunity to have taken it.

"But I do not know why Henry would have taken the SIM card."

Cheryl didn't know why either, but she did have some guesses. If he had something to hide, surely he would want to disguise his number when he sent the text to Lydia.

But if he had something to hide, why would he send the texts to Lydia at all?

Cheryl's head was spinning. It seemed like the more answers she uncovered, the more questions she had.

A woman's voice called out something in Pennsylvania Dutch from the other room.

"I am sorry, I need to go help my maam," Thomas said, glancing toward the kitchen.

"Of course. Thank you for talking with me."

Cheryl headed back out to her car and sat there for a few moments, processing what all she had just learned. How in the world was she going to find that SIM card? Just in case, she pulled out her phone and tried calling the number again, but her call was immediately sent into the voice mail box, and a computer-generated message told her that the mail box was full. No dice.

She started the car and began her drive home, but then she thought of something. She turned it around in her mind until she realized she was right about it.

She couldn't believe she'd missed something so obvious. She wanted to smack herself on the forehead. But since she was driving, she kept her hands on the wheel, and at the next opportunity, she made a U-turn and headed back toward town.

CHAPTER TWENTY

A few minutes later, Cheryl sat in Chief Twitchell's office. The fluorescent lights above his desk popped and crackled. He stared at her over the rim of his glasses, incredulous.

"I want to track the phone by tracking the signal," Cheryl said again. She knew he'd understood the first time, but he didn't seem to know how to respond, so she was trying again. "The card has been used recently, so the company should be able to find it by tracing which cell phone towers it's pinged, right?"

Cheryl knew that every time a phone was used, the signal was sent from one of the cell phone towers that broadcasted signals all over the area, generally the closest one. The phone company should be able to tell which tower was pinged, which would show approximately where the call was sent from.

"I suppose." Chief Twitchell was watching her, shaking his head.

"So how do we go about getting those records?"

The police chief cracked his knuckles and then sighed. "Cheryl, as I told you before, this is a closed case. I looked into those phone records as a favor to you, but I can't keep wastin' the department's resources chasin' down every harebrained idea you have about a boy who ran away."

She tried not to let that last line sting. "But if we could just figure out where the SIM card was, roughly, that would make it so much easier to find the person sending the texts. Then we could know for sure whether he did run away or not."

He sighed.

"So I just need you to get in touch with the phone company and see what they can tell you about where the SIM card is."

"I don't think we're going to be able to get that information without a court order," Chief Twitchell said.

"Okay, how do we get one of those?" Cheryl said, putting on a false sense of positivity.

"You start by getting a lawyer."

Cheryl's heart sank. Would it really have to come to that?

For a moment, Cheryl stared at the faux wood grain of his desk. That couldn't really be what it would take, could it? She was almost positive that wasn't really how it worked, that he was just saying that to get her to drop it. And she understood that he believed the answers were obvious and the case cold. But she couldn't just drop it like he wanted her to.

"There's no way you could pull some strings for a friend?" She tried her best to look ingratiating.

"I'm sorry I can't be more help," Chief Twitchell said. Cheryl wasn't sure she believed him, but she suppressed her frustration and nodded anyway. "And I hate to see you spinning your wheels looking all over town when I know what you're going to find. He's just another Amish runaway, pure and simple."

Cheryl felt her frustration bubble over into anger. It was one thing to not put any real effort into an investigation. It was entirely another to not put any effort into an investigation because the boy was Amish.

Before she could stop herself, she snapped.

"Even if he did run away, where did he go?" she said, her voice raised.

The police chief reared his head back.

"There's a family out there who has no clue what happened to their son. Just because he's Amish doesn't mean he's not worth caring about. So maybe he did leave. Why has no one heard from him? Why is there no trace of him, even three years later?"

"That's not my concern, Cheryl. The case has been closed."

Cheryl had to restrain herself from lashing out. Her temper had gotten her into trouble before, and she knew from experience that shouting was not the best way to get what she needed. But it was difficult.

"But there is new evidence in the case. The texts should be enough to get it opened back up."

He shrugged. "Unless the family requests for the case to be reopened, my hands are tied."

Cheryl was pretty sure that wasn't how police cases worked, but knew she would get nowhere by arguing.

"The texts are probably just a tasteless joke," Chief Twitchell said. His voice was now placating, like she was a silly child and he was trying to get her to behave.

"Maybe they are," Cheryl said, though she didn't believe that at all. "But even if they are, it's worth finding out for sure." She sucked in a breath. "I believe someone out there knows what happened to Mark Troyer. And I am going to figure out who it is."

She grabbed her purse and stood up. Chief Twitchell didn't say anything as she walked out of the office.

Oh dear. She should not have lost her temper like that. She knew it even as she walked away from his office. It certainly was not a great example of Christian love, never mind making sure the police wouldn't be anxious to help her in the future. But it was hard not to get upset when it was a boy's life you were talking about.

Cheryl went home and made herself dinner, and then she went to bed early. She tried to sleep, but her mind kept spinning in a thousand different directions. One minute she couldn't stop thinking about the fund-raiser, about how Naomi had not wanted her help. It hurt a bit, if she was honest. But then she thought about Levi, about their conversation on the steps and how it had made her feel better. He was a good man, a faithful man—pretty much the opposite of Lance.

Cheryl rolled over, looking for a cool spot on her pillow, and forced her mind to drift away from that fraught topic, but instead her mind went back to the conversation with Chief Twitchell this evening, which only made her blood pressure rise. She *would* find who was sending those texts, with or without his help. Even if Mark *had* run away, it would help so many people to find out what had happened to him.

Finally, Cheryl gave up. She headed to the kitchen for some warm milk. She pulled the milk out, but the dishwasher was running and most of her mugs were in it, so she dug around at the back of the cabinet for one of the strays that rattled around back there. She pulled out one she hadn't used before with an owl on it and noticed something inside.

Smiling, she set the mug down. She knew what this was. She pulled out the folded piece of paper and smoothed it.

Cheryl,

Don't forget that God knows more than we ever will and cares more than we ever can.

Aunt Mitzi

Aunt Mitzi had hidden several notes for Cheryl before she left, and somehow they were always exactly what Cheryl needed. She may not know what had happened to Mark, but God did. Thank goodness He was the one in charge, Cheryl thought as she drank her warm milk. She prayed for wisdom, and for insight, and for His help. A few minutes later, she headed back to bed, knowing her search was in His hands.

CHAPTER TWENTY-ONE

On Friday, Cheryl opened things up at the Swiss Miss, and once Lydia arrived she left for Lester Coblentz's studio. She'd found the address out on Pleasant Valley Road listed on his Web site. There was a sign at the side of the road shaped like a guitar with the words Coblentz Guitars painted on it. She pulled into the driveway and saw a sturdy farmhouse with neat green shutters and a barn painted a nice soft gray and trimmed with modern-looking windows and doors. Cheryl stopped in front of the barn, which she could see had been converted into Lester's studio. The lights were on inside, she saw through the door, so she stepped inside.

"Hello?" Cheryl called. She was in a small waiting area with a desk and some comfortable chairs, all done in mid-century modern style. The walls were hung with exquisitely crafted guitars. Her voice echoed in the high-ceilinged room.

"Hi, there." Cheryl heard a man's voice and footsteps from the other side of a divider. She waited, and a moment later a man with graying brown hair cut close to the scalp appeared. "I'm Lester," he said, holding out his hand.

"I'm Cheryl Cooper. Pleased to meet you," Cheryl said.

Lester wore jeans and a checked button-down shirt, and he had a warm smile and wide blue eyes. He gestured for her to sit in one of the padded chairs, and he sat down behind the desk. "Are you interested in a guitar? We make them all by hand here," he said, showing her a winning smile. "From reclaimed wood wherever possible. But we can customize according to your needs."

"I'm afraid that's not why I'm here, though they really are beautiful," Cheryl said, looking at the fine grain on the display models hung on the wall. There were both acoustic and electric models on display, and she was no expert, but they looked like well-made instruments that could be appreciated as art on their own. "I am trying to find out about an Amish boy named Mark Troyer. He was interested in sculpture and woodworking, and Roxanna over at Artistic License gave me your name. She wondered if you might have heard of him."

Looking around now, Cheryl could see why Roxanna had thought of Lester. Mark's woodworking was right up there with Lester's. The form might be different, but they both created art.

"Mark Troyer, huh?" He looked up, like he was searching for something. "I'm afraid not."

"Do you ever take on interns or workers to help you here? It seems likely he was interested in becoming an artist, and I think he may have been looking for some practical experience. And this seems like something he would have been very good at," she said, gesturing at the guitars.

"Sometimes my brother comes in to help me," Lester said. "But I'm afraid the markup on these guitars isn't really high enough for me to be able to hire a lot of help. Mostly I make each one by hand."

Cheryl felt her hopes deflate. It had seemed so possible when she'd stepped in here, almost too perfect.

"They are really gorgeous," she said. "The work you put in really shows."

"Thank you," Lester said, ducking his head.

"Can I ask you another question?" Cheryl said, and he nodded. "Roxanna also told me that you used to be Amish."

He ducked his head again. "Well, I started out that way. My parents actually left the church and joined an evangelical church nearby when I was eight. I still keep in touch with many of my Amish family and friends from my early days, but I didn't exactly leave on my own."

"That must have been quite a change, starting a whole new life when you were eight," Cheryl said.

"It sure was," Lester said smiling. "I think it was probably the hardest thing my parents ever did, leaving the Amish world behind. But the more they studied the Bible, the more they took to heart the passages about not hiding your light under a bushel. They felt like we are supposed to be living in the world and sharing Christ's message of grace with those who need to hear it, not hiding away in a closed community. I have to say, I see it the same way, so I'm thankful for the choices they made. But I know it must have been difficult for them."

Cheryl nodded. She could see the point he was making and had always thought Christians were supposed to be in the world but not of it. But she couldn't even imagine how hard that must have been for them to leave their community behind.

"The Amish boy I'm looking for may have been trying to leave the church as well," Cheryl said. "Do you ever run into kids looking to make a break from the Amish world?"

"I do, on occasion," Lester said. "And I'm sympathetic. I try to help if I can. But it's not something I really make a habit of. And I'm afraid I don't know this Mark boy you're asking about."

Cheryl's heart sank. This man was being as helpful as he could, but she could see she wasn't going to get any answers here.

"Thank you so much for your time," Cheryl said. "You really do make beautiful guitars."

"Please let me know if there's anything else I can tell you. And I will be sure to let you know if I hear anything about this Mark."

"Thank you so much." Cheryl handed him a business card and then headed back out to her car.

She'd struck out again. Now she'd heard from all of the artists Roxanna had mentioned, and none of them had heard of Mark. She was running out of places to look. She drove back to town, praying for wisdom and guidance.

As she drove, she had an idea. Was there any chance Mark had been using a different name once he left Sugarcreek? Could that have been why none of them had heard of him? But what name would that have been? And surely any of the artists would remember an Amish boy, even if he had been using a different name. She shook her head. It didn't seem likely.

When she got back to the store, there were a handful of customers. While Lydia rang up the purchases of a group of women who were stocking up on Christmas ornaments, Cheryl helped a mother and her grown daughter who were interested in the selection of handmade local cheeses.

A few minutes later, the shop was quiet, and Cheryl filled Lydia in on her conversation with Lester Coblentz.

"I guess that means he did not work with any of the artists then," Lydia said. Cheryl nodded. Another door closed. She didn't want to focus on the negatives, though.

She noticed that Lydia's puzzle box was sitting on the stool behind the counter.

"Have you had any luck getting that open?"

"A little." Lydia picked up the box and set it on the counter. "I brought it in to show you. Thomas helped me get the first panel open again," she said. She indicated a section of wood about an inch wide on the bottom of the box. She pushed it very hard with her fingers, and Cheryl gasped as it slid over. Now that that had been moved, she could see a panel on the side of the box. "This is supposed to slide this way," Lydia said, indicating the direction of the grain. "But the wood is warped here"—she indicated the edge of the box—"and it is stuck."

"That's good, though," Cheryl said. "You got it open a bit."

"But I do not know if we are going to be able to get it open the rest of the way," she said, shaking her head. "Thomas is very good at figuring these things out, and he thinks the wood is too warped."

Cheryl reached out for the box, and Lydia handed it to her. She slid the panel that Lydia had gotten open back and forth, but she was right, the panel underneath it was jammed. She examined the box carefully again, and now she could see another seam.

"I think that part must be a drawer." Lydia pointed to the section Cheryl was examining. "But you need to get the other parts open to move it. I will keep trying," Lydia said. "And if I cannot get it open today, we will cut it."

Cheryl pressed her lips together. Now that she could see how this box was supposed to work, she was even more reluctant to destroy it—she loved puzzles—but like Lydia she really wanted to know what was inside.

"So?"

Cheryl looked up. Lydia seemed to be expecting something from her.

"I am told you went to my house again yesterday," Lydia said.

Cheryl wanted to slap her forehead. She couldn't believe she'd forgotten to bring that up before this. "Yes, I did. Did you hear why?" She set the box down gently on the counter.

"Thomas said you were asking about his cell phone." Lydia looked at her expectantly.

Cheryl told her about her conversation with Thomas. It was clear she had heard about the visit from Thomas's side of things as she nodded.

"So you are looking for a SIM card, not a phone," Lydia concluded. "That is what I gathered from what Thomas told me." She lowered herself down onto one of the stools. "That is harder than finding a phone, is it not?"

"It probably will be," Cheryl agreed. "But I'm not giving up. After I talked to Thomas last night, I went to talk to Chief Twitchell to see if I could figure out who is actually paying the bill for the phone line. The number is registered to Elam"—Lydia nodded; she must have heard that part—"but since he isn't allowed to use a cell phone anymore, it probably isn't him. But Chief Twitchell couldn't help me figure that out without a court order, so I don't really know what else to do except keep calling the number to try to see if the phone rings."

Cheryl looked to see how Lydia took these things, but the girl seemed to be staring at something far away.

"Lydia?"

"Elam can use a cell phone," she said.

"What?" Cheryl struggled to understand. "But he is Amish. I mean, you're Amish too obviously, but he's baptized, isn't he? Once you're baptized, you have to stop using forbidden technology, don't you?"

"He is." Lydia nodded slowly, a bit absently, like she was trying to figure something out. "And most people aren't allowed to use them once they are baptized. But Elam works with animals."

Cheryl tried to make sense of this explanation and couldn't so she let Lydia go on.

"He is very skilled with animals, especially horses and cows. He is not a veterinarian because he has not been to school, but he treats animals around here, and better than most fancy veterinarians. If an animal is very sick, someone might call a large animal vet, but for most things Elam can handle it."

"And he is allowed to use a cell phone because of this?" Cheryl loved her cat Beau, and she had taken him to a vet a few miles from here to keep his shots current a few months back, but she couldn't see why this would qualify Elam for a special exemption to the cell phone rule.

"If one of our horses is hurt, that is a big problem," Lydia said. "We cannot use them for our buggies or in the fields."

For the second time in this conversation Cheryl felt silly. Of course it was a big deal if a horse was sick for the Amish. They couldn't just drive him to the vet like she did with Beau. They relied on their animals as more than companions; they needed them to survive.

"So he is allowed to use a phone in case there is an emergency," Cheryl said.

"Yes. Much like midwives are allowed to use cell phones in our district so they can know when a woman goes into labor, Elam is allowed to use one so people can get ahold of him if there is an emergency with an animal."

Cheryl rested her arms on the counter and leaned over, trying to sort this all out in her mind. This was an interesting loophole. She had assumed when she moved here that the Amish were ignorant about modern technology, but she now knew that they weren't ignorant, they simply chose not to indulge in it. But she also knew that many of them used technology at their jobs that they weren't allowed to use in their everyday lives. It wasn't the technology itself that their culture banned, it was the reliance on it in everyday life.

"So you're saying Elam has a cell phone."

"He did not mention that?"

Cheryl shook her head. Elam had told her he didn't use a cell phone, hadn't he? Had he ever come out and said that, or had

Cheryl just assumed? She couldn't be sure. Why wouldn't he tell her about his work phone, in any case?

"He is only allowed to use it for work, though. He cannot use it for personal reasons."

But just because he wasn't technically allowed to do so, that didn't necessarily mean he hadn't sent an extracurricular text from his line. "What is his phone number?"

Lydia pulled her cell phone out of her pocket and scrolled to his number and then made the call. Cheryl held her breath while it rang, and then she heard a man talking in Pennsylvania Dutch. Lydia answered him in that language, and they had a quick conversation. Cheryl couldn't understand a word they said, but she could hear from the tone of Elam's voice that he was not happy about the call. Lydia ended it and set the phone down.

"He was mad that it was me," Lydia said, but she did not look at all guilty. "But this means that he has his own SIM card in his phone, right?"

"Yes, it does. He has it in his phone for now, at least." The fact that he had answered when Lydia called his number did mean that he didn't have the missing SIM card in his phone at the moment, but what was to say that he didn't have the SIM card and switch it for his own when he wanted to place a text, and then switch it back afterward? Elam was one of the people who had had the easiest access to the SIM card—the broken phone with the card in it had been kept in his brother's room; no one would question Elam poking around there, and even if he had been caught taking the SIM card out of the old phone, it had been his phone to start with. It was entirely plausible that he had the SIM card.

"Do you know what kind of phone he has?"

"I remember him talking about going to the store to get the newest model." She named a brand, and Cheryl recognized it as one of the models that would be compatible with the SIM card.

"Lydia," Cheryl started. She had to phrase this carefully. "Can you think of any way to find out if Elam is the one sending the texts?"

"I do not know," Lydia said. She looked down at her phone and turned it around in her hands. Then she looked back up at Cheryl. "But I will do my best to find out."

Lydia had planned to work until mid-afternoon, but as soon as Esther came in, Cheryl shooed her off to try to talk to Elam. They both thought there was a chance he would be honest with his sister in a way he wouldn't with an outsider like Cheryl. Esther and Cheryl worked in companionable silence for a while, helping customers pick out gifts and ringing them up.

As they worked, Cheryl thought through everything she had learned, everything she still needed to know. If Mark hadn't run away to work with one of the artists, where had he gone? If he wasn't involved with gambling, why had there been a betting slip in his car? Who was this Englisch girl who had been in the car with him, and why had no one been able to place her in all this time? She thought again about Mark's father Saul, about his temper, about the fact that he'd been very clear he didn't want Cheryl looking into his son's disappearance. Why was he so adamant about that? Despite Naomi's assurances, Cheryl couldn't shake the sense that he was hiding something, that he knew something about what had happened to his eldest son. But how could she find out what? How could she get him to tell her what he knew?

Cheryl was pretty sure she wasn't going to have much luck showing up and demanding Saul talk to her about Mark's disappearance. But Joanna had made it clear that she wanted to find out what had happened. Joanna would be willing to talk with her. She'd have to be careful about what she asked, but...

"Esther?" Cheryl called. The girl looked up from the display of potholders she was rearranging. "Do you mind if I run out for a bit?"

"Not at all," the girl said.

"I won't be too long," Cheryl said, stepping into the back to grab her coat and purse.

"You do not need to rush," Esther said. "I will be here."

She dashed out the back door and into her car.

Chapter Twenty-Two

S oon she was pulling up in front of the house Naomi had taken her to the other day. The name Troyer was spelled out on the mailbox.

Cheryl held her breath as she knocked on the door, and she was quickly ushered past the living room, where Cheryl saw puzzle boxes and carvings much like the one Lydia had, and into the kitchen where Joanna and Matilda were working. There was flour everywhere. Joanna seemed to be rolling out dough into a thin layer, and Matilda was using a pizza cutter to trim it into thin ribbons.

"Hello, Cheryl." Joanna brushed her hands on her apron and smiled. "It is good to see you. Please excuse the mess. We are preparing noodles for a fund-raiser for a sick boy in our district."

"Oh, Jonas Esch." Cheryl tried not to let her frustration with that situation show. "I met him."

"Goodness. You know more about what is going on in our church than most of us," Joanna said. "And it is good to see you. Do you have news?"

Cheryl could see pure, unadulterated hope in her eyes, and she suddenly felt terrible. Joanna was obviously hoping she'd come here with answers.

"Nothing solid yet," she said, and the light in Joanna's eyes dimmed a bit. "But I am learning a lot, and I think I might be getting closer," Cheryl said. Or at least, she was trying. Matilda finished cutting a sheet of the dough into noodles and gathered the pasta with her hands. Behind them, Cheryl could see a large pot of water bubbling on the stove.

Joanna didn't answer, just nodded. Cheryl tried to figure out how to approach this. She couldn't just come out and ask Joanna if her husband had done something to hurt her son. She decided to take a broader approach.

"I was trying to piece together the timeline for Mark's last night, and I was hoping you could tell me more about what everyone was up to that day."

Joanna laid down her rolling pin and cast her eyes upward, like she was thinking. Matilda looked at Cheryl and then quickly looked away.

"I will try to remember," Joanna said. She paused for another moment and then nodded. "I had been working on canning the tomatoes in the kitchen downstairs."

Cheryl had heard that some Amish houses had a kitchen in the basement specifically for canning so that a woman could work on that project without having to clean up to make each meal. It sounded very convenient.

"I remember that because we had quite a large harvest and I had not finished that day, and when Mark didn't come home that night I was worried and went downstairs to work on it so I could stay busy while we waited. I was down there until the middle of the night and he still did not come home, and I was sick with worry." She slid the sheet of dough she'd rolled out across the floured counter, and Matilda started cutting it into strips.

"When did you realize he was gone?"

"When he wasn't home by morning, I was very upset. Saul was sure he would come back that day, that he must have stayed with a friend, but when he never came home that morning, even Saul started to be concerned."

"What did you do then?"

"Saul hitched up the buggy and drove around to ask the neighbors if anyone had seen him. No one had. We spent the whole next day asking everyone who knew him if they'd seen him. Then we heard that his shirt had been found in the garbage can behind the Honey Bee, and that is when I decided to go to the police."

"Did Saul support that decision?"

"We do not like to bring the police into our affairs unless it is necessary," Joanna said carefully. "Saul preferred to honor that."

"Do you think there was any reason why he didn't want to get the police involved?"

Joanna looked down at the counter and then picked up her rolling pin and started rolling out another lump of dough with quick, vigorous strokes. Next to her mother, Matilda was keeping her eyes focused on making her noodles straight and thin, but she appeared to be listening.

"We do not like to bring the police into our affairs," Joanna said again.

Cheryl couldn't tell if there was more Joanna simply wasn't saying. Amish women, in her experience, deferred to their husbands. Was that what was happening here? But Joanna *hadn't* actually deferred to him when her son was missing. She had gone to the police against his will. Was she protecting him now? Would she hide information that could possibly lead to finding her son, if it meant not betraying her husband? Cheryl couldn't tell, but she could see that she was not going to be able to get any more from Joanna from this line of questioning.

"What about your husband? What was he doing the last day you all saw Mark?" Cheryl tried to keep her voice neutral, like she wasn't particularly interested one way or the other.

"I do not remember exactly, but it was September so I would guess he might have been in the fields."

This was vaguer than Cheryl had hoped for. "Do you think we could ask him?"

"I will ask him tonight," she said. She reached for her rolling pin and started working on flattening another lump of dough. "He is working in the barn right now and does not like to be disturbed."

Was that a trace of fear in Joanna's voice, or was Cheryl simply looking for reasons to be suspicious? She couldn't be sure.

"It would be great if you could," Cheryl said. "And do you know where he was that night?"

"After supper, he went back out to the barn. One of the cows was about to give birth, and he was monitoring her."

"Was he out there by himself?"

Joanna tilted her head, and Cheryl quickly added, "I mean, did he call someone like Elam Troyer to help with the birth?"

"Oh. No. It was a simple birth. Elam is only called when complications arise."

So no one could vouch for Saul's whereabouts the night Mark had vanished. He was supposed to have been in the barn, but did that mean he'd been there the whole time?

"What about everyone else? What was everyone else up to that day?"

Joanna finished rolling out a sheet of dough and started to slide it toward Matilda, but Matilda had laid down her pizza cutter and was taking off her apron.

"I just remembered I need to take that basket over to the Hochstetlers before it gets too late," she said. And then, quickly, she hung her apron on a hook, picked up a wicker basket piled with loaves of bread and cheese, and stepped out of the kitchen toward the hall.

Cheryl and Joanna watched her go. Her departure had seemed quite abrupt to Cheryl. Was that just how she was? Or was there a reason she had left so suddenly? She looked to Joanna, who shrugged.

"I think it could have waited until after we finished the noodles." Joanna stepped over to where Matilda had been working. "I guess she must have thought they needed the food early so Ellie could get dinner started. She is always thinking of things like that."

Cheryl wasn't sure it had been that simple. The departure had seemed too abrupt, the timing too strange... Was there a reason

Matilda hadn't wanted to discuss her family members' where-abouts that evening? Did she know something about Saul? If she did, would she keep it secret all this time?

"Joanna, does Matilda ever use a cell phone?" Cheryl tried to keep her voice level. Was there any chance she knew something and hadn't wanted to keep quiet about it any longer?

"Oh no. Matilda was baptized years ago."

"How many years ago?"

Joanna gave her a strange look, but thought back. "It was soon after Mark..." She stumbled over the word *disappeared*.

If that was true, it seemed unlikely that she was behind the texts, but Cheryl had come to understand that mothers didn't always know what their children were up to. Joanna was sure Matilda didn't use a cell phone, but that didn't mean much.

"Can you tell me what Matilda was doing on Mark's last day?"

"She was here canning with me most of the day. That afternoon she brought a pie to Mary Hershberger, who had just had a baby. She was back by dinnertime."

"Is there any chance she might have made any other stops while she was out?"

Joanna was cutting the noodles into long, thin strips with sharp, efficient strokes.

"I do not think so. Matilda is very... Well, she has always liked to follow the rules. She does not bend them or like to see others bend them. I do not think she would tell us she came right home if she did not."

That may be, and it matched up with what Lydia had said, but her sudden exit made Cheryl suspicious that she knew something she wasn't saying.

"What do you mean she doesn't like to see others bend the rules?"

Joanna set a fresh pile of noodles aside and started rolling out another lump of dough. "Just that she always helped me keep the younger children in line, as they say. She helped me correct their behavior. She is a very big help."

Cheryl thought about this. "Would you say she has a close relationship with her siblings?"

Joanna got the dough flat and thin with surprising ease. "I suppose not." She laid down her rolling pin. "They get along fine, but I would not say they are close. But it still hit her really hard when Mark"—she stumbled again—"went away. It hit us all hard."

She scooped her noodles up into a pile and set them aside. "I keep hoping she will find a *goot* man and settle down, but she seems more interested in her books than anything else."

"So Matilda likes to read?"

"Oh yes. She is at the library many times a week. She is always learning new things." She picked up the pizza cutter again. Cheryl wondered how many noodles they were making. There was already a large pile waiting by the stove. "Sometimes I think she would have liked to have gone to college. But she never says anything about it. My Matilda would not do something like that. It is not allowed, you know."

Cheryl nodded. Matilda sounded eager to please and follow the rules, responsible and hardworking. If she did know anything about Mark, Cheryl wasn't going to find out about it now. She asked about the other members of the family, and Joanna filled them in on what her younger children had been doing. Cheryl chatted with her for a little while longer, and then when she realized that Joanna was moving into preparations for her own family's dinner, she thanked her and said good-bye.

It wasn't a wasted trip, Cheryl thought. She hadn't found out anything for certain, but things were pointing more and more toward Saul being involved somehow in his son's disappearance.

She turned her car back toward the shop, puzzling over the encounter. About halfway to town, surrounded by open cornfields, she heard her phone beep. She'd gotten a text. Cheryl pulled off to the side of the road and dug her phone out of her purse. When she'd freed it, she glanced down at the screen.

Her breath caught. It was from the same number as the other mysterious texts.

You're getting close. Please don't stop now. There is not much time.

Chapter Twenty-Three

Not much time for what? Cheryl's heartbeat sped up. What would happen if she didn't find him soon?

She immediately called the number back. The phone rang once, twice, and then the call was ended. She tried again, but the call was declined quickly. Whoever had the SIM card in their phone apparently did not want to talk to Cheryl.

She sat on the side of the road, jittery from the excitement. So whoever it was knew that she was involved in the search for Mark, knew her cell phone number, and knew that she was getting close. Someone had been following her progress and thought she was on the right track. She leaned back and pressed her head against the headrest. If only she felt the same way.

But how would they know? Was this message from one of the people she'd talked to today? Had Elam found out that she knew about his work cell phone?

Cheryl dialed Lydia's number, and when she picked up, she quickly explained about the text she'd just gotten and asked Lydia to call Elam's work cell and see if the call went through. If it did not, it was possible he still had the missing SIM card in his work phone. She also asked her to find out where Elam was right now. Was he at home, where his wife Miriam might be able to tell them what he had been up to, or was he out working somewhere, where he might be able to send a text message unobserved? Lydia seemed shocked and delighted by the news, and she promised to get back to Cheryl as quickly as she could.

Cheryl felt there was a very good chance that the person sending the texts was Elam. But what if she was wrong? What if someone else had that SIM card? Who else could it be? What did it mean, there was not much time?

Lydia's face flashed into her mind again. But Lydia wouldn't send her on a wild goose chase, would she? Was there any reason Lydia would want Cheryl to uncover what she already knew? It was true that she would have had even easier access to the cell phone the SIM card had come from than Elam did, since it had been in her brothers' bedroom. Could she have taken the SIM card and been using it to... send texts to her own phone? Cheryl shook her head. That didn't make any sense.

Cheryl was getting more confused the more she thought about it.

Just as she was about to pull back on to the road, she got a call back from Lydia. Elam was out at a job, she said. He was not home, where Miriam might have seen him send a text. It could very well have been him.

Cheryl pulled back out on to the road, feeling more and more sure she was on to something.

CHAPTER TWENTY-FOUR

Saturday dawned clear and cold. It was a beautiful morning, and the shop was packed with tourists. A tour bus had rolled up right as she opened, and Cheryl enjoyed chatting with the ladies on the tour, hearing about where they were from and the people they were selecting gifts for. It was a group from a church in Cincinatti, she found out, and they were delighted to hear that she was a member of Silo Church.

Through it all, Cheryl was able to put on a good face, but she was distracted, thinking about Elam, about what he knew about Mark and wasn't telling her. The more she thought about it, the more certain she was that he was behind the text messages. But she needed a way to prove it, to catch him at it. And, more importantly, she needed to find a way to get him to confess whatever it was that he knew about Mark. And she needed to do it soon. The last text had said that she was running out of time. She didn't know what would happen if she didn't find him in time, but she knew she needed to find answers quickly.

With all the business and crowds, the morning flew by, and before she knew it, Esther was pulling on her apron and starting her shift.

"Goodness. It must have been busy this morning," Esther said, gesturing at the picked-over shelves.

"You can say that again," Cheryl said. There were still half a dozen shoppers wandering around the store, but the crush of the busload of passengers had dissipated, no doubt moving on to Yoder's Corner for lunch. Esther tied her apron strings behind her back and immediately started to tidy the shelves. "How was your morning?"

"Busy," Esther said. "We all went over to my maam's cousin's house to get the tables set up for the fund-raiser this evening."

"How did that go?" Cheryl was able to keep any trace of bitterness out of her voice, even though she knew that if they'd hired a caterer, that would have been taken care of for them.

"It went fine. My maam and Elizabeth are still there decorating. It will be lovely. Elizabeth is so good with this sort of thing."

Cheryl thought it would take a truckload of decorations to get that dusty old barn looking lovely, but she knew better than to say so. She knew that her style of decorating was different from that of her Amish friends, who preferred things a little more, well, simple, than she did.

"I am looking forward to it," Cheryl said. Well, she was looking forward to seeing her friends at the fund-raiser, so that was close enough to the truth. "I was planning to bring some cookies for the potluck. Do you think that will work?" She would pick them up from the Honey Bee after work. Kathy's cookies would taste better than anything she made at home anyway.

"That will be lovely." Esther deftly arranged potholders and hand towels into a neat stack. "Thank you for coming. It will mean so much to my maam and to Sylvia."

Cheryl smiled. She didn't know how much Esther knew about Cheryl's own plans for the event, but it was very nice of her to encourage Cheryl anyway.

She was about to say more when the door opened, and Lydia walked into the shop, the wooden puzzle box under her arm.

"I have decided to cut it open," she said without preamble. A few of the customers turned and looked as she strode across the shop toward them, but quickly went back to their browsing.

"Are you sure?" Cheryl tried to hide her excitement. The second text had said they needed to get the box open; there had to be a clue in there. At least, Cheryl hoped so.

"Yes. I am tired of waiting, and I need to know what is inside. My daed has a saw at home, but the blade is dull. I thought I would take it to Weaver Lumber and have them cut it with one of their power saws."

"Good idea. Please let me know if there is anything inside," Cheryl said.

Lydia shifted on her feet. She seemed to be waiting for something. Cheryl waited for her. Finally, Lydia said, "I was wondering if I could have a ride. My brother Thomas was coming to town and brought me this far, but it will take me a good long while to walk to Weaver's."

Cheryl laughed. How had she missed that was what Lydia was waiting for? "Of course." She often forgot what a hassle it was for her Amish friends to get around, relying mostly on buggies and bicycles. She looked back at Esther, still working on the display but watching them.

"Esther, do you mind..."

"Please go," Esther was saying, shooing them out. "I cannot stay late today because I need to help with the fund-raiser, but I will be here for a while longer. I will take care of things here."

Cheryl thanked her and grabbed her purse. On the way, Lydia told her that she'd been unable to get in touch with Elam yesterday, which they both thought was suspicious in itself. Surely he'd gotten her message? She'd gone to his house and left it with Miriam herself. But he hadn't responded. Their eyes met briefly, both knowing what this could mean. A few minutes later she and Lydia were stepping inside Weaver Lumber.

The man Cheryl had spoken with on her last visit—Larry Weaver—was behind the counter again, but Moses Schrock was nowhere in sight. The man seemed confused by the sight of Cheryl and Lydia entering together, but after Cheryl greeted him, Lydia said something to him in their dialect, and he answered, gesturing toward the counter. The clean smell of sawdust hung in the air, and Cheryl fought to keep herself from getting distracted by the beautiful samples of hardwood flooring and cabinet fronts around the shop.

"He wants to take a look at the box," Lydia explained as she placed the box on the counter. Cheryl always felt like such an outsider at moments like this. It almost felt like being in a foreign country sometimes.

Larry picked up the box and turned it over in his hands, indicating the keyhole. He said something else in Pennsylvania Dutch, and Lydia nodded and pointed out the part of the puzzle she had figured out so far and where the wood was warped, the pieces sticking. He examined the box silently for a few minutes and shook it, trying to make the pieces work. Then he looked up. "We will cut it."

Lydia nodded, and he gestured for them to follow him through the door behind the counter and into the back room. They stepped into the back, a big, warehouse-like space with stacks of lumber piled high all around. The floor was polished concrete, and fluorescent lights hung from the high, lofted ceiling. Men in Amish dress moved around in the space, but no one seemed to notice them.

"This way," he said, leading them toward a table saw along one wall. He set the box down on the flat surface of the saw and started making adjustments to the angle of the blade. "You came in here the other day to talk to Moses Schrock," he said.

"Yes," Cheryl said. "Thank you for letting me interrupt his work. It was very helpful for me."

He didn't seem to respond to these words, but kept talking.

"I heard you asking him about the night Mark Troyer disappeared." He twisted a handle, and the base of the saw lowered. "I wanted to tell you something about that night, but I was busy with a customer."

Cheryl remembered that he had been occupied with another customer when she was talking with Moses. She waited for him to go on. In typical Amish fashion, he seemed in no hurry to get to the point.

"The last day Mark came to work, I saw that there was a girl waiting outside the shop. I thought it was strange. This does not happen often."

Cheryl could imagine that this wasn't exactly a popular hang-out for local women.

"I saw that when Mark left, the girl stopped him."

This caught Cheryl's attention. "What did she look like?"

"I do not usually notice what girls wear. It is all the same to me. But I studied this girl for a while because something about her looked familiar and I was trying to understand why. She wore jeans and a brown sweatshirt that was far too big."

The hair on Cheryl's arms stood on end. Jessica Stockton had mentioned that the girl in the car had been wearing clothes that were too big. Could this have been her?

"Why do you say there was something familiar about her?" Jessica Stockton had told her the same thing. What was it that made people think they might recognize her?

"I do not know. I could not figure it out."

Cheryl wished he could tell her more, but in any case, she now knew that in all likelihood, Mark had met up with the Englisch girl here, at his work, whoever she was. That was more than she had known before. Had they been planning to drive to the bus station from here? But if so, how had they ended up on the side of the road clear over by the Troyers' farm? That was the opposite direction of Columbus.

Larry now moved the box, positioning it under the saw blade. He brought the still blade down partway to check where it would cut through the wood and then nodded and raised the blade again.

"Oh yes. And she had glasses," he said. "Thick, black glasses."

He flipped a switch, and the saw blade screamed.

Thick black glasses. Where had she seen… And then, it clicked into place. The solution was so simple she couldn't believe she hadn't seen it before.

She knew someone who wore thick, black glasses. Someone who would have cared very much about Mark's disappearance. She thought back to her visit to the Troyer farm yesterday, to the strange way Matilda had reacted when she'd started asking where the family members had been Mark's last day. Hadn't Joanna said Matilda had been out the evening of Mark's disappearance? She'd been bringing food to neighbors. But was that all she'd been up to? The girl had been evasive; Cheryl had thought that maybe Matilda had been avoiding saying anything because she knew something about her father that she didn't want to share. But had Matilda been trying to avoid revealing where *she* had been that night?

If the girl who waited for Mark that night, the girl Jessica had seen in the car, was Matilda, that explained why she had looked familiar to both Larry Weaver and Jessica Stockton. And it also explained why Jessica said something about her was off. She was wearing Englisch clothes, but she was not used to wearing them. They were probably not hers. She was hiding behind unfamiliar clothes, trying not to be recognized for some reason.

Larry lowered the blade, and the saw cut into the wood, slicing cleanly through one end of the box.

Suddenly, Cheryl was certain of it. The "Englisch girl" was Matilda. It had to be. Even though she was a stickler for rules, she had been willing to break them to dress in Englisch clothes. She must have wanted very much to not be found out.

And then the saw shut off. The noise ended. They waited a few moments while the dust settled, and then Larry picked up the sawed off end of the box. The interior of the box was revealed.

Inside, the box was lined with dark velvet. It would have been a nice place to store jewelry or other treasures, especially since the box was designed to lock. But with the side cut off like this, you could now see that there was a false bottom to the box. Underneath what appeared to be the bottom was a hidden compartment. And now you could see that there was something hidden inside that.

Carefully, Lydia reached into the compartment. She gently tugged, and the contents came out into her hand.

She looked down, trying to make sense of it. It took Cheryl a minute to register what it was.

"Oh my goodness."

Cheryl couldn't believe her eyes.

Chapter Twenty-Five

Cheryl looked at the object Lydia had just pulled from the false bottom of her puzzle box.

"A key," Lydia said, turning it over in her hands. It was a large, flat silver key. She looked up at Cheryl quizzically. Cheryl recognized what that key was, even if Lydia didn't.

"It's a car key," Cheryl said. It hung from a keychain; Cheryl pointed to it and Lydia held it up to show her it had the logo of Greyhound.

"This is the bus company," Lydia said, her voice rising. "But what could he have meant..."

"There's something else," Cheryl said, pointing back to the box. Lydia looked, and they both saw a few pieces of paper folded flat on the bottom of the compartment. She slid them out and unfolded them quickly, her hands shaking.

"What is it?" Lydia asked, staring down at the creased paper.

Cheryl leaned in closer and looked at the papers. On top was a note that simply said:

> I need something more reliable where I'm going. You're more likely than anyone else I know to want to try driving, so it's yours now. Sorry you'll have to wait a few years.
>
> —M

While Cheryl was trying to understand what it meant, Lydia flipped to the next paper in the stack. It took Cheryl a moment to make sense of it, but she had seen papers like this before. She looked to make sure, but yes...

"It's the title for his car."

Both Lydia and Larry stared at her.

"See what's underneath." Cheryl had a sneaking suspicion she knew what it would be and nodded when she saw that it was the car's registration.

"They're documents that tell the government who owns a car," Cheryl quickly explained. "And look." She pointed to a line on the title. "According to this, he is signing the title over to you. You just need to sign here."

Lydia's mouth hung open. "But who is this? This is not Mark."

She pointed to the line on the title that listed the seller's name. It was listed as Mark Troyer Puryear.

Puryear. That was the name of the sculpture artist Mark had admired. A book about his art had been found in Mark's car. But—Cheryl had wondered if Mark had been using a different name after he left. It had never occurred to her to ask if he had been using a different name *before* then.

"It looks like he registered his car under a different name."

From the other end of the big warehouse, she heard the sounds of men talking and a forklift moving, but all three of them were focused intently on the paper in front of them.

"But why?" Larry asked. He seemed as confused as Lydia by all that was going on.

Why indeed. Cheryl shrugged. "My guess is that he had been planning to leave for a while. He had to have gotten identification, a social security card, and a driver's license, at least, to get insurance to drive this car. Did anyone ever see the name he used on those documents?"

"I do not know."

Cheryl guessed, based on what she saw here, that Mark Troyer Puryear had been the name he had taken for himself long before he left. Chances were very good that he had been planning his departure for a long time.

"What does this mean?" Larry asked. "Why would Mark leave his cousin these papers?"

"Ja, what does it mean?" Lydia asked. Excitement and confusion showed on her face.

"I'm not positive, but..." Cheryl looked again to make sure she was seeing it right, and then she said, "I think it means Mark wasn't just giving you a puzzle box for your birthday. He was giving you his car."

Lydia watched her for a moment, trying to make sense of this. "But that means..."

Cheryl nodded. She had just worked this out herself. "It means that he planned his departure." She pointed to the keychain with the image of the greyhound. It was the image she'd seen in neon lights on the side of the bus station. "You said he liked puzzles, and it seems that this one was a doozie."

Lydia was still staring at her, waiting for her to explain.

"He left his car at the bus station for you to find."

A slow grin spread over Lydia's face.

"This is proof, then. He left on purpose. Nothing horrible happened to him," Lydia said. As understanding dawned, her voice was almost giddy. "I was right. He is out there somewhere."

Cheryl was pretty sure Lydia was right about that. But once again, it seemed like every answer she found simply led to more questions.

"Do you know what happened to the car?" Cheryl asked.

"I do not know." Lydia shook her head. "I guess the police took it. I do not really even care." Pure joy lit up her face. "I only care that this means my cousin is out there somewhere."

It warmed her heart to see how pleased Lydia was, despite being told she should have been given a free car. She didn't know too many Englisch teens who would gloss right over that and wonder where their missing cousin was. But that didn't answer so many of the questions Cheryl still had.

"But if he had been planning to leave for a while, why in the end did he just vanish like that?" Cheryl asked. "Why didn't he tell anyone where he was going?" She still didn't understand.

"And, most importantly, where is he now?" Lydia added.

Cheryl didn't know the answers to those questions.

But she was pretty sure she knew someone who did.

"Let's get going," Cheryl said. "There's someone I think we need to talk with."

Cheryl and Lydia drove straight to Joanna and Saul's house, but Joanna said that Matilda was out. She had gone over to Naomi

Miller's house on her bike to drop off some tablecloths and a milking bucket Naomi wanted to use for the fund-raiser that evening. Cheryl could not understand what possible purpose a milking bucket could serve, but she was even more curious about the event tonight now.

They took off, headed for the Millers' house. But when Cheryl and Lydia got there, Naomi was already over at her cousin's barn, helping to set up for the fund-raiser. Elizabeth told them that Matilda had come and gone more than an hour ago. She didn't know where she had been planning to go after that. Cheryl asked Elizabeth to please have Matilda contact her if she heard from her again.

Cheryl and Lydia piled back into the car and drove up and down the back roads around the Millers' farm, searching for the girl on the bicycle. The roads were good and straight, but the dips and hills made it difficult to see down them very far. Where could she have gone?

"This is why everyone needs a cell phone!" Lydia lamented as they circled around the edge of the Hershbergers' property. Cheryl wasn't so certain that Matilda would answer her phone right now, even if she had one. Or maybe she did have one, and she had kept it well-hidden. In any case, Cheryl thought there was a very good chance Elam and Matilda had been working together somehow. Matilda, she was increasingly certain, had been there on the night Mark had disappeared and had probably taken the SIM card from Elam's old phone, and Elam had been using the card in his work phone to text Cheryl and Lydia. Cheryl just had to find Matilda. If they couldn't track her down, she could try to find Elam and demand answers.

But then she looked at the clock on her dashboard and realized that she needed to go back to the shop and relieve Esther.

"I'll try to get ahold of her," Lydia promised as Cheryl dropped her off at her house. "And Elam as well. And if we cannot find them right away, they should both be at the fund-raiser tonight."

Lydia picked up the broken pieces of her puzzle box from where they rested on the car floor, and then, before she shut the car door, she leaned back.

"We are getting close, Cheryl," she said, her eyes bright. "We are going to find him, I just know it."

Cheryl agreed with her. Things were starting to make sense. They had to be close to figuring out where Mark was.

"Call me if you get in touch with either of them," Cheryl said. "And I'll see you at the fund-raiser." She waved as Lydia slammed the car door and ran into the house.

Cheryl turned the car and headed back to the shop. She said good-bye to Esther, who hurried to get home but promised to see her at the fund-raiser.

There were a number of customers in the shop, and Cheryl spent the next hour helping them select gifts and ringing up purchases, but her mind was far away. She couldn't do anything to get ahold of Matilda or Elam right now, but there was something she could do, and she had a strong suspicion it would help lead her to Mark.

Finally, the shop was quiet, and she sat down at the computer. She started with a basic search for the name Mark Puryear, but though that yielded results that were partially right, she didn't find anything that led her to Mark. So she pulled up the phone numbers she had for each of the art schools she'd contacted before. She dialed the schools, but it was Saturday afternoon, and the offices were closed. She left a message on the voice mail for each school, asking if any student named Mark Puryear had ever been enrolled. She wasn't hopeful that she would hear back from any of them before Monday, and she turned to her list of artists.

She had corresponded with most of them by e-mail, but she didn't want to wait for them to read and respond to e-mails. It took some digging through their Web sites and e-mail signatures, but she soon located a phone number for each of them. She started with Lester Coblentz.

"Hello, Lester," Cheryl began when he picked up. She tried to figure out how to word this question. "This is Cheryl Cooper. I came by your studio yesterday."

"Of course. I do hope you find that Amish boy. I suspect he's doing just fine, but I know how much it would mean to his family to know where he is."

"I know it would. And that's actually why I'm calling. It turns out he might have been using a different name than the one I thought."

"That wouldn't be surprising," Lester said. "A lot of them do pick names that sounds less, well, obviously Amish." He laughed. "I stuck with Lester Coblentz, but if I had to do it all over again, I might have gone for something more Englisch, like Jazz, or Mars."

"Jazz or Mars?" Cheryl laughed. "Those aren't exactly typical Englisch names."

"Don't forget I'm an artist. I'm expected to be *out there*," he said, laughing.

"Well, the name I think Mark might have been using isn't quite like that," Cheryl said. "Mark's favorite artist was named Martin Puryear."

"Then the kid has good taste. I love Puryear myself. His work is all about redemption."

Cheryl felt out of her element. From the pictures she'd seen of Martin Puryear's work, it mostly just looked like pieces of wood nailed together. "Yes, well, I found something that made me think he might have been going by the name Mark Puryear. Is there any chance you had a boy with that name helping you?"

"I'm afraid not." Lester did sound genuinely disappointed. "I wish I could help, but I don't know of him. But if I do hear about someone going by that name, I will let you know."

"Thanks so much." Cheryl hung up, disappointed but determined to try the other artists. She had to leave a message for Max Wiley, and she asked him to call her back as quickly as he could. If talking to the artists turned up no leads, Cheryl wasn't sure what more she could do, but she would figure something out.

Cheryl heard customers in the front of the shop, and she went and helped them, ending the day with a tidy sum in the cash register. If this week was any indication of how the month of December would go, Cheryl might need to look into getting Lydia and Esther to work more hours. She closed the shop and tidied up, putting out the fire in the woodstove and unplugging the Christmas lights. Cheryl dropped by the Honey Bee to pick up a couple dozen cookies to bring to the fund-raiser and then stopped by her house to change.

She would confront Elam tonight, she decided as she drove down the hilly country road. She would tell him that she knew he was the one sending the text messages. Even if he denied it, she would find a way to get him to admit it, and—

Her cell phone rang. Normally, she would have kept driving, but she thought it might be Lydia, so she carefully pulled her phone out of her bag. The call was from a number in a different area code. She recognized it as one of the numbers she'd called earlier this afternoon. She slipped on her headset and quickly answered the call.

"Hi there, is this Cheryl Cooper?" It was a man's voice.

"Yes, it is," Cheryl said.

"This is Max Wiley returning your call," he said. He had an accent that indicated he'd spent time in the northern Midwestern states.

"Thanks so much for calling me back," she said, slowing down as her headlights caught an orange reflective triangle. That was a warning an Amish buggy was on the road ahead of her. "I'm sorry to bother you again, but as I said in my message, I think there's a chance the boy I am looking for might have been going by a different name than I thought."

"That's why I called back so quickly," the man said. "In your e-mail, you asked about an Amish boy named Mark Troyer, and I didn't know him, but your voice mail mentioned a Mark Puryear. I do know him."

"You do?" Cheryl couldn't believe it. Was he really talking about the same person? Could she really—after all this time—have finally found someone who had known Mark after he disappeared from Sugarcreek?

"Sure. Good kid. Hardworking. And a good artist in his own right, as I recall. He liked to draw and make carvings out of the wood we had lying around. He even helped me make some shipping crates for getting my pieces to shows. Just threw them together like it was nothing."

This sounded like Mark. But how could she be sure?

"And now that I think about it, I think he did say he had grown up Amish, but you wouldn't have known it. I totally forgot all about that when you e-mailed me before. I just knew I hadn't heard of a Mark Troyer, but yeah, Mark Puryear, I did know him."

"When did he work with you?"

"Oh, probably three years ago or so. Yes, it was the autumn before my grandson was born—I remember that because Mark talked to my son about what it was like to have babies around the house. Helped calm his fears, for sure. The boy turns three in January, so that has to be it."

That was right after Mark disappeared. And Roxanna had said that Max lived up by Toledo; that was a three-hour drive if all went well. That was far enough away that it would have made sense for Mark to be worried about his car dying on the drive. Even if he got there safely, the weather in Toledo, perched right on the shore of

Lake Erie, was harsher than the weather inland. If the car had been in bad shape, the winters up that way might well have done it in. And he could have feasibly taken a bus to get there.

"When did you last talk to Mark?" Cheryl asked. Her heart was beating faster, and she felt her palms start to sweat.

"Oh, goodness. Let's see. He stayed on in the area clear through the spring, I think. Lived over in a little room he rented in town. Worked delivering pizzas or something to make extra money."

Cheryl came up on the buggy and slowed down even further, and she swung wide as she drove up alongside it. She didn't recognize the people inside, but she could see that it was a family with several kids riding in the back. The kids waved.

"He was studying for his GED in the fall when he wasn't helping me, and he got that by Christmas if I remember right. And then he started applying to art schools. I wrote a recommendation letter for him. He got in to a few of them. He decided to go to one just outside of Chicago, I think."

"Do you happen to know how to get in touch with him?"

"I don't think so," he said. "I dropped my phone in the pond fishing a while back, and I lost all the numbers that were on there. I'll dig around and see if I can find it. Maybe I have some contact info from him in my e-mail somewhere. I'll see what I can find."

"Thank you so much." Cheryl couldn't believe it. She was so close. Even if this man didn't have his contact information, now Cheryl could focus on looking into art schools outside Chicago for a Mark Puryear. If she could figure out what school he'd enrolled in, she had no doubt she could find him. Cheryl wasn't sure how long art programs were, but even if he'd graduated, the school might have a record of his most recent address. "I really appreciate it."

"I'll let you know what I find out," he said and then hung up. Cheryl took off her headset and set her phone down in the console.

Cheryl thought through everything she'd learned as she continued the drive to the farm. Something niggled at the back of her mind. When Mark left, he had boarded a bus and headed for Toledo. Cheryl thought about the things that had been left in the car. There was the Martin Puryear book. It made sense that he had that, knowing how much he had loved the artist. If he had been heading out on a bus, he would have been traveling light and no doubt needed to leave the heavy hardcover tome behind. She understood why he had the CDs. Every teen loved listening to music. But the betting slip with the number 87 written on the back...

All this time, she'd been distracted by the betting slip itself. But could the number have been the clue she needed to follow?

A moment later, she turned into the driveway that led to the Esches' house and barn. She stayed to one side, far from the horses and buggies lining up along the edge of the driveway, hoping her headlights wouldn't scare the animals. She turned off her engine and picked up her phone again. She pulled up a browser window and did an Internet search for the bus company that left from the terminal in Columbus. It only took her a moment to find the page that allowed her to search for bus schedules. She searched for a bus route that would take her from Columbus to Toledo and held her breath...

She couldn't believe it. There was a bus that ran between the two cities. It was bus route 87. It left Columbus at 8:05 every evening.

Mark may or may not have been involved in gambling, but she was sure now that that hadn't been what the slip in the car had been about. The scrap of paper had been nothing more than a place where he'd recorded the time and line of the bus he was planning to take.

All the pieces were starting to fall into place. She needed to talk to Matilda about why she had been in Mark's car that night and see what else she wasn't telling. But Matilda wasn't the only one she needed to talk to.

Cheryl was so close she could almost taste it. She just needed to find out where Mark was now. And to do that, she needed to pin down Elam. And chances were, he was right over there inside the Esches' barn.

Cheryl was smiling as she stepped out of her car and looked toward the old barn, lit up against the dark night.

She would find the answers she was looking for tonight, she was sure of it.

CHAPTER TWENTY-SIX

Cheryl walked toward the Esches' barn, her box of treats in hand. Around her dozens of Amish men and women carrying covered dishes were headed toward the open doorway of the barn. In the dark it was hard to make out faces, but Cheryl knew that Naomi and her family were here somewhere, and so was Lydia and, more importantly perhaps, her cousins Elam and Matilda. But right now Cheryl was thankful for the inky blackness. It made her feel less obviously different than the people streaming in toward the party.

Cheryl took a deep breath, adjusted the box of cookies, and headed toward the barn door. She was surprised how bright the interior of the barn was. Light spilled out through the open door. She stepped inside and realized they must have gathered every kerosene lantern in the county to light this place up. There were lamps on tables, along the edges of the hayloft, even perched on rafters—Cheryl didn't even want to know how they'd gotten them up there—and the result was a soft, warm glow that spread over the whole space.

There was a line of tables pressed up against one side of the barn, and Cheryl could see from here that it was piled with whole roasted chickens, mountains of potatoes and green salads, bowls of buttered noodles topped with cheese, and nearly a dozen loaves of homemade bread. On a separate table there were enough cakes, cookies, and pies to keep them all full through Christmas.

The middle of the room was taken up by square tables—gathered, Cheryl knew, from Amish homes all over the district—pushed together to form rows and draped in white linen tablecloths. Wooden benches were pulled up along both sides of the tables, and they were dotted with poinsettias in simple silver buckets. Tea candles were threaded through evergreen boughs that were draped along the tables. The rustic rough wood of the barn walls made the festive tables seem even more striking.

The result was breathtaking. It was simple—understated and tasteful—but absolutely beautiful. Cheryl felt a wave of shame crash over her. She had wanted to trick this place out with cut-crystal vases and thousands of dollars worth of exotic flowers. It would not have turned out nearly as beautifully as this—and, judging by the smells coming from the food tables, Cheryl doubted that a catered meal would taste as good either.

In front of the tables, closer to the door, there was plenty of room to move around and gather, and clumps of Amish women stood in groups, chatting in Pennsylvania Dutch and laughing.

"There you are." She was grateful to see Naomi standing in front of her. Her friend gave her a warm smile and guided her forward to a rack where she could hang her coat and then to a table by the door where there was a wicker basket for donations. Cheryl was shocked by how low the price of admission was, and she tossed some extra money in in addition to the cost of her meal. "I am so glad you came."

"This is beautiful," Cheryl said, gazing around the barn. "It's totally transformed."

"I do think it turned out nicely. Elizabeth is quite skilled at decorating," Naomi said, smiling at her handiwork. And then, realizing she might have offended her friend, she quickly added, "Of course, it would have been even lovelier if we had brought in a decorator as well."

Cheryl didn't even have the heart to tell her that it was a florist she was thinking of. She felt humbled all over again.

She'd been worried that it would be too cold in here, but between the press of bodies and the kerosene-powered space heaters tucked away throughout the room, it was nice and toasty.

"It couldn't possibly have turned out more beautifully," Cheryl said. She held up the box of cookies. "Should I just put these on the table?"

"Oh yes. Right this way." Naomi led her through the crowded room to the dessert table. Cheryl scanned the room, looking for Lydia, anxious to give her an update, or for Matilda. She did see Elam on the other side of the room, standing with a group of men, but she didn't see a good way to break away from Naomi and go over and confront him right there. She would find a way, though, before the evening was out.

She felt curious eyes on her as they walked through the room. Naomi had made it clear that she was welcome, and she had plenty of friends here, but she knew she still stood out.

"Elizabeth," Naomi called, and Cheryl noticed that her daughters Esther and Elizabeth were stationed behind the food tables,

monitoring them. Cheryl so often only saw Esther; it was interesting to see the sisters together. Elizabeth was so quiet she tended to
fade into the background, but she really was striking, with her dark
hair and big, doe-like eyes. "Is there an extra plate back there?"

"I believe there is. Hello, Cheryl," Elizabeth said, nodding
shyly, and then quickly squatted down out of sight to rummage
around underneath the table. "Here we are." She popped up again
holding a plain white dish, much like the others on the table.

"Thank you, Elizabeth."

Naomi turned to Cheryl. "Would you like to put them on
this?"

Cheryl nodded gratefully. She already stuck out enough here.
She didn't need her offering to look silly too. Esther and Elizabeth
arranged the cookies on a plate, and while they worked, Cheryl
told Naomi what she had discovered on the way over.

"That is wonderful," Naomi said. "You are so close, Cheryl."
Naomi tossed the cookie box in a garbage can.

"I am going to find answers tonight, I can feel it," Cheryl said.

"I am so glad." Naomi brushed the crumbs off her hands and
looked around the room. "Now then. Come meet my cousin Ellie.
She has come in from Holmes County for a visit so she could be
here. Sylvia is her youngest sister."

Cheryl smiled and started to follow Naomi across the crowded
room, but just then Lydia came up next to Cheryl and touched her
arm. "Matilda is over here," she whispered, but in a voice so loud
Cheryl wasn't sure why she had bothered. She bobbed her head
toward one side of the barn. "Now is our chance to talk to her."

She started to pull on Cheryl's arm. Cheryl was glad to see she wasn't the only one in Englisch dress tonight. Lydia was in black pants, a chunky sweater, and ankle boots.

"Excuse me, Naomi," Cheryl said, gesturing at Lydia, and Naomi smiled, understanding that Lydia needed her. "I would love to meet your cousin Ellie later, though."

"Of course," Naomi said and waved them off.

Lydia pulled Cheryl through the crowd, and Cheryl tried to keep up, but as they got to the midpoint of the barn, she hesitated. She heard something.

"Lydia. Wait." Cheryl stopped and pulled back. She started digging into her purse.

There it was again.

Her phone was alerting her that she had received a text message.

She dragged her fingers around the bottom of her purse, searching, and then finally felt them strike against the hard plastic side of her phone. She grasped it and pulled it out.

Around them, people were still moving and talking, laughing and chatting, and yet somehow the world around Cheryl had frozen. She didn't hear or see anything else as she looked down at the message on her phone.

You are so close. You will find Mark through the art school with the new name.

"It's from the same number," she said, holding up her cell phone. This was it. Somehow the texter knew she had found out Mark had gone off to art school. Someone must have overheard her filling in Naomi. But who could...?

In a room this size, it could have been anyone. In any case, she now knew that whoever had sent the message had to be in this room. Was probably watching Cheryl and Lydia now. Cheryl stopped and looked around the room.

"Where's Elam?"

He was nowhere to be seen. They looked around, checking in every corner, but he was not there.

"He's gone," Lydia said.

Cheryl was sure now that Elam Troyer was the one who sent it. He'd been there on the other side of the barn a few minutes ago, and now, just as the new text had come in, he had disappeared. She had to confront him somehow. He had the missing SIM card in his work phone right now. She had to find him, before he had the chance to change it back out for his normal SIM card.

Quickly, she touched her cell phone screen and placed a call to the number that had just called her. Then she stopped and waited. She held her breath as all around her people continued to move and talk.

And then, somewhere off on the other side of the barn, there was a sound so foreign, so strange in this Amish gathering, that for a moment Cheryl didn't recognize it.

And then she realized what it was. It was the sound of a cell phone ringing.

CHAPTER TWENTY-SEVEN

Cheryl tried to follow the noise through the crowded room, and she was thankful the ringing continued. Where was he? Elam had to be in this room somewhere.

"Over there," Lydia said, pointing to the side of the barn where the food tables were. She was momentarily thrown. What was Elam doing over by the food?

But when she saw where Lydia was pointing, Cheryl's heart stopped. Someone was hunched over, fumbling with something in her hands, trying desperately to silence a cell phone.

Someone who wasn't Elam Troyer.

At first Cheryl couldn't believe it. But then, as the girl finally managed to switch the noise off, she shoved the phone back into a fold of her dress and looked around guiltily, as if to see if anyone had seen. Cheryl couldn't believe it, but she knew she had found the texter.

"Elizabeth?" Lydia said, looking at Cheryl, confusion on her face for a moment. And then, without another word, she took off, and Cheryl followed just a step behind. They reached the food table in a matter of seconds, before Elizabeth Miller had finished rearranging her apron.

"You were the one sending the texts about Mark?" Lydia asked. The confusion in her voice echoed the confusion Cheryl felt. But she... But how...

Elizabeth kept her gaze low so the brim of her bonnet prevented her from meeting their eyes. She didn't say anything for a minute.

"Was it you, Elizabeth?" Cheryl asked.

Elizabeth kept her head low, but her voice was surprisingly confident when she finally spoke. "Let's go outside."

She then said something in their dialect to her sister Esther, who had been watching the scene unfold, her eyes wide. Esther said something back, but Elizabeth didn't really answer, just slipped out from behind the table and gestured toward the back door of the barn, which was down beyond the far end of the table. Cheryl and Lydia followed a few steps behind her.

The night air was frigid, and Cheryl wished she had had a chance to grab her coat, but she saw that Elizabeth was leading them toward a bonfire across the yard, burning bright against the dark night sky. There was a group of men huddled together on one side, and the women acknowledged them quickly and then gathered in the dim light on the far side. The fire radiated heat, and they moved close to it. The warm, woodsy smell of smoke hung in the air.

"Was it you?" Cheryl asked. Elizabeth hesitated, and then she nodded.

A thousand questions raced through her mind—how did she know where Mark was? Why send the texts? Why now? Why had she tried so hard to stay anonymous? What were they running out of time for?

But Lydia started with the most obvious one: "Where is he?"

Elizabeth held her hands up to the fire, thinking, for long enough that Cheryl began to wonder if she was planning on answering them at all. But then, finally, she spoke.

"He goes to art school," she said. Cheryl registered this information.

"In Chicago?" she asked.

Elizabeth nodded. So she had been right. Given a little bit more time, she would have found him herself. But that wasn't what mattered now. What mattered was—

"So he's okay?" Lydia said. Her eyes were still wide. She was obviously trying to process the news.

"He is doing great," Elizabeth said, a smile on her face. She looked like she was about to say more, but Lydia didn't give her the chance.

"But what happened? Where has he been all this time? Why did he leave without telling us? And"—she looked directly at Elizabeth now—"how do *you* know all this?"

Elizabeth hesitated again, but her expression didn't change.

"Maybe you could start at the beginning," Cheryl suggested.

The flames popped and danced, casting uneven shadows on their faces. Elizabeth finally nodded.

"Mark left because he wanted to be an artist," Elizabeth began. Cheryl nodded. She'd figured out as much on her own. "He had been planning it for a while. He had decided on a day, and then when the day came, he left a note behind for his family..."

"There was no note," Lydia said, shaking her head.

"Yes," Elizabeth said. "There was. His daed found it, and his parents rejected him. He never heard from them, even though he tried to contact them many times."

"No," Lydia said again, more firmly this time. "There was no note. His daed never found anything."

"His mother, Joanna, did not ever see one," Cheryl added. "She did not know where he was."

"She went to the police," Lydia added. "Everyone was looking for him. We thought he might be dead. If Uncle Saul found his note, or letters he sent later, why wouldn't he say something?"

Elizabeth hesitated. "I do not know. But I know it did not take long for Mark's daed to cut him off. I have always assumed he was simply too hurt."

She let her voice trail off. Cheryl considered this. Could Saul have found a note from Mark and destroyed it before anyone else found out? He had a temper. He had moved quickly to disinherit his eldest son. He had been so adamant that Mark had left and had told Cheryl to not look into it any further. Was that because he had something to hide after all? It was entirely possible.

But something about it didn't totally add up. Even if he had been angry with Mark, wouldn't he at least tell his wife about what he was doing and why? Cheryl had seen how distraught she was, even all these years later. Could he have known what happened to Mark this whole time and kept it from her?

"Are you sure?" Cheryl said.

She shrugged. "I do not know why his daed did what he did," Elizabeth said. "But I do know that Mark tried to tell his family that he was leaving. And when he didn't hear from them, even after he sent many letters, he realized they did not forgive him for leaving, and he stopped trying. It still hurts him to think about that."

Cheryl absorbed this, but she continued to puzzle. Even if Saul had found the note and kept it quiet, that still didn't answer all the questions about what happened the night Mark had left. There was still the Englisch girl on the side of the road, and—

"Matilda," Cheryl said.

Both Lydia and Elizabeth turned to her, waiting for her to go on.

"We need to talk to Matilda."

Lydia's eyes widened as understanding dawned. She nodded. "Wait. I will go get her," she said and held up one finger, and then she ran off.

For a moment there was an awkward silence, and Cheryl watched Elizabeth, a hundred questions running through her mind. Elizabeth kept her face down, so her kapp hid her expression.

"You did not use your own phone number to send the texts."

Elizabeth shook her head. "I did not want anyone to know it was me."

"But why?"

Elizabeth hesitated. "Maybe we should wait until Lydia gets back. Then I will only have to explain it once."

Cheryl nodded. She wasn't sure she could wait that long, but she would try. She tried a different line of questioning.

"How is it that you are the only one who knew where he was this whole time?" Cheryl asked.

Elizabeth looked up shyly from under the brim of her kapp.

"Mark and I were close," she said simply.

Cheryl waited for her to go on. By all accounts, Mark had been close to Lydia and Elam too, but he had not told them about his plans. Why Elizabeth?

"We were, well..." She stepped back a bit as the fire popped and sent up a shower of sparks. "We both knew it could never work. He was a few years older, and he was planning to leave anyway, but, well, if things had been different..."

"You were romantically involved?"

Elizabeth nodded. Cheryl could see her cheeks turning pink even in the low light from the fire. Cheryl had heard from several other girls who had thought Mark was interested in them. Was this another case of a young girl misled by a handsome face? Another young girl—Elizabeth was just eighteen now; she would have been only fifteen at the time—tricked into believing a good-looking, artistic boy cared about her? In all her conversations about Mark, no one had ever mentioned Elizabeth. No one had seemed to know anything about any connection between them, romantic or not, not even Naomi.

"We talked a lot, whenever we could. It was... We understood each other, I guess. We had a lot in common." She kicked at the dirt with her toe. "I know it doesn't seem to make sense. He flirted with so many girls, but it wasn't like that with us, not at first anyway. We started out as friends, talking about art and other things no one else seems to care about around here. But then, well..." She shrugged. "Anyway, like I said, we both knew it wouldn't go anywhere, not with him already making plans to leave, so we kept it very quiet. But he told me all about his plans."

Cheryl thought about this. Could Mark really have kept everyone else—his family, his best friends—in the dark about his plans to leave everything behind, but opened up to this girl no one even realized he was friends with?

Cheryl studied Elizabeth. The light from the fire carved out every hollow in her face, and while it would have made some people look sinister, it only made Elizabeth more beautiful. She was gorgeous, there was no denying that. And, Cheryl realized, she was thoughtful and sensitive as well as startlingly bright and insightful. She could see how Mark—by all accounts outgoing and confident, but idealistic and artistic at heart—had found a kindred spirit in her. But she was quiet and no doubt used to being overlooked. Cheryl had done it herself a few times in the past few days, talking to Naomi and forgetting that her eldest daughter was in the room. If Elizabeth had found a kinship with Mark, there was a good chance no one would even have noticed unless she called it out. And no one had thought to.

And then there was the fact that Mark obviously *had* kept in touch with her. He had discussed his plans with her. She was the only one, it seemed, who knew where he was.

Cheryl looked around again, searching for Lydia. What was keeping her? There was plenty of noise and movement inside the barn, but no sign of the girl returning.

Cheryl struggled with how to formulate this next question. Would Elizabeth be honest with her, knowing how close she was with her mother? "Were you—are you planning to leave Sugarcreek as well? To meet up with Mark?"

Elizabeth's eyes widened, and she laughed. "Oh no," she said. "Oh, goodness no." Then, after a pause, "For a while, when I was younger, sure, I thought maybe someday..." She shook her head. "But his life is not the life I want. We are just friends now. Actually, he is..."

"Cheryl! I've got her!" Lydia appeared, stepping out of the open door of the barn, followed by Matilda, who trudged beside her, her head down, as well as someone else. Cheryl squinted, and as they got closer, she could see by the light of the bonfire that it was Joanna. She felt a rush of gratitude for Lydia. She was sensible to bring the boy's mother here to hear all of this firsthand. As they got closer, she could see that Joanna looked bewildered, and her eyes moved quickly from Cheryl to Elizabeth and back to Lydia. Matilda kept her gaze on the ground and shuffled in behind the others.

"What is this about?" Joanna asked. "Lydia says you have had news of Mark?" The sheer, unbridled hope in the woman's eyes was enough to make tears spring up in Cheryl's.

Cheryl looked at Elizabeth, waiting for her to say something. Elizabeth looked down at the ground and then up at Cheryl, who nodded.

"I know where Mark is," Elizabeth finally said. "He is safe. He attends an art school in Chica—"

But the rest of her words were drowned out by the noise Joanna was making, somewhere between a cry and a laugh. She had tears brimming in her eyes.

Chapter Twenty-Eight

Is it true?" she said, her hands clutched together.

Elizabeth nodded, and then Joanna let out a whoop, and tears began streaming down her cheeks. Matilda's eyes also brimmed over, but she stood still, as if frozen. Joanna was letting out a string of words in their dialect, and Cheryl couldn't understand them, but the meaning came through loud and clear: Joanna was giving thanks to God for this news.

It took Joanna a minute, but then she finally calmed down enough to ask for information. Cheryl and Elizabeth quickly filled her and Matilda in on what Elizabeth had told them so far about her relationship with Mark and about how she'd kept in touch with him. Lydia looked at Elizabeth, incredulous, as Elizabeth revealed this, but she didn't say anything, and Elizabeth went on to talk about how Mark had been hurt by the fact that his family had never responded to his letters so that he eventually stopped trying.

"Wait," Joanna said. "What do you mean? There were no letters. There was no word. Just one day he was gone, and we didn't know what happened. He did not leave a note."

"Actually, I think maybe he did leave one," Cheryl said.

There was a moment of awkward silence as three pairs of eyes turned to Matilda. It had not been Saul after all.

"Matilda," Cheryl said. "We know you disguised yourself as Englisch and met up with Mark after work the night he disappeared. Larry Weaver saw you there. And I know that instead of heading directly to the bus station to catch his 8:05 bus, he ended up driving back out this way, presumably to bring you home. We know his car broke down along the way, and when Jessica Stockton stopped to see if he needed help, she saw you in the car."

She didn't need to add that Jessica hadn't known it was Matilda at the time; they knew now that it had been.

"So you must have known what he was planning somehow," Cheryl continued. "And the only way I can figure that you knew about his plan to leave that night was if you had found the note yourself."

Matilda didn't say anything for a moment. Her shoulders rose, and she seemed to shrink back into herself somehow. Her thick, dark glasses stood out against her unusually pale face. The rest of those gathered watched her. Joanna held her breath.

Finally, cornered, Matilda gave just the slightest bob of her head. Joanna gasped and held her hand to her mouth. Cheryl felt for her. She had gone from unbridled joy at hearing news of her son to deep disappointment, learning that her daughter was the reason she had not known where he had been this whole time.

"He left a note for us, and you took it?" Joanna said, her voice so quiet it was barely audible over the roar of the fire.

"I did find it," Matilda said, reaching out for her mother's arm. "And I went to him that night to try to stop him. To try to convince him to stay. I did not want to let him walk away from this, from us..."

"But you did not tell us?" Joanna said, like she couldn't quite believe what she was hearing. "You did not show us the note, even after he left?"

"I hid it because I knew how much it was going to hurt you, knowing that he had rejected our family and rejected our faith. I thought it was for the best," Matilda said, her voice rising. "I thought it would be better for you to think, to assume..."

They waited for her to finish, but she didn't. She just stood there, her chin up, hands on her hips. She didn't seem ashamed. Instead, she seemed almost, well, defiant. Certain.

"You thought it was better to think that my son had left us without saying good-bye—or to think that he was dead—than to know that he had chosen a life outside our church?"

Cheryl could see that Joanna was trying to keep her voice calm, but anger, disbelief, and grief all seemed to bubble just below the surface.

"The rules of our district are quite clear," Matilda said. "We are not to condone sin amongst our members. Mark chose the Englisch life over ours, and I wanted to protect you, so when his letters came in..."

"I do not care what you think the rules say. I care about my son," Joanna said, as close to angry as Cheryl had ever seen her. "He was not baptized yet. He would not have been under the *bann*, even if he did leave. You had no right..."

"But he was misguided. He rejected our faith and chose the outside world. I could not let him influence the younger children that way." Her voice wasn't hateful or mean-spirited. It was just—it was like she was convinced she was right and couldn't understand why no one else saw it her way.

And maybe that was true. In all likelihood, she had acted in the way she had thought best for the family. Lydia had said that she tended to see everything as black-and-white.

"That was not your decision." Joanna's eyes were wide, her mouth open, like she could not believe what she was hearing. "And are you telling me that you found more than just the note he left behind? There *were* other letters too?"

Matilda nodded, conviction making her bold.

"Did you know where he was this whole time?"

"No, I did not know where he was," Matilda said. "When his letters arrived, I burned them. I did not stop to see where he was writing from." She adjusted the stem of her glasses. "But it seems that Elizabeth here did know where he was. Why isn't anyone asking her why she did not tell anyone this whole time?"

Slowly, each of them turned from Matilda to look at Elizabeth. Cheryl had been hoping to get there herself. Why had Elizabeth kept the information from Mark's family, even when the police were called in?

"I had promised Mark that I would not tell anyone," Elizabeth said simply. "I promised I would not tell what he was planning, and then, after he was gone, he thought that you had gotten his note and had rejected him. He made me promise that I would not tell, that I would never reveal where he was."

"But why did you not simply tell him we did not get his note?" Joanna asked.

"I did not know what had happened." Elizabeth looked confused. "I did not realize then that Matilda had taken it. I thought, just as he did, that your husband had gotten it and rejected him."

"But she went to the police," Cheryl said. "Didn't you realize then that Joanna didn't know what happened?"

"I knew *she* didn't," Elizabeth said. "But I thought—well, I assumed Mark's daed did."

And there it was. Cheryl, too, had assumed that Saul might have kept the news from his wife and family. They all knew now that he hadn't, that he had been as much in the dark as everyone else, but she could see Elizabeth's justification for keeping quiet. Joanna seemed not to know how to respond to that. Surely she could see how that could have been possible, plausible even. But that was not what had happened in this case.

"I did not know it was Matilda who kept the news from you," Elizabeth continued. "Mark did not know either. For the past three years, he has thought you didn't want to hear from him."

At that, Joanna's eyes brimmed over with tears again.

It was not a perfect explanation. It seemed to Cheryl that several people—Mark among them—had made assumptions and decisions that they should not have made. Maybe—no, likely—it should not have taken three years for his whereabouts to come out. So much hurt could have been avoided if people had simply questioned a bit more. But it was too late to do anything about that, and she still had questions for Elizabeth.

"You knew Mark had left the car for Lydia, then?"

"Yes." Elizabeth hesitated again, toying with the edge of her apron. "He told me what he had hidden in the box for his cousin."

"But why didn't he just tell me? Why not just give me the keys?" Lydia asked.

"He thought this was more fun. A nice birthday surprise," Elizabeth said. "And of course he never imagined that you wouldn't get it open."

Cheryl believed that. If that box hadn't been left out in the rain, they all likely would have known what had happened to Mark years ago, with or without a note. She cringed, just thinking how different things could have been.

"But when he didn't hear from Lydia, why didn't he follow up with her?" Cheryl asked. "Why didn't he reach out to her, send her a hint or something?"

"He assumed she had turned her back on him, just like the rest of his family."

Cheryl couldn't understand how Mark could have believed something like that. If he and Lydia really were so close, what could possibly make him think that she would simply turn her back on him, just like that, because he had chosen to leave their community? But then Cheryl realized, as Naomi had reminded her many times over the past few months, that she didn't fully understand the Amish and their ideas about community. Could staying in the community be seen as more important than keeping in touch with your family? Cheryl didn't see how, but clearly Mark had seen that as a possibility.

She would need to ask Naomi to explain that again later. But there were still so many things that Cheryl didn't understand, so many things she wanted Elizabeth to explain.

"Why now?" Cheryl asked.

Elizabeth looked startled, thrust back to the present.

"After three years of silence, of protecting him, why break your promise now?" The heat from the fire was intense, and Cheryl stepped a little to her right, away from the flame.

"But I did not break my promise," Elizabeth said. "I did not tell anyone how to find him. Well, not until tonight. But you'd already figured that out."

While this was technically true, this was not a full explanation.

"But you sent me the texts," Lydia said. "And then Cheryl too. You wanted us to find Mark."

"You told me to find him before it was too late," Cheryl added. "What did you mean by that?"

Elizabeth pressed her lips together. "I do not want to say... I... you know enough to track him down. You do not need me to tell you. All I needed to do was get you moving, and you figured the whole thing out," she said, looking at Cheryl.

Cheryl understood now. If Elizabeth didn't actually come out with the words herself, if she only pointed them in the right direction, then she would not have technically broken her promise to Mark. But she did want Mark to be found, and badly, for some reason.

"That's why you didn't use your own SIM card. So you could anonymously point us in the right direction and not break your promise."

"Exactly." Elizabeth seemed pleased Cheryl had understood. But she still had so many questions.

"But how did you get the SIM card from Thomas's phone?" Cheryl asked.

Lydia's mouth dropped open. "It was when you helped Maam after Beatrice was born," she said, realization dawning.

Elizabeth nodded. "He showed me his broken phone, hoping I would want to buy it. I did not want to and knew no one else would either. I knew he would not miss it. Mark had just told me that he had a baby on the way, and I was trying to figure out what to do. So..."

"So you swiped the SIM card," Lydia said with clear admiration on her face. "I can't believe you did. I didn't think you had it in you."

"I did not think so either," Elizabeth said, laughing. "But it was easy, and no one seemed to notice."

Baby Beatrice was six months old. So Elizabeth had been planning this the whole time, no doubt trying to figure out how to do it.

"Again, why now?" Cheryl asked.

Elizabeth looked from Cheryl to Joanna to Lydia and back to Cheryl.

"Please, Elizabeth," Joanna said. "If you have more news of Mark, please tell me."

"You said, 'before it's too late.' Too late for what?" Lydia added.

Elizabeth pursed her lips. She thought for a minute, and then she shook her head.

"Before his baby is born," she said quietly.

"What?" Joanna's hand flew to her mouth. "What do you mean?"

"Mark is married," Elizabeth said. "He got married last year. To an Englisch girl he met at school. And now they're going to have a baby. The baby is due in January, and after that they will move to Rome so Mark can study art there. He didn't want me to say anything when he got married, and I said I would not, but now that a baby is coming and they are leaving, I just couldn't keep quiet." The words she had been so hesitant to speak before now came out so fast Elizabeth seemed to have a hard time keeping up. "I thought his family was mad at him for leaving, but I also thought it would not be right for there to be a baby and have his family not know. I thought you could not stay mad at him when there was a baby. I hoped if you found out about it, you might want to see him and the baby, and maybe you could all start speaking to each other again."

They all just stood there for a moment, taking in what Elizabeth had just said.

"Mark is married?" Lydia said, her eyes wide. "And about to become a daed?"

"Yes."

Lydia's face broke out in a wide smile. "That is *wunderbar*."

Elizabeth nodded, offering a shy smile. It *was* wonderful news.

Cheryl could see that Joanna was still processing the words, and then she saw the woman's shoulders shake and her hand come to her mouth, and she saw her crying huge tears of joy.

"My Mark? A baby?" she asked, her eyes bright, her smile wide.

Matilda simply stood there, unmoving. She had obviously heard the words, but did not seem to be reacting.

Elizabeth nodded. "I just... I thought you should know. It would not matter how upset I was at my maam, I would still want her to know she had a grandchild. I could not imagine keeping that from her. It doesn't matter how upset you are at her, your mother still loves you like no one else. It would not be right to keep her from knowing."

She dug her toe into the ground again. "But I did not want to break my promise to him. So..." She shrugged. "The anonymous texts."

"Oh my." Joanna was still absorbing the news about her new grandchild. "Oh, goodness. Oh, I must tell Saul. He will be so glad. To think, all this time..." She laughed through her tears.

Then she turned and took Elizabeth's hands in her own. "Thank you, Elizabeth. You have given me a very great gift today." She let go of Elizabeth and turned to Cheryl and nodded at her and then at Lydia. "And thank you too. Thank you for believing the messages she sent you and for looking all over for answers. I would not have this wonderful news today if you had not worked so hard to find my son. I cannot thank you enough."

"Don't thank me, thank Cheryl. She did all the work," Lydia said, bouncing up and down on her toes. "I'm just glad we know what happened. When do we get to see him?"

"As soon as possible," Joanna said quickly, and Lydia nodded her agreement. "He must come home. We will have a big dinner. We will gather all the relatives. Oh, I cannot wait to see him. And to meet his wife. He has a wife!" She laughed, like she couldn't quite believe it.

"Mother, are you sure...," Matilda started, but Joanna cut her off.

"Of course I am sure," she said sharply. "It is as Elizabeth says. A mother loves her children and wants what's best for them, no matter what."

"But is this what's best for him? Living with this Englisch woman..."

"With his *wife*," Joanna said sternly. "And if this is what he has chosen, then yes, it is what is best." She gazed at her daughter for a moment, considering her words. "Naturally, if I had had my choice, I would want Mark to remain in our community. But even more than that, I want him to be the person *Gott* made him to be. If that is an artist, with an Englisch wife and baby, that is all right with me."

"Is everything all right out here?" They all looked up, surprised to see Naomi crossing the yard toward them. "Elizabeth, you were not at the food table, and Esther told me you were out here, and—"

She broke off when she saw that Joanna was crying, and Lydia was still bouncing around.

"What has happened?" she said. She looked to Cheryl for answers, but all Cheryl could do was laugh.

"I'll fill you in inside," Cheryl said. "Right now, I think Joanna needs to go in and find her husband."

Naomi caught her eye, questioning.

"She has some good news to share."

Naomi's face broke into a wide grin. "Then it is a very good night indeed."

As soon as they were back inside, Cheryl told Naomi about what they had learned, and Naomi rejoiced with her over the news that Mark was safe. Lydia had used her cell phone to call the number Elizabeth had given her, and now Joanna and Saul were outside talking on the phone to their son.

As Cheryl relayed the short version of the story, Naomi cast glances over at her eldest daughter, who had taken her place behind the food table once again, but was avoiding looking their way.

"My Elizabeth?" Naomi said, shaking her head. "Are you sure? She had a relationship with Mark Troyer?"

"That's what she told me," Cheryl said. "And she was the one who sent the texts."

"And she knew where Mark was this whole time?" Naomi's voice was incredulous.

"I'm afraid so."

Naomi set her jaw and shook her head. "She knew, and she did not think to tell anyone."

"Well, she had promised not to," Cheryl said.

"That is no excuse," Naomi said. "Three years of heartache, and all because she did not say what she knew. I am not proud of my daughter."

"It wasn't all her fault," Cheryl said, doing her best to stick up for the girl. "She wasn't the one who burned the note he left and the letters he wrote after that."

"This is true. Matilda will no doubt be in very big trouble."

Cheryl suspected that was an understatement; she wondered if church discipline might even be involved.

"But Elizabeth is also in very big trouble," Naomi continued. "I will be having a long talk with her about this after this fund-raiser is over tonight."

Cheryl looked around. It seemed crazy, but in all the excitement of the last hour, she had almost forgotten they were at a fund-raiser. Around her, people were seated at the long tables enjoying heaping plates of food. Jonas Esch and his mother and father were talking with Naomi's husband Seth. Cheryl saw Sarah Schwartz, her stomach so big she barely fit on the bench, sitting next to a man Cheryl assumed must be her husband. He had his hand on her knee and was smiling at her, listening as she talked to a friend to her left. She saw Hannah Hilty among a group of teen girls who were clearing away dirty dishes and ferrying them to the house to be washed. The Hoffmans were sitting with their adult children, and Greta Yoder was surrounded by her grandchildren.

Cheryl also caught a glimpse of Levi at a table a few rows away, sitting next to his brother Caleb. Levi caught her eyes and gave a smile and then looked away.

"When will you announce the total amount you raised?" Cheryl asked.

Naomi tilted her head and looked at her. It was a now-familiar gesture that Cheryl knew meant her friend didn't understand what she was talking about.

"You know, count up the money from the ticket sales and donations and let everyone know how much came in?"

Naomi hesitated. "We will not do this," she said.

"But how will everyone know how successful the fund-raiser has been?"

Again, Naomi looked at her as if she had two heads.

"Look around." She gestured around the room, packed with Amish families eating, talking, laughing. "See how many people are here to show my cousin and her family that they care? Of course it is successful."

Cheryl thought Naomi didn't understand her point. "But did you raise enough to buy the medical equipment Jonas needs?"

"I do not know," Naomi said, shrugging. "I do know that we did not raise enough tonight to take care of his medical expenses for the rest of his life. I am sure of that," she said. "But that wasn't really the point. The point was to help with some of the bills, but also to show his family that we are here. We know their need. And we will take care of them."

"But what about your medical fund?" Cheryl asked. "Will that have enough money to cover his expenses?"

"Maybe not." Naomi said, but she didn't seem at all concerned. "But Gott does. We will trust in Him. Gott will provide."

Cheryl absorbed this. Sometimes her friend's ways confused her. And then other times they turned everything she thought she knew upside down. It was really that simple to Naomi. God would provide. Period.

Did Cheryl trust Him like that? God was big enough to take care of Jonas Esch. He was big enough to take care of her problems as well.

"I am so thankful for your offer to help with this fund-raiser," Naomi said, bringing her back to the present.

"I am glad you told me no," Cheryl said, and Naomi just nodded.

Naomi's way—the Amish way—was to bring the whole community together. To show their love for their neighbors, one family at a time. To focus on not just this one night, but a lifetime of living together and helping one another.

Cheryl looked around, taking in the homemade food, the handcrafted decorations, the families gathered around the tables. She saw an entire community coming together to care for its own. Putting more value on its people than on the bottom line. Prayerfully, humbly asking God to bless this sick boy.

It was simple. And it was beautiful.

"Thank you," she whispered. She wasn't sure who she was saying it to—to Naomi or to God—but it didn't really matter. All she knew was that her heart overflowed with gladness tonight.

Epilogue

Cheryl stood back, away from the family, trying to stay out of the way. Lydia, Elam, and the rest of the Troyer cousins were there, chatting anxiously. Mark's younger siblings stood behind their parents, waiting quietly. Joanna was craning her neck down the driveway, holding baby Samuel on her hip. Saul put his hand on her waist, comforting her, drawing her back.

They'd all been waiting in the house a few minutes ago, but somehow they'd slowly migrated out here, where they would be able to see the car approach. Cheryl pulled her coat tighter around her, but no one else seemed to mind the cold.

"They will be here soon," Saul said.

Back inside the house, there was a table piled high with food and another topped with gifts for Mark and his wife and their baby. Thinking about the bounty that awaited the couple, Cheryl couldn't help but think of the story of the prodigal son Joanna had referenced last week. The family might as well have killed the fatted calf.

Cheryl felt like she was intruding being here, but Lydia had needed a ride to get here in time after her shift ended, and Lydia insisted that she stay to meet Mark. It had been because of Cheryl that Mark had been found, after all, Lydia insisted. Surely she could stay to meet him. Still, she tried to remain in the background, wanting to give Mark's family the space to greet their long-lost son on their own.

From the right, off in the distance, there was the sound of a car motor. They all turned, and soon a small white hatchback came into view down the road.

"Is that him?" Thomas asked.

Cheryl held her breath as the car came down the road toward the house and slowed just before the driveway.

"It's them!" Lydia cried, and everyone seemed to tense, eager with anticipation.

The car turned into the driveway and bumped along the rutted lane. A cloud of dust blew up behind the car.

The car stopped, and the motor turned off. The driver's door opened, and slowly, uncertainly, a tall man with blond hair stepped out. He went around to the other side of the car and helped a tiny woman with a swollen belly out of the passenger seat.

For a moment, no one spoke. No one even moved. And then Joanna let out a shriek and ran to her son. Suddenly everyone else seemed to be moving, laughing, running toward him.

Cheryl stood back and quietly watched as, one after another, these usually stoic Amish pulled Mark in for a hug or clapped him on the back. She smiled as the women introduced themselves to his wife, touching her belly and wiping away tears. Cheryl let her own tears fall freely as she saw their pure, unbridled joy at his return.

"Let's have a feast and celebrate. For this son of mine was dead and is alive again," the long-lost son's father had said in the verses in Luke. *"He was lost and is found."*

"Cheryl, you must come meet him," Lydia called, and hesitantly, Cheryl stepped forward.

Mark had been found, and she was glad of that. But she was also grateful that this community had taken her in and made her feel at peace in her new home. Being here with her Amish friends, she knew that she was blessed beyond all measure.

Author Letter

Dear Reader,

I always enjoy writing mysteries—I love figuring out where all the pieces of the puzzle fit—but I especially loved escaping to the beautiful world of Sugarcreek, Ohio. I live in New York City, and Sugarcreek is everything New York is not: serene, peaceful, slow, centered around faith. At the end of a long day, I loved getting lost in this world.

This story was especially meaningful for me because I started working on this book when my second daughter was only a few months old. She lay beside me, her little coos and cries keeping me amused for many long hours while I worked on this story. I cannot even begin to imagine what it will be like when my daughters are teenagers and they start to make decisions about their futures. I pray that they will hold on to the faith my husband and I are teaching them. I pray that they will make wise choices. I pray that when the time comes I will have the strength to let them go off into the world.

My own children will not have to choose between my lifestyle and the rest of the world, as Mark Troyer did, but there will be many tough decisions in their futures, and I hope I will help them through these choices. And, like Joanna Troyer, I know that I will love my children, no matter what.

I hope that you enjoy reading this story as much as I enjoyed writing it!

Blessings,
Elizabeth Adams

ABOUT THE AUTHOR

Elizabeth Adams lives in New York City with her husband and two young daughters. When she's not writing, she spends time cleaning up after two devious cats and trying to find time to read mysteries.

Fun Fact about
the Amish or Sugarcreek, Ohio

I always imagined the Amish to be completely ignorant about technology—I mean, they don't even have electricity! I assumed they didn't know anything about refrigerators, let alone computers, televisions, or iPads. Smartphones? I guessed they'd never heard of them. But then I saw some photos of Amish girls on bikes, cell phones pressed to their ears, and they intrigued me. They looked just like the teenagers I see every day, focused more on their screens than on what's going on around them. I did some research and discovered that many Amish teens have cell phones, and even some adults do as well. Many Amish use computers for their jobs. Some even use small battery-powered gaming devices or video players on occasion.

It's not that the Amish are ignorant about technology, I discovered. It's that they make careful and conscious choices about which technologies they will allow into their lives and how they will be used. Many Amish are allowed to use technology in their jobs but not at home. They are not afraid of technology, but they do not want to be distracted by it. They do not want their lives to be ruled by screens, which often distract from the people around you. They are hesitant about anything that might make them forget to put God first.

The more I learned about the thoughtful way most Amish choose which sorts of technology to allow into their lives, the more I wished the rest of us made these sorts of conscious choices about how technology will be a part of our lives. It has made me rethink how much technology I will allow my children to partake in. It turns out the Amish are far wiser than I first thought.

Something Delicious from Our Sugarcreek Friends

Joanna Troyer's Fund-Raiser Noodles

2 cups flour   3 eggs
½ teaspoon salt   Water

Mix flour and salt in a large mixing bowl. In a separate bowl, beat eggs until frothy and then add the eggs to the flour mixture. Blend until a dough forms. If needed, add a bit of water, a few drops at a time, until it's smooth. Use a rolling pin to roll out into a thin disc. Using a sharp knife or pizza slicer, slice into thin strips. Allow the noodles to dry for at least half an hour. Cook in boiling salted water until desired consistency, usually around ten to fifteen minutes, depending on the thickness of your noodles.

Read on for a sneak peek of another exciting book
in the series Sugarcreek Amish Mysteries!

O Little Town of Sugarcreek
by Amy Lillard

Brisk cold nipped at her nose as Cheryl Cooper walked down the street. It was going to snow...and in time for Christmas. What a lovely thing, a white Christmas, her first Christmas in Sugarcreek. She placed the kitty carrier on the ground in front of the Swiss Miss and unlocked the door. Beau meowed as if to say he was happy to be there. Despite the increase in traffic Cheryl was expecting, she was glad to have him with her.

She picked up the carrier and walked inside, shutting the door firmly behind her but leaving it unlocked. It was a quarter of nine and she liked to get to the shop with plenty of time to enjoy another cup of coffee and let Beau explore before their ten o'clock opening. This allowed the locals to come and shop before the tourists arrived. For all intents and purposes the store looked closed, but everyone in Sugarcreek knew they were welcome as long as there was a light on.

It was Thursday and Howard Knisley, the bus driver for Annie's Amish Tours, had promised that tourists would soon be flocking to Sugarcreek in droves. Cheryl always loved when the buses arrived. People came from all over to this little town to visit with the Amish and shop in the quaint stores. It was as close to a fairy-tale as she had ever seen. Yes, she had enjoyed her time in this town known as the Little Switzerland of Ohio.

She would admit that she had been a little skeptical when her Aunt Mitzi had asked her to come to Sugarcreek and take over her shop. Aunt Mitzi was now in Papua New Guinea, fulfilling a life-time call to do mission work in the remote villages there.

Now Cheryl wondered how she'd stayed away from Sugarcreek so long.

She flipped on the lights as she made her way through the shop, pausing for a moment to note that the string of brightly colored Christmas lights hanging from the shelf behind the counter were not working. She sighed, wondering if she should climb the ladder and look at them before the store opened or if she should just wait until later.

Beau sniffed around at the edge of the counter and Cheryl thought he must have caught the scent of a stray piece of fudge. Leave Beau to find anything she had missed during cleanup.

Cheryl shook her head at her cat, then she placed Aunt Mitzi's jewelry box on the counter while she shrugged out of her coat. Her aunt's Christmas card and a letter had arrived a couple of days ago. The letter included a request that Cheryl would have the items in her jewelry box appraised. Aunt Mitzi wanted to sell some of the pieces to pay for a new water purification system for the mission.

Today promised to be a busy day, but Cheryl thought she could slip away around lunch when Esther Miller, the young daughter of her friend Naomi, would arrive for her shift. Cheryl didn't think it would take long to get the value of the items. A new "cash for gold" type of place had recently opened three doors down from the Swiss Miss. So she would run down there before she ate and get the appraisals her aunt requested.

Folding her coat over the crook of her arm, she grabbed up the jewelry box and headed for the back room. Couldn't be too careful considering the number of strangers they had in Sugarcreek right now. So she locked the jewelry box in the safe when she took out the money for today's business.

She was no more than halfway finished with her recount when a knock sounded at the door. Just a tap against the windowpanes.

Cheryl looked up from her counting to see her good friend Naomi Miller standing at the door. Naomi was a tiny thing dressed in her stern Amish clothing—a wool cape to hold out the cold and a black bonnet on her head as was the way of the Amish women. She blew on her hands as she waited for Cheryl. She pointed down, letting Cheryl know that she had brought her cart full of goodies to sell.

Of all the Sugarcreek residents, Naomi was the only one reluctant to come in when she knew Cheryl was there but the store was closed. Strange really, considering the Amish oftentimes walked into each other's homes without a knock or a second thought.

Cheryl returned her smile and waved for her to come inside. "Good morning, Naomi," Cheryl greeted her.

"Good morning," Naomi returned, pulling her painted cart into the store. It reminded Cheryl a little of a child's wagon except it was light blue and decorated with flowers painted down both sides. "I brought some more jams and spreads. The bus driver promised a big group today, so I wanted you to have plenty on hand."

"That's terrific." Cheryl finished the count and placed the cash drawer into the old-fashioned register. The thing was a definite antique, but it only added to the charm of her aunt's little shop.

Naomi pulled her cart around the front side of the counter. The cart was stacked with the jars of jellies, jams, and fruit butters that Cheryl couldn't keep on her shelves. Strawberry, strawberry rhubarb, crabapple, blackberry, and raspberry jalapeno, just to name a few. Though Cheryl had to admit the strawberry jam was by far her favorite. "I think it's going to be a really good day."

Naomi was the last person that Cheryl thought she would end up befriending when she moved to Sugarcreek. But there they were, the *Englisch* shopkeeper and the Amish jam maker becoming as good of friends as anyone could find. Naomi's daughter, Esther, worked a few days a week at the Swiss Miss, allowing Cheryl time to get away for lunch and to focus on paperwork in the back room without having to worry about customers.

Naomi nodded her head toward Cheryl. "It looks like it's going to snow outside, ain't so?"

"I was just thinking the same thing myself." Cheryl chuckled as she walked her friend to the door.

Naomi turned to look in the shop one more time, and a small frown puckered her brow. "Those lights are out, *ja?*"

Cheryl nodded. "They worked yesterday when I left. I guess one of the bulbs wiggled loose during the night."

"I could send Levi to take a look at it," Naomi offered.

"That's very kind of you," Cheryl started with a small shake of her head, "but I imagine Levi has more important things to do than check my Christmas lights."

"Perhaps that is so, but you are our friend and it is no trouble to help."

Cheryl couldn't stop her wide smile. That described her friends. They seemed to care more about others than they did themselves. Such was the way of the Amish, she supposed, but she found the custom to be charming as well as godly.

"In humility consider others better than yourselves. Each of you should look not only to your own interests but also to the interests of others."

The Amish followed the verse in Philippians faithfully.

Cheryl stood at the door and watched her friend hustle through the cold into her waiting horse and buggy. She admired the Amish for their slower pace of life. For their determination to hold the world at bay and for their devout faith. It was hard enough to be a Christian in today's world, but so much harder to do it the way the Amish did.

As promised, Howard the bus driver brought a busload of tourists on his big blue bus. They swarmed about the town like a cloud of happy locusts buying up everything in sight.

The bell over her door jangled, and Cheryl looked up from her task of helping a young girl find a present for her picky stepmother. The store was so crowded, she wasn't sure if the place could hold another body. But her puckered forehead smoothed itself as she caught sight of Levi and Esther, followed by Lydia.

"*Ach*, it's busy, ja?" Esther said, tying her red and white apron around herself.

Cheryl told the young woman to give a shout if she needed anything, then she moved away, allowing the customer to examine the quilted potholders and Bible covers for herself. "There's a large tour bus here today," she explained, smiling at Naomi's youngest daughter. Esther was sixteen and had finished her formal schooling as the Amish only attended school until the eighth grade. Now the young girl was in *rumspringa*, although she was very reluctant to stray far from her Amish roots. Her best friend, Lydia Troyer, who also worked at the Swiss Miss, didn't have such reservations about experiencing the world. Lydia hardly appeared to be Amish at times, coming to work in borrowed jeans and no prayer *kapp*, her hair in a ponytail and fancy shoes on her feet. But Esther clung to the old ways. Occasionally she would wear a pair of Englisch jeans under her plain dress, but Cheryl had yet to see the teen without her pristine white head covering.

"*Maam* said you had some lights you needed looked at."

Cheryl smiled as she focused her attention on Levi Miller, the oldest of the Miller children. "Yes," she said, hoping he attributed her breathlessness to the fact that only moments before she had been crouching on the floor. She cleared her throat and pointed to the strand of lights behind the counter. "Those there."

Levi's eyes, though an impossible dark blue, grew darker still. He turned to look in the direction she pointed and gave a small nod. "I will see what I can do to fix them."

"It's okay if you don't have time," Cheryl said, offering him an out from his mother's promise. "Weatherman says there's snow coming. If you have to get back to the farm, I understand."

He shook his head and shrugged out of his heavy wool coat. In the traditional way of the Amish, the garment was solid black and very plain with only a couple of loop fasteners to hold it closed against the wind. "*Ne*," he said with another shake of his head. "I'll fix it for you."

"Thank you," Cheryl said then left him to return to her customers.

But Cheryl found it hard to concentrate on work with Levi so close. *Stop being ridiculous*, she chastised herself. Regardless of how handsome and hard-working he was, one fact would always remain: he was Amish and she was Englisch. Okay, that was two facts, but neither worked in their favor. There could never be anything between her and Levi.

"Cheryl."

She jumped when he came up behind her. "Y-yes?" As lunchtime approached, the crowd had shifted toward the eateries in town, leaving Lydia, Esther, and Cheryl a little time to straighten the shelves before the second wave hit.

Levi held the dead string of lights in one hand. "You are going to need a new set." He had put on his coat and hat, ready to go back into the cold.

"Thanks, Levi. I'll get another later." When, she wasn't sure since it was just a few days until Christmas and she still had a lot of work to do. Oh well, it wasn't important for the back counter to be festively lit.

"I will get it for you."

"Give me a minute, and I'll get you some money." Cheryl started toward the office, but Levi stopped her.

"There is no need, Cheryl Cooper. I can take care of that. I will be back in a while to finish the job."

She smiled. "Thank you," she said.

Levi merely nodded and made his way to the door.

Instead of watching his broad shoulders disappear out of sight, she turned and went to the back room to retrieve the jewelry box and her coat. Three customers still lingered in the shop, but Cheryl knew the two girls could handle it long enough for her to walk down to the Gold Standard, the shop that had just opened. Once she talked to the owner, she would stop by the Honey Bee Café, pick up a sandwich to go, then hustle back before the crowd struck again.

"Lydia," Cheryl called as she used one hand to scoop her hair out of her collar. "I'm going out for a bit, but I'll be back shortly."

"Ja," Lydia replied. "Okay."

The bell on the door chimed over her exit, and once again Cheryl was in the cold December air. She tucked her chin into the collar of her coat and wished she had thought to put on her scarf and hat before venturing out, but she didn't plan on being gone long. She quickened her steps and in no time at all was in front of the designated store.

A twin set of real pine wreaths hung, one on each door, the ends of their deep red bows fluttering in the wind. What appeared to be hand-painted letters spelled out The Gold Standard on each of the plate-glass doors. Despite the cheesy name, the intricate gold lettering somehow lent a fancy air to the place.

A blonde-haired woman stood on this side of the main counter as if waiting for whoever had been helping her to return.

The inside of the store was toasty warm, and Cheryl's feet sank into the plush red carpet. The beautiful floor covering just added to the expensive ambiance of the place. Rich cream painted walls, immaculate glass counters filled with tray after tray of sparkling jewelry. The store was large and full, and it was almost more than she could take in all at one time.

Just as the thought crossed her mind, a petite man came out of the open doorway and met her gaze. "I'll be with you in a moment, ma'am."

Cheryl nodded as he turned his attention back to the customer he had been helping.

She could hear the murmur of their voices, but not their words over the music filtering in from the mounted speakers. The "Nutcracker Suite" always brought back so many fond childhood memories. She was more than happy to enjoy the music and allow them the privacy of their conversation. She pretended to be interested in the many items of fine jewelry for sale as she waited for him to help her.

"This isn't over." The blonde snatched a satin bag off the counter, whirled on one heel, and started for the door. She caught Cheryl's gaze for the briefest of moments, then she was gone.

There was something familiar about the woman as she brushed past Cheryl on her way out. But before she could figure out what it was, the man had turned his attention to her.

"May I help you?"

Cheryl stirred and finished her trek to where the man stood. She set the cherry wood jewelry box on the counter between them. "Yes, I have some antique pieces I'm interested in getting appraised and possibly selling." She made a mental note of his name badge— Dale Jones.

The man's eyes lit up like a kid at Christmas, then the look disappeared as quickly as it came. "Let me have a look." He pulled the box closer and lifted the hinged lid.

"*Hmm*...I see," he murmured. He pulled a velvet tray from under the counter and laid it flat next to the box. Ever so gently he started to remove the treasured pieces, laying them side by side.

A strand of pearls Cheryl thought belonged to her grandmother, a wedding ring encrusted with diamonds from some long-ago ancestor, a thick tricolored bracelet that looked a little newer than the others. One by one, the slender man removed each piece, muttering to himself as he placed them on the velvet.

He examined the pieces one at a time until he had touched each one at least twice. Finally he looked up and met her gaze. His brown eyes were masked, and his full, black-as-tar mustache twitched above his hidden lips. "You want a group price?"

"Yes, please."

He dropped his loupe then stated a number far below what Cheryl was expecting.

She swallowed back a cough. "Thank you," she said as politely as her shock allowed. "I'll give that some consideration and get back to you." She shouldn't lie, but it was also not a good idea to wallop a stranger upside the head a week before Christmas. Now she understood why the woman ahead of her had been so upset. For all the luxuriousness of the store, it seemed they thrived on undercutting the customer.

Cheryl reached for the cameo and placed it back into the box first.

Dale Jones clutched her fingers before she could grab another piece. "You don't like my offer?"

"No, Mr. Jones. I don't." She quickly scooped up the jewelry, not giving it the loving touch such treasures deserved. But she had them all back in the box and the lid shut in record time. She slid the box from the counter and headed for the exit.

He shouted another number as she pushed the door open, this one a mere hundred dollars more than his insult from before.

"No thank you," Cheryl said. "Good day."

The cool air chilled her flushed cheeks as Cheryl made her way back to the Swiss Miss. She was all the way to the shop entrance when she realized she had forgotten all about getting a sandwich. A quick peek into the heart-shaped window told her that the girls would be fine on their own for a few more minutes. Only two customers milled around the store.

She checked the traffic and dashed across the street after two cars and a horse and buggy had passed.

The hominess of the Honey Bee was as welcome as a crackling fire on a cold winter day. Cheryl made her way to the counter and placed her order. Thoughts of Dale Jones and his insulting low offer filled her as she waited. Surely he hadn't expected her to dicker with him, had he? Had he deliberately undercut her, hoping he could take advantage of her?

Surely not. It was Cheryl's understanding that Dale Jones was a relative of August Yoder's. Hadn't the storeowner vouched for him?

Yet the low-ball offer still rang in her ears. After Christmas she would drive to Columbus and get a couple more appraisals before she decided to accept an offer. Hopefully, Aunt Mitzi would be able to wait until then.

A sharp poke registered in her upper arm. She was surprised to discover that she was clutching the jewelry box to her as if she were surrounded by muggers, the corner pressing into one tender bicep. She relaxed a bit, but her teeth were still on edge.

"Miss Cooper?" the young girl behind the counter said. Cheryl didn't know her name. Most likely the girl was just there to help out for the holidays. "Here's your order."

Cheryl flashed her the best smile she could muster, dropped a tip into the jar on the counter, and took the paper sack.

She would just lock the jewelry box into the safe, eat lunch, and forget she ever made the mistake of asking Dale Jones for a price on her aunt's jewelry.

Back at the Swiss Miss, she opened the door to the shop and breathed in the comforting familiar smells—lemon wood polish, chocolate, and spice.

She resisted the urge to close her eyes and just bask in it. She had work to do, lunch to eat, and a stack of paperwork waiting in her office.

Beau yowled from somewhere behind the counter. Levi was balanced on the stepladder hanging the new string of Christmas lights he had promised. He had taken off his jacket and hat once again, and Cheryl did her best not to notice his broad shoulders as he stretched to reach the hooks just under the molding, or to rest her gaze on the quaint indentation in his hair where his hat rested. Lydia was showing an elderly lady all the different patterns on the embroidered dish towels.

"She should be back anytime," Esther said to the man standing at the counter. "You are welcome to wait."

The man's back was to her and Cheryl couldn't see his face, but there was something so very familiar about him. His light brown hair curled softly against the collar of his camel-colored overcoat, his hands buried in his pockets. He shrugged and turned just enough that she caught sight of the cashmere scarf he wore. An emerald green scarf so like the one she had bought Lance last year as part of his Christmas present.

"Lance?" she murmured, her voice barely above a whisper. It couldn't be. What would Lance be doing here? They had broken up. Splitsville. No more.

He turned at her voice, his hazel eyes sparkling green with joy. It was Lance. Here. In Sugarcreek.

What was he doing here?

She didn't ask. Couldn't. Her words were paralyzed in her throat. Stuck there while she floundered like a fish out of water.

"Darling!" he exclaimed. He opened his arms and started toward her, his intentions clear.

Rooted to the spot in her surprise, Cheryl could only stand there as he wrapped his arms around her and rocked her from side to side.

She could feel everyone's gaze on her as she scrambled for the right thing to say. To do. How did a girl greet the man who had so recently broken her heart?

"Oh, I have missed you so much," he said, planting a small kiss on the top of her head.

Finally she gained her movement and pulled away from him. "What are you doing here?" she managed.

He flashed her that killer smile, the one she had fallen for, hard and fast. "I've come to take you home for Christmas."

MEET THE REAL PEOPLE OF SUGARCREEK

Sprinkled amid our created characters in Sugarcreek Amish Mysteries, we've fictionally depicted some of the town's real-life people and businesses. Here's a glimpse into the actual story of Bye Bye Blue Art Studio.

When we launched this series, Bye Bye Blue was a real art studio and gallery that shared the building with the Honey Bee Café. Shortly before this book went to press, we learned that Bye Bye Blue was giving up its lease to become an online gallery and traveling art school. They host classes at businesses all over the area. But we liked having an art studio in this location, so we changed the name and kept it there!

A Note from the Editors

We hope you enjoyed *Sugarcreek Amish Mysteries*, published by the Books and Inspirational Media Division of Guideposts, a nonprofit organization that touches millions of lives every day through products and services that inspire, encourage, help you grow in your faith, and celebrate God's love.

Thank you for making a difference with your purchase of this book, which helps fund our many outreach programs to military personnel, prisons, hospitals, nursing homes, and educational institutions.

We also create many useful and uplifting online resources. Visit Guideposts.org to read true stories of hope and inspiration, access OurPrayer network, sign up for free newsletters, download free e-books, join our Facebook community, and follow our stimulating blogs.

To learn about other Guideposts publications, including the best-selling devotional *Daily Guideposts*, go to Guideposts.org/Shop, call (800) 932-2145, or write to Guideposts, PO Box 5815, Harlan, Iowa 51593.